ALSO BY ROGER SMITH

Mixed Blood

WAKE UP
DEAD

WAKE UP
DEAD

A THRILLER

ROGER SMITH

HENRY HOLT AND COMPANY

NEW YORK

Henry Holt and Company, LLC
Publishers since 1866
175 Fifth Avenue
New York, New York 10010
www.henryholt.com

Henry Holt® and 🎲® are registered trademarks of Henry Holt and Company, LLC.

Distributed in Canada by H. B. Fenn and Company Ltd.

Library of Congress Cataloging-in-Publication Data

Smith, Roger, 1960–
    Wake up dead : a thriller / Roger Smith.—1st ed.
        p. cm.
    ISBN: 978-0-8050-8876-2
    1. Cape Town (South Africa)—Fiction.   I. Title.
    PR9369.4.S65W35 2010
    823'.92—dc22   2009021779

Henry Holt books are available for special promotions and premiums.
For details contact: Director, Special Markets.

First Edition 2010

Designed by Meryl Sussman Levavi

Printed in the United States of America
10 9 8 7 6 5 4 3 2 1

For Natalie and Maxwell Smith

WAKE UP
DEAD

THE NIGHT THEY WERE HIJACKED, ROXY PALMER AND HER HUSBAND, Joe, ate dinner with an African cannibal and his Ukrainian whore.

The African, languidly elegant in a hand-tailored silk suit, was blue-black with tribal scars on his cheeks. He spoke beautiful French-accented English, and he could have recited the Cape Town phone book and made it sound poetic. The whore had yellow braids, the dark roots cross-hatching her skull like sutures on a cadaver. She didn't say much, spent most of the meal hating Roxy for her naturally blonde hair and perfect American teeth.

When the cannibal paused his monologue to eat or drink, Joe Palmer tried to fill in. After the francophone eloquence, South African Joe sounded like a truck driven without a clutch.

They were at Blues in Camps Bay, overlooking the ocean, and even though they sat down to eat at nearly nine, the last of the golden light still washed the beach and the slopes of Table

Mountain. Cape Town is twinned with Nice on the French Riviera, and on a night like this Roxy could see why.

She spaced out during the meal. Picked at some rock cod, drank one more glass of Cape white wine than she normally allowed herself, and let the rhythm of the African's voice carry her without listening to his words. A necessary skill she had acquired in her years with Joe. But something nagged at her, a shard of memory that pierced her hard-won detachment.

Then she remembered.

The man sitting opposite her, taking delicate bites of duck l'orange, had been caught on a news camera during one of his central African country's endless civil wars. He'd cut the heart out of a living enemy, pulled the still-beating organ from the man's chest, and taken it straight to his mouth and eaten it. Grinned at the camera while he chewed.

No French accent was going to smooth that image away. Roxy lay down her knife and fork and sipped her wine, staring out at the moon rising over the waves. Then Joe gave her the look, invisible to anyone else, and she knew that the men needed a few minutes to talk business. Weapons or mercenaries. Or both.

Roxy stood. "Let's go to the bathroom."

"I don't need," the whore said, clearly new to this part of the game.

The cannibal elbowed her beneath her plastic tits. "Go and piss." Coming from his mouth it sounded almost like a benediction: *Go in peace.*

The bottle blonde battled brutally tight Diesel knockoffs and six-inch heels and dragged herself to her feet. Roxy moved through the tables of Cape Town's rich, tanned, and mostly white diners. The Ukrainian teetered after her. All eyes were on Roxy. She could still do that—draw the looks—even though thirty was a memory.

They walked into the tiled and scented bathroom, Michael Bolton dribbling from the ceiling speakers. Roxy went into a stall, shut the door and sat down. She didn't need to pee, but she needed a minute on her own. Just to keep herself cool and in the moment, as they say.

When she came out, the woman was doing a line at the basins. "You want?"

Roxy shook her head as she rinsed her hands. She hadn't touched blow in years.

"Where do you meet him?" Sniffing, wiping her nostrils, looking at Roxy in the mirror. "Your husband?"

"In a place pretty much like this." Roxy dried her hands and did one of those meaningless things that women do to their hair in front of bathroom mirrors.

The whore tried a smile, revealing pre-Glasnost dentistry. "Maybe I too get lucky. If you can, so I can."

"Sure." Roxy said.

Thought, *Like fucking hell, Chernobyl-mouth.* But was she so different from this woman? True, she'd never hooked, but her years as a model had been filled with rich men who had paid for her time and affection in other ways.

Just as Joe did now.

She left those thoughts in the bathroom.

Disco De Lilly's curse was that he was just too drop-dead gorgeous. Everybody told him so, from when he was a kid right up to today. His beauty, as beauty can, had opened doors for him. But it had also caused him no end of fucken trouble.

As he sat in the passenger seat of the stolen Nissan, his butt muscles unconsciously clenched at the memory of that first night in Pollsmoor Prison. An ordeal that had left him torn and terrified until he'd found his protector. Then his eighteen-month stretch had entered a different dimension of hell.

"Wanna catch up?" Godwynn MacIntosh held out the small glass pipe, still bubbling from the heat of his lighter flame.

Disco took a hit, held the meth in his lungs, then coughed out a billow of smoke. He needed it to settle his nerves, put the image of prison out of his mind, and help him focus on the job.

Godwynn grabbed the pipe back, and as he inhaled the last of the meth it made the *tik-tik* sound that gave the drug its local name. Where Disco was tall and slender, Godwynn was chunky and squat. And dark. Not something to be proud of on the color-conscious Cape Flats, where the birth of a dark child was no reason to break out the box wine and party.

Buzzing now, Disco entertained himself with the thought that if he and Godwynn were coffees, he'd be a cappuccino and Goddy a double espresso.

He laughed.

"Ja? What's so fucken funny?" Goddy asked.

Disco shook his head, eyes fixed on the Benz parked three cars in front of the Nissan, on the curve. Goddy had come to Disco's backyard hut two hours earlier. Told him Manson, head of the Paradise Park Americans gang—Goddy's boss—had said he better not fucken come back if he wasn't driving a Mercedes-Benz 500 SLC. This year's model.

So they had headed over to Camps Bay with its sidewalk bars and rip-off restaurants. The fancy cars were drawn to the beachfront strip like ticks to a stray dog's asshole.

Goddy was sitting up straighter. "Check this out."

Disco watched the couple approaching the Benz. The man, big, flabby, and white, was dressed in black pants and a light shirt—no tie—suit coat draped over his left arm. The woman was blonde, and there was something in her walk like those skinny girls on the Fashion Channel. Except she wasn't skinny; she was built good.

"Think he's packing?" Goddy asked.

Disco saw the man's fat squeezed into his tight shirt like a sausage. No place for a gun. He shook his head. Goddy ducked under the dash, fiddling with the wires hanging loose from the steering column, trying to get the Nissan started.

Disco watched as the big man tossed a coin to the car guard. The Benz's alarm chirped, and the turn signals flashed yellow for a second. The man held the passenger door open for the blonde, who slid in with a nice show of leg in the streetlight. He chucked his coat onto the rear seat of the Benz. The coat had covered the small silver case he carried in his left hand. The whitey popped the trunk and threw the case inside, shut the lid, got into the car, and fired up the V8.

"The sardines is opening the can," Disco said as the Benz's roof slid back, revealing the two heads: one blonde, one dark.

The Nissan coughed into life, and Goddy came back up from under the dash. "Can't they make it no easier?"

The Benz slid out into Victoria Road. Goddy allowed another car to pass, and then he followed. Disco felt the tik in his veins and the Colt tucked snug against his washboard belly.

Time to go to work.

"You could of made a bit more of a fucken effort, Roxanne," Joe said. The flat accent still grated on her ear after five years in Cape Town.

Roxy said nothing.

"Christ, I wish you'd get over it. I mean, for fuck sake, how much bloody longer . . . ?" He was driving too fast, as always. Overtaking a car on a blind curve near Glen Beach.

She held her tongue. Knew it pissed him off when she ignored him. Waited for the rage that stalked Joe like a shadow.

But he only shook his head and muttered, "Ah, what the fuck . . ."

Roxy guessed he'd made a sweet deal with the African and was riding the glow, not wanting to sour his good mood. She watched his hands on the wheel of the Mercedes. Beautiful hands. If you didn't see the man they were attached to, you would think they were the hands of a pianist or a surgeon. Not an overweight bruiser who sold death for a living.

The night was hot and windless as they drove up the lower slopes of Lion's Head, toward Bantry Bay, Table Mountain a flat black cutout against the moonlit sky. The next few minutes passed in silence. She watched the moon paint the ocean silver, and she could see the V-shaped wake of a cruise ship as it left Robben Island behind on its way to open water.

For a stupid moment she caught herself imagining she was on that boat.

"I'M TAKING THE driver, okay?" Goddy kept the taillights of the Benz in sight as they wound their way up to the houses of the rich.

"Ja. Cool."

Disco thought of the blonde in the car ahead, the dress falling away from her legs as the white fuck opened the door for her. Pity they weren't going to be able to take her with them.

Then he thought of prison and turned to Goddy. "Hey, brother, you not gonna fucken shoot them, okay?"

The Benz slowed, signals flashing.

Goddy slowed, too. "Chill," he said. "Only if I got to."

JOE'S HAND MOVED on the steering column, and she heard the muted ticking of the turn signal. He stopped the car in their driveway, pressing the clicker on the key chain to open the high gates. Nothing happened. He tried again, the car idling, headlights hot on the wooden gates that refused to move.

"Bloody motor's still playing up." He reached for the door handle.

As Joe lifted himself out of the car, the dark man came out of the shadows, the gun an extension of his arm. Roxy heard her door opening, and she felt something cold against her cheek and a rough hand on her shoulder. Tugging her.

"Get out. Fucken move it!"

The second man, waving a gun, dragged Roxy from the car, her dress riding high on her thighs. She saw his face in the spill of streetlight. Saw he was as beautiful as a Calvin model. Her right shoe snagged and stayed in the car as the man pulled at her. She stumbled to the ground, grazing her knees on the brick paving, telling herself: *This isn't happening. This is stuff you read about in the papers, stuff that happens to other people.* She could see Joe grappling with the man on the driver's side. Macho Joe.

A shot, deafening in the still night.

Time ramped.

The men were in the Mercedes, and it was reversing away and speeding off, fishtailing. For a second all she could think was that they had her shoe, her Manolo Blahnik. The pair given to her by the designer himself after a show in Milan. Then she saw Joe lying on the driveway on his back, arms flung wide like he was tanning by the pool. Roxy stood, hobbling on her one heel. Kicked the shoe off and ran to him.

"Joe!"

She knelt beside him. There was enough light from the carriage lamps flanking the gates to see he was bleeding from the right leg, above the knee. But he was moving, trying to get up.

"Fucken bastards." Joe gripped his wounded leg with his left hand, using his right arm for balance as he struggled to his knees.

Something lay on the bricks next to Joe, something that gleamed oily and black in the light. A gun. Dropped in the struggle. Before Roxy allowed herself to think, her hands found the pistol and lifted it. Joe's eyes tracked the movement, staring up at her as she stood, her hair a halo against the streetlight. She pointed the gun at him, amazed that her hands weren't even shaking.

He produced a very Joe-like half laugh. "Roxy?"

She shot him right between the eyes.

chapter 2

BILLY AFRIKA KNEW HE WAS HOME WHEN THE TRIBAL WOMAN SET off the metal detector at Johannesburg airport.

He'd hitched a ride on a Brit cargo plane from Baghdad to Dubai. Then flown Emirates to O. R. Tambo in Jo'burg, a flight crammed with South Africans returning from shopping sprees in the duty-free desert paradise. They wandered the aisles of the airbus like zombies, still feverish from days of burning plastic.

Billy was in domestic departures for his late-night connection to Cape Town. A lean brown man, midthirties, wiry hair buzz-cut to his scalp. Watching the world through the green eyes inherited from a German father he'd never known.

He stood behind the tribal woman as they went through security. She was barefoot, wrapped in an embroidered blanket, braided hair heavy with beads, her legs and arms thick with wire bangles. Didn't make the metal detector happy.

As Billy lifted his duffel bag from the conveyor belt, he saw the woman being led off to be body searched. Later he glimpsed her talking Zulu into the latest Nokia, standing against a backdrop of floodlit Boeings.

He had been maintaining since he'd flown out of Baghdad. Focused his mind on his immediate mission, letting his anger fuel him. By the time he was seated on the 737 he was feeling closer to his normal, controlled self than he had in a week.

Until Abdul leaned down and told him to fasten his seat belt. Of course it wasn't fucken Abdul, just some Muslim flight attendant from Cape Town with a black mustache and bad breath.

But sweat pricked Billy's forehead, and he caught his hands clutching the armrests as he felt the percussive whump of the explosion smashing into the left side of the BMW, piercing the armor plating and decapitating the Iraqi driver, sending his head into Billy Afrika's lap. Abdul had looked up at him, mouth twisted in a smile, like he was about to crack funny about Sunni women and desert donkeys. The force of the blast buckled the chassis of the BMW, bending Billy's door open and allowing a partial target: him.

A round smacked his Kevlar vest. The lead car was lost in smoke, but he could see the third car pulled over, the men inside laying down covering fire. He batted Abdul's head away and took a quick look into the rear, checking on the asset, the VIP he was meant to be protecting: the Swede or the Dane or whatever he was. He wasn't. He lay smeared across the seat. A closed-coffin case.

Billy kicked the door open and went out firing the Czech submachine gun, specially modified for close-quarters work. A ricochet bounced off his helmet, leaving his ears ringing. He sprinted to the car behind and almost made it when the second explosion lifted and tumbled him, tearing off his helmet, flak jacket, and boots, before flinging him to the ground.

When he opened his eyes four hours later, in the Twenty-eighth Combat Support Hospital, he was looking at the peeling pink nose of the albino Afrikaner Danny Lombard, the whitest man he had ever seen.

"There's good news, and there's bad news," Lombard said.

"What's the good news?"

"Your ball bag is still there."

"And the bad news?"

"Your ass has been fired."

"Why?"

"Somebody gotta take the blame for losing the asset. Not gonna be one of the Yanks."

Billy shrugged. The movement made his head throb. "I'll talk to the recruiting people back home." He saw the albino's face. "What?"

It got worse.

The South Africans had been recruited by a security broker in Cape Town who had hooked them up with an American outfit in Iraq, Clearwater Tactical. Clearwater paid the broker, who paid them, deposited the money in their bank accounts back home each month. Or was supposed to. But they were each thirty thousand down, and the broker wasn't taking calls.

Multiply thirty thousand dollars by seven, and you got the reason Billy was risking his ass in Iraq. Two hundred and ten thousand rand. When he'd been a cop in South Africa, it had taken him over three years to earn that kind of money.

Billy thought of the man buried out on the windswept Cape Flats, and the promise he'd made him. Felt things starting to seep through the crumbling wall he'd built around himself these last two years.

He'd checked himself out of the hospital with a couple of bruises and a killer headache. He was going home. Back to Cape Town.

The 737 hurled itself off the runway and into the night sky. Billy Afrika knew what he had to do. And who he had to see.

The broker. Joe Palmer.

*   *   *

ASIDE FROM THE surprisingly small entry wounds in his forehead
and leg, Joe looked pretty much the way he always looked first
thing in the morning: white and unhealthy and butt naked. His
flabby gut sagged, and his penis drooped sadly toward his hairy
thigh. His left eye was closed. The right eye stared up at Roxy,
heavy-lidded, lazy. Like he was winking at her. A tag dangled
from the big toe of his left foot. Roxy noticed that he badly
needed a pedicure.

"Jesus, can't you cover him at least?" Dick Richardson, Joe's
lawyer, stood at Roxy's side by the freezer drawer.

The morgue attendant, a young brown man in a stained
white coat, shrugged.

"And why the hell aren't we in a viewing room?" asked Dick.

"Viewing rooms is full."

Roxy was still numb after the events of the night, and anyway, she'd seen Joe looking worse. The attendant watched her
like she was edible, waiting for her to speak.

"Yes. This is my husband."

He made a note on a clipboard and shoved the drawer closed.

"Hell of a business," Dick said as he took her arm and led
her away. "This bloody city is out of control."

He held open a door the color of clotted cream and let her
walk out into the corridor.

A bedlam of bodies on gurneys, cops, harried morgue offi-
cials trying to deal with the deluge of the dead and the grieving
families they had left behind. Industrial-strength disinfectant
fought a losing battle against the sweet smell of human flesh
gone bad.

Dick moved in to take her arm again, but she edged away
from him. He had graying sandy hair, and yachtsman's wrinkles
fanned out from his pale eyes. Cultivated a passing resemblance to a younger Robert Redford.

"Sorry you had to go through this. I asked the police if I couldn't do it, but they insisted you identify Joe."

"It's okay."

They stopped at an office, where Roxy had to sign for Joe's personal effects. An asthmatic woman with faded yellow skin wheezed as she dumped a bulging plastic bag onto the counter. The woman removed each item for Roxy to identify. Joe's shoes, socks, underwear, suit pants, belt, and bloodstained white shirt. His wallet was there, with his driver's license and credit cards, but the wad of cash she'd glimpsed the night before when he'd paid for the meal was missing. As were his wedding band, cell phone, and the Patek Philippe watch she'd bought him for his last birthday.

Bought with his money, but still.

Roxy didn't bother to query the missing items. If the living were targets in this city, then why not the dead? She signed the form, and the woman sucked on an inhaler and crammed the clothes back into the bag. Roxy took the bag and followed Dick out into the corridor.

"There were things missing, weren't there?" he asked.

She shrugged. "I don't care."

"In this place you're lucky if they only steal your phone or your money. Last week they sawed the foot off some poor bastard who died in a car accident." This got her attention. "Probably sold it for *muti*." Coming out as *moo-tee* in his nasal accent. "Witchcraft, you know? Bloody savages."

He held another door open, and they were out in the brightness of the Cape Town morning, the hard African sun showing all the blemishes of the Salt River morgue and the shabby buildings around it, out on the fringes of the city.

Roxy slipped on her sunglasses. As they walked toward Dick's Range Rover his cell phone warbled, and he mouthed an apology and took the call. Roxy stood and looked up at Table Mountain, looming above the squalid buildings, a soft white cloud boiling over the flat top like spume as the wind drove in from the south.

It was still early, just gone eight in the morning. She hadn't slept the night before, lay on the bed in the spare room—unable to face the bedroom that still smelled of Joe—staring out into the dark, until the sun touched the rocky face of Lion's Head. Lying awake when Dick called her at seven, told her the police wanted her to formally identify Joe so they could start the autopsy. Dig the bullets out of him.

Roxy walked over to a trash can on the sidewalk. Junk overflowed onto the pavement, so she set the plastic bag on top of the mound of garbage beside the can. A homeless couple lurched out of a nearby doorway and hurried toward the trash, leaning like sailors on a storm-swept deck. She turned back to the car. Dick was still talking into his phone, his free hand patting down the sandy hair that lifted in the wind.

Roxy heard shouting and looked back. The couple fought over the bag. The man tore Joe's shirt out of the woman's hands and unballed it, holding it up against his chest, the cloth flapping like a bloody flag of defeat.

Roxy saw Joe's body surrounded by cops and emergency teams, flashing lights washing the road red and blue. And she saw herself, wrapped in a paramedic's blanket, telling her story. There had been two men. No, she never really got a look at them. It had all happened too fast. One of them shot Joe twice, and they fled into the night in the Mercedes.

Carefully editing out how, after she had fired that shot, she had thrown the gun over the cliff, into the scrub far below. Manufacturing widow's tears as she watched the paramedics sliding Joe's body into the morgue van like they were taking out the trash.

She was still shocked at how easy it had been, how light the gun had felt in her hands, how the recoil had flowed effortlessly up her arms and into her shoulders. How the lies had flowed from her tongue.

chapter 3

FIRST THEY MADE HIM DIG HIS OWN GRAVE.
Because they were young—at sixteen Piper was the old-
est, and Goose with the withered arm was just twelve—they
were impatient and the grave was shallow. Then they beat him to
the ground with their fists, kicked him as he folded himself into
a ball in a vain attempt to protect himself. Piper kneeled over him
and applied the blade, even at that age expert at understanding
the difference between wounding and killing.

The honor of pouring the gasoline fell to the feebleminded
Elvis, who giggled and showed his missing front teeth as he
doused their victim. Piper lit a cloth and threw it. They all
stepped back and watched the flames leap, laughing as he
screamed and writhed.

After a minute they rolled his burning body into the grave.

Two of them, black against the bleached sky, worked the
shovels, the other three pushed at the sandy soil of the Cape
Flats with their hands and feet. The earth pressed down onto

his limbs, filled his mouth and his nose, and covered his eyes until he saw nothing but blackness.

Billy Afrika fought himself up through the dark.

Found himself in bed at the backpackers' hotel, light slicing through the shuttered windows.

Drenched in sweat, he pulled on a T-shirt and jeans to cover the scar tissue that patterned his legs and torso like the hide of a piebald horse, and went out onto the wide balcony that ran the length of the building. Eyes squinting against the sun, he drank air and gripped the railing, his fingers locked around Victorian wrought-iron filigree.

It was years since he'd had that dream.

He'd slept much later than he intended, and traffic snarled beneath him. The backpacker on Long Street, the low-rent tourist district of downtown Cape Town, was cheap, anonymous, and noisy. Beer bottles and dirty ashtrays littered the plastic table beside him. Jet-lagged, he'd battled to fall asleep the night before, kept awake by the mating calls of French and German kids, drinking and smoking weed with hard-eyed local girls the color of toffee. A watering hole on an African sex safari.

Calmer, Billy went back into the room, stripped to his briefs, and lowered himself to the wooden floor. After a hundred push-ups he felt a different kind of sweat dripping from his body. He pushed on, muscles warm and fluid.

Two hundred.

Lifting onto his fingertips.

Three hundred.

Sweat plopping to the wood beneath his eyes. Without breaking his rhythm he put his left hand behind his back, flattened his right palm to the floor and continued one-armed.

Three fifty.

Swapped in midair, right hand behind his back.

Four hundred.

Rolled himself up to a sitting position, feet hooked under

the frame of the bed, fingers laced behind his neck. Five hundred sit-ups. Fast. His scarred body a blur of muscle and sweat.

Then he lay back on the floor, staring up at the pressed metal ceiling high above him, letting the sweat cool, drawing air into his lungs through his nose. The terror had drained from his body. As he felt his pulse rate slow, he carefully packed away the fragments of his past.

THEY WERE IN Dick's Range Rover, stuck in the morning traffic between Woodstock and downtown. Roxy had opened her window, not minding that the hot wind blew her hair into her eyes. Dick reeked of the aftershave a TV commercial told him would make him irresistible. It had lied.

He maneuvered into a gap in the traffic, searching for words to fill the silence. "Jesus, I still can't get my head around this. Can't believe Joe's gone. He was one of a kind."

"Yes, he was," she said.

No, he wasn't, she thought. He was like most of the men she'd been with since she was a teenager. Like the man sitting next to her, looking at her as if she was a beautiful accessory, a floating trophy ready to move from one rich man's bed to the next. The way she'd allowed them to look at her. The way she'd looked at herself.

No more.

"How are you for cash, Roxanne?"

"I dunno. Joe took care of that." Playing dumb. Men like Dick liked dumb.

"Look, all his bank accounts will be frozen until the legalities of the estate have been observed. But I was holding some money in trust for him, which, under the circumstances, could be made available to you. About a hundred and fifty thousand rand."

Around twenty thousand dollars.

"Thanks, Dick. I really appreciate it."

"No problemo. Give me two days, max." He beamed, like a golden labrador about to bury his snout in a woman's crotch. "Now, can I take you to breakfast? The Mount Nelson is fabulous on a day like this."

His insensitivity almost made Roxy laugh. "Some other time, okay?"

"Sure." Hiding his disappointment behind a grin. "You need anything, you just shout. Twenty-four seven. Anything at all."

She stared down at a small car stopped next to them at a light. A child—a girl with wispy blonde hair—was strapped into a car seat in the rear, having an animated conversation with a soft toy. She looked up and saw Roxy and covered her face with her hand, shy, but one eye still peeping. Roxy felt a moment of almost overwhelming sadness, followed by a flash of the same fury that had made her squeeze the trigger and kill her husband.

Then, as the Range Rover surged off into the traffic, leaving the girl behind, it was as if the anger was left behind too, and Roxy had a sudden sense of her own freedom. A soft voice nagged, telling her that things couldn't be this easy. She should feel something. Guilt. Fear.

But she didn't. Not yet.

She felt clean. Cleaner than she had in years.

chapter 4

THE CAPE DOCTOR, THE GALE THAT TORE IN OFF THE INDIAN
Ocean, blew Billy Afrika back to his past, way out on the
Cape Flats. Table Mountain a distant mirage.

Back in the apartheid days of the sixties and seventies, the
Afrikaners—ashamed of the mixed-race people who had swum
out of a shared gene pool and spoke their language—had dumped
them out here. Their labor had been welcomed in the city and
suburbs by day, but by night they had to hustle their brown asses
back to these windswept ghettos—a grid of cramped houses and
airless apartment blocks.

A decade and a half after apartheid ended, things hadn't
changed much.

Billy hadn't intended coming back here so soon, but Strategic Solutions, Joe Palmer's recruiting agency, was locked and de-
serted, mail piling up behind the glass doors in its downtown
offices.

He'd put a call in to an ex-colleague, a cop with a weakness for gambling and jailbait, who promised to track down Joe's home address in exchange for a hundred bucks. Would have the address for him at the end of the day. Time, then, for Billy to go back to the place where those nightmares were born.

Time to return to Paradise.

He drove a rental Hyundai down Main Road, which carved Paradise Park in two. White City, to the left, was the turf of the Americans, who wore the tattoos of the 26 prison gang. Dark City, facing off across Main, was ruled by their enemies, the 28s. Two armies separated by a narrow road and truces fragile as tik smoke.

And when the wind blew the truces away, the yellow sand of Paradise Park ran red with gangbangers' blood.

Billy passed the open lot where he'd been torched and buried twenty years before. Not vacant anymore. Home to a tik dealer whose rusted trailer drew schoolkids like flies to shit. The trailer squatted in the shadow of a ghetto block as uncared for now as it had been back when Billy lived there as a kid. Only the 26 gang graffiti was fresh.

At sixteen, when he'd left the burn unit—weak and scarred—he'd dragged himself up the piss-fouled stairs, to a squalid apartment where his naked mother had entertained some rubbish with a soul patch and prison tattoos. She lay on the sofa, a bottleneck in her hand, pulling on what they called a *barry* back then. Barry White. White pipe. Weed mixed with a crushed button of Mandrax.

She hadn't been near the hospital in the months he'd lain there silently screaming, stinking beneath the salve and the bandages.

His mother had raised herself on one elbow, breasts sallow and heavy, squinting at Billy through the fumes and said, "Where the fuck you been?"

That had been the extent of her sympathy.

Billy's journey down memory lane was interrupted when a

car sped out of Vulture Street—Dark City side—nearly collecting him before it shot off down Main. It was a new BMW 7 Series, sporting extras like fat tires, louvers, mud flaps, and a feature that definitely didn't come standard: a man tied to the rear bumper by his ankle, bouncing as he was dragged, leaving a strawberry smear on the dusty blacktop.

On the sidewalk a group of schoolkids, in the grip of the munchies after visiting their dealer, bought cotton candy from a one-legged simpleton. The kids pointed at the Beemer. Laughing fit to puke. The simpleton danced on his good limb—empty trouser leg flapping—clapping and whistling through his missing front teeth, enjoying the free entertainment.

Whoever said there's no place like home had got it one hundred percent fucken right.

Billy was heading in the same direction as the Beemer, but he stayed well back in case the rope snapped and sent the man under the wheels of his car. All along Main Road people seeped out of houses to watch the procession.

The road ran dead into a garbage dump, a huge landfill that sprawled out toward the airport. Two houses backed onto the dump, in no-man's-land between 26 and 28 turf, staring up Main Road. Not a popular place to live, and one of the houses was derelict. The second house was in better shape but still dilapidated, even by Paradise Park standards.

This was Billy's destination. And that of the driver of the BMW.

As the Beemer stopped, Billy saw that the man who had been dragged—his clothes bloody shreds, flesh raw and livid where the skin had been scraped off—was moving, lifting a torn arm as if some kind of salvation was within his grasp.

Billy left the Hyundai, hearing Céline Dion belting out "The Power of Love" from inside the BMW. There were three men in the car, which rose on its springs when the driver stepped out.

Shorty Andrews said, "Billy Fucken Afrika." Head of the

Dark City 28s, he stood six-six and weighed around three hundred, bulging out of his T-shirt and striped baggies, arms a canvas of gang tattoos. His voice as high and sweet as a castrato's.

Billy said, "Shorty," as he looked down at the man on the road. "Who's the hamburger?"

"Some fucker lives my side but steals shit over in White City. We got a ceasefire going, Manson and me. And you know fucken Manson, any excuse to start shooting. I got me a wife and kids now. Can't let a cunt like this start another war."

Shorty nudged the bleeding man with a giant Nike. The man whimpered. Shorty kicked him hard, then turned to the two men who stood beside him. "Osama, Teeth, go fetch Doc before this fucker dies. I want him walking round still."

The two men went toward the house and banged on the front door.

Shorty said, "So, when you get back, Barbie?"

Barbie. Nothing to do with the doll. Barbecue. Cooked meat. Cape Flats humor. The name given to him when he came out of the burn unit. It had been a while since he'd been called that, almost made him feel at home.

"Last night."

"And how is it over there?"

"A fucken mess. But it's not my mess, you get me?"

"Ja, I hear you, brother. But they pay a man good?"

"Ja. The Yanks they liked this brown skin. Said I blended in nice with the local inhabitants."

"Good to know a brown man got some use somewheres." Shorty laughed.

A blue Ford sped by, braked, threw a noisy U-turn, and slid to a stop, flinging dust at them.

"Where's the circus?" Shorty said, " 'Cause here's a fucken clown."

Detective Ernie Maggott left the Ford and walked over to them. A small, coiled spring of a man, jammed inside a check shirt and no-name-brand jeans, a violent eruption of pimples flaring across his putty-colored face and neck.

His eyes flicked over Billy, then he looked down at the bleeding man. "The fuck's this?"

"What you'd call an internal matter," Shorty said.

Maggott spat a laugh. He shook a half-smoked Camel out of a pack, hand shielding his mouth from the wind as he lit the cigarette. He exhaled smoke up into Billy's face.

"Didn't think you'd come back this side."

Billy stayed cool. Said nothing.

Shorty's two men were walking back, followed by Doc, who was on the downhill side of sixty. Flabby, with skin the color of strong tea left to stand. What hair he had left crept across his skull in an uneven fuzz. He had the cautious walk of the permanently drunk.

Doc looked at the bloody man, then up at Billy. "Not even a fucken postcard, Barbie?"

Billy shrugged.

Doc shook his head, sighed. "Shorty, what in God's name you expect me to do with this?"

Shorty said, "Patch him up, Doc. Get him back on the streets. He gonna be a lesson to the fuckers out there."

Doc set a course for the front door, moving carefully. He flapped a shaking hand.

"Bring it inside then."

Osama knelt, produced a switchblade, and cut the rope tied to the man's ankle. He and Teeth each grabbed the man by a foot and dragged him into the house. Billy could hear him crying.

Maggott was still standing too close, and he dribbled smoke into Billy's face. "Gonna go put flowers on Clyde's grave?"

"Maybe."

"Or you gonna go Pollsmoor side? See Piper's got all he needs to be nice and comfy. Food and bed. TV. Enough young flesh to fuck."

Billy kept silent, as if he was watching all this from a distance.

Maggott drew the last life out of the Camel and spoke around a mouthful of smoke.

"You sleep at night, knowing you couldn't finish that bastard?"

"Like a baby," Billy lied.

The cop flicked his burning cigarette butt at Billy. It bounced off his shirt, sparking, and fell to the ground.

Maggott shook his head. "Fucken chickenshit."

He walked back to his car and drove away, smashing through the gears like he hated them. Billy stepped on the Camel and killed it, his eyes far away.

Shorty said, "Don't worry with him; he's sexually frustrated. His wife finally left him."

"The little nympho from the meat factory?" Billy asked, coming back from wherever he'd gone.

"Ja. Miss Sausage 2002." Shorty laughed. "Would you marry somebody won a fucken competition like that?"

Osama and Teeth sloped from the house and got into the Beemer. Shorty squeezed himself behind the wheel, looking like an inflated airbag. He flashed Billy a peace salute and drove away, the rope snaking after the car, a bloody umbilical cord.

As Billy walked into Doc's house, he heard the mutter of a TV—the muted thwack of a ball on a bat and a thin cheer. He took in the mess around him. Sagging sofa, plates of half-eaten food black with flies. The familiar squalor was almost reassuring.

In the early nineties Doc and a syphilitic nurse had performed backyard abortions, fishing for fetuses with wire coat hangers. A couple of their patients went septic and died, and the nurse had turned state witness. Doc was struck from the medical register and spent eight years in prison, which left him alcoholic and palsied.

Now he stitched up gangbangers and, it was rumored, trafficked in human body parts. He also dealt in illegal firearms, mostly acquired from the cops who confiscated them from the gangsters. The cops sold them to Doc, who sold them back to the 'bangers and dug lead out of the survivors.

Billy heard a low moan from the kitchen, where Doc did his surgery, then the old alky ambled in.

"He gonna make it?" Billy asked.

"Man, he's mincemeat. But you know these tik heads. They too fucked up to know when they dead." Doc lifted a bottle of brandy from the table and waved the dregs at Billy. "You learned to drink yet?"

Billy shook his head. "No. But don't let me stop you."

"No chance." Doc lifted the bottle, chugged back what was left, and wiped his mouth on the back of the hand. "So, Barbie, what's up?"

"I need me a gun."

"Ja, and why don't you go buy you one? You licensed."

"I'd rather go under the counter."

"Not like you."

"Things have changed."

"You know what they say, Barbie: you can't change nothing but your underpants." Doc coughed up a wet laugh. "Sit your ass down, lemme see what I can do for you."

He wandered off into the dark bowels of the house.

Billy stayed standing, watching the cricket on TV. Doc was addicted, spent hours boozing in front of games stretching over five days sometimes. And mostly ending in a draw. Like gang wars, just less bloody.

Doc came back and held out something wrapped in cloth. Billy opened the cloth and saw the gleaming barrel of the Glock 17.

"Okay?" Doc asked

"Sweet." Billy checked the action. Smooth. "How much I owe you?"

"For you, five hundred."

Billy handed over the cash and slid the automatic into the waistband of his jeans, covered it with his loose shirt. Doc's eyes were on the TV. A batsman had smashed a ball into the crowd.

Billy took a moment before he spoke. "You seen them? The woman and the kids?"

Doc shook his head, still watching the game. "You know me. I don't get out too much."

"You hear anything, then? Why they still living White City side?"

Doc fixed him with those eyes like poached eggs. Eyes that had seen it all and had lost interest. "Barbie, all I wanna hear is the cricket score. Understand?"

Billy nodded, turned toward the door, Doc following him. "You keep it cool now."

"Always, Doc." He patted the Glock under his shirt. "Thanks for this."

Doc shrugged and closed the door after Billy, who stood awhile looking out over the dump. Hovering seagulls mocked the lines of broken people who prospected for anything to convert into cash for food and shelter and tik.

chapter 5

SHE PULLED THE TRIGGER, SAW THE BULLET ENTER JOE'S FORE-head.

As Roxy floated on her back in the pool, eyes closed, she didn't force the image away. Just stopped paddling and sank beneath the water as she saw Joe fall, dead by the time he hit the pavement. She drifted slowly upward and felt the sun on her face as she broke the surface.

Opened her eyes to Lion's Head, the rocky peak that flanked Table Mountain. The house clung to a cliff on its lower slopes, an engineering marvel. Joe's pride and joy. She kicked once and flowed to the side of the infinity pool, water merging seamlessly with ocean and sky. With an easy motion she pressed her hands down on the edge and lifted herself out, sitting naked and dripping on the tiles.

As she felt the sun warming her body, she caught her fingers tracing the bruises beneath the ribs on her right side. A month ago they were as purple as pulped berries, but they had faded to a mottled yellow-brown, blending with her tan.

The numbness that kept reality at a distance since last night was receding. A word came to her: *culpable*. No, fuck *culpable*. She was a killer. A murderer. Roxy was shocked by what she had done the night before. Shocked that she had killed her husband, sure, but astonished that she had managed to do something so out of character. So fucking vivid.

Life had always been something that happened to Roxy. It was easy, when you were beautiful, to just lie back and let the current catch hold of you and wash you up someplace you never even knew existed.

But she had never expected to end up here.

She felt a surge of panic. Pure terror. Knew she was going to pay for what she'd done. Big-time.

Told herself to calm down. Take it easy. Nobody suspected her. Crime was epidemic in this absurdly beautiful city. She'd been here long enough to know that most of the criminals and their victims lived out on the Cape Flats, the ghetto that had turned its hatred and fear in on itself. But crime touched the privileged, too. Home invasions and hijackings left tanned and well-fed corpses in the sitting rooms and driveways of the suburbs that adorned the slopes of Table Mountain.

The cops the night before had seemed bored. She had felt they were going through the motions, the crime already solved for them, even if the hijackers had disappeared into the sprawl of the Flats. All she had to do was keep cool. Let Joe's estate be processed and buy herself a ticket out of here. She'd overstayed her welcome, anyway. Came for a summer and stayed five years.

Back when she was modeling, Roxy was always being touted as the next somebody, but her career hadn't caught fire the way it was meant to. She did okay, but by the time she was twenty-eight she knew that she wasn't going to have a fragrance named after her, and she felt ancient next to the starved fifteen-year-olds who haunted the studios and catwalks.

So Roxy migrated south to Cape Town, where the modeling scene was big, but not flooded with the huge names like Europe and the States. Catalog work and the odd TV commercial came her way. But she wasn't going anywhere.

Then she met Joe Palmer in a beachfront bar, an older guy with the confidence that money bought. He gave her a pair of Cartier earrings on their first date, and they were married six months later.

She'd never loved him.

Learned to hate him later.

Roxy stood and wrapped herself in a printed cloth, shaking the water from her hair. It was hot, the dry heat that scorched Cape Town this time of the year. The wind had died during the morning, and she could see a smear of brown smog hanging over Robben Island and the Flats.

As she walked up the staircase to her bedroom, Roxy found her fingers probing her bruised ribs again. Remembered flying down these stairs, hitting, rolling, ending up unconscious on the tiles below. She stopped at the door to the room at the top of the stairs. The pink room. Thought about opening the door, closed since that night a month ago. Went as far as touching the doorknob with her fingertips. Knew she wasn't ready to turn it.

Roxy withdrew her hand and went toward her bedroom.

DISCO DE LILLY woke up looking straight into his mommy's eyes.

She said, *Why you mess up your life like so?*

Lying there, staring at the framed photograph that hung on the wall of the wooden *zozo* hut—all that was left of his mother, dead these fifteen years—he flashed back to the smack of the gunshot, saw the white man grabbing his leg, sinking to his knees.

Panicked, Disco stood his bare ass up from the bed and turned his back on the photo he couldn't bring himself to remove.

But he still heard his mommy: *You know where you going? Straight to hell.*

Never mind hell; unless he got his shit together, he was going straight back to Pollsmoor Maximum Security Prison.

And Piper.

The sun blasting in through the window told him it was past midday as he pulled on a pair of jeans, slung low on his narrow hips. He grabbed for his cell phone and dialed Goddy's number. Call disallowed. Out of fucken airtime.

Disco opened the door of the hut and sat on the step, shirtless, preparing his first pipe of the day, already feeling the itching on his skin, his body crying out for the meth. His perfect torso was etched with tattoos. Not the elegant, swirling curlicues that adorned the blond surfer boys who rode Cape Town's waves, these were the crude prison variety, carved into his skin with razor blades and sharpened wire. Ink made from melted plastic, shoe polish, and the blackened innards of batteries. Dollar signs, playing cards, bleeding hearts, poker dice, a coiled snake with the head of a penis.

The work of Piper. Disco the helpless supplicant as he lay on the bunk in the communal cell in Pollsmoor.

Disco pulled on the pipe. Exhaled. Sucked the pipe empty, oblivious to the hot glass burning his lips. Trying to suck his way to oblivion. A blank place without memory.

He couldn't.

Disco made another pipe and fired it up. Battling to hold back a sewage spill of fear. He absorbed the smoke, feeling the rush by the time he exhaled.

Better.

The fat woman from the main house waddled out to string up washing on a sagging line. She was barefoot, wearing a frayed nightdress, buttons straining against her massive breasts, her coarse hair wound tight around pink rollers. A little black mongrel bared its teeth and snarled at Disco from behind the woman's hairy calf, peering past the varicose veins that grew like jungle vines up her legs.

The fat bitch spoke around the clothes peg she held in her mouth. "Hey, go put you a shirt on. You scaring little Zuma." She laughed and made wet kissing sounds as she stroked the dog with a calloused foot.

She wobbled over to where Disco sat. "Where's your fucken rent money?"

"Tonight, Auntie, okay?"

"Gimme a hit."

She grabbed the pipe and vacuumed up what was left, her tits threatening to escape the housecoat. Her naked gums smacked wetly as she exhaled a stream of smoke. "Or you can pay me the other way."

She was looking at him the way the 28s had looked at him that first night at Pollsmoor: like he was a piece of meat. Her left hand opened the folds of the nightdress, and Disco saw she hadn't bothered with underwear. Her stink filled his nose as she pushed herself close to his face.

He jumped to his feet, remembering the god-awful day a month back when he had done what she wanted, her brutal thrusts rocking the wooden hut, leaving the picture of his mommy hanging askew.

Never again.

"I'll have Auntie's money tonight." He fled into the *zozo*.

"Don't think I didn't see youse in that Benz last night, little fuckers!" she shouted as he slammed the door.

Disco looked at himself in the cracked mirror that leaned against the wall, lamenting the mess Piper had made of his body. Not only had Piper broken him and poisoned his soul, but he'd marked his one asset: his looks.

Forever ended the dream that had kept Disco alive—the

dream that his mommy had given him. That one day he would be a big-time fashion model, vibing for the cameras.

BARBARA ADAMS DREADED the walk up the short pathway to her house. But there was no other way to her front door, just this gate in a tired fence and the few squares of concrete pavement thrown onto the parched grass that fought a losing battle against the sand of the Cape Flats.

It was especially bad today. The heat, the angle of the sun, the hard glare bouncing back off the small white house, all reproduced vividly that day, two years before, when she and her children watched as her husband was gutted like a pig, right here on the pathway.

She saw Clyde Adams sinking to his knees on the yellow sand, staring up at her in disbelief as he tried to stop his intestines from bulging out between his fingers.

She saw that thing grab Clyde by his hair—the dark, straight hair he had been so proud of—and slit his throat. He had held her husband's body upright by his hair for a moment; then he let go and Clyde crumpled to the sand, his left foot convulsing, the shoe kicking up a small cloud of dust.

Then he was still.

Barbara found herself standing where her husband had died. Her hands holding the plastic shopping bags clenched tight, nails stabbing into her palms. She forced herself to breathe and walked to the front door and let herself into the house, a thin woman with black hair and olive skin who had forgotten she was pretty.

When she saw who was inside she paused, collected herself.

Billy Afrika sat on the sofa. Her thirteen-year-old daughter, Jodie, dressed in a T-shirt and sweatpants, sat next to him, bare feet folded under her, showing him her photo album. The one with blonde fairies on the cover.

Billy looked up.

"I thought you were dead," Barbara said, sounding disappointed he wasn't.

BILLY STOOD AND followed Barbara as she went through to the kitchen, put the bags on the counter, and started unpacking the contents. Three skinny chops, wrapped in plastic, went into the fridge along with a wilted lettuce. She put a couple of cans of beans and a packet of rice into the cupboard above the sink. Barbara had to slam the cupboard door closed, and it sat skew on its hinge. The house was clean but rundown.

Barbara's hair needed to be cut, and her clothes hung on her spare body. Billy saw that one of her shoes had split along the side, exposing the pale flesh of her toe. With the money he had sent her—a fortune on the Flats—she shouldn't be living like this.

At last she turned to face him. "So? Large as life, Billy."

"Looks like it."

She made a sound that may have been a laugh, then splashed tap water into a glass and drank it down in one draft.

"We never heard nothing from you."

"But you got the money?"

A nod, not looking at him as she rinsed the glass and up-ended it on the draining board. She didn't offer him anything.

"Sorry about these last two months," Billy said. "I'll sort it."

Barbara shrugged. "You home for good?"

"I dunno."

"You mad to come back here."

She walked past him into the sitting room. Jodie was gone, and he could hear R & B moaning from a bedroom. A girl in heat over a boy. Barbara chose the chair next to a table dominated by her wedding photograph. Billy couldn't look at her without seeing a smiling Clyde Adams.

"Barbara, why you still living here?"

"And where must I go?"

"Move to the suburbs."

She shook her head. "The only time you get away from here is in a bag, Billy. You know that."

The girl singer was approaching some sort of climax.

"Jodie, turn that down!"

A groan, but the volume was lowered.

"What's happened to the money I sent?" He watched her eyes. Old cop habits die hard.

"What you mean?"

"Why you living like this?"

For the first time she looked away from him. "Clyde had his debts. I had to pay them off."

"Bullshit, Barbara. There wasn't a man more chicken of debt than him."

Color flared in her cheeks. "Do you dare to sit in my own house and call me a liar?"

"Why don't you tell me what's going on?"

"Better you go, Billy."

"Clyde wouldn't want this."

"Clyde is gone."

Billy found his eyes on the photograph of a smiling Clyde, felt rivulets of sweat running like acid across the scars on his ribs. Looking at the photo, but seeing Piper's smile as he dropped the bloody knife to the sand and raised his hands in mock surrender, standing over Clyde's body.

Feeling his own finger tightening on the trigger of the automatic.

But not squeezing it.

Billy looked up from the photograph when Barbara stood and left the room. Too proud to cry in front of him. He heard a bedroom door close. Billy scribbled his cell number on the back of the Emirates boarding pass he found still folded in his pocket. Put it on the table beside the picture and walked out.

A boy of ten, dressed in school uniform, kicked a tennis ball in the sandy patch of garden, foot to knee to head to foot. Never letting the ball touch the ground. Billy waited until the ball angled off the boy's head, bouncing too high for him to control, coming to rest in the sand.

"Shawn."

The kid looked up at him.

"Let's walk," Billy said.

"Why for?"

"I want to ask you something, is why."

The boy shrugged and followed him out the gate, tossing the ball in the air. Billy leaned against the Hyundai, felt the harsh sun unsoftened by the gauze of dust.

"Who comes here? To visit your mommy?"

Shawn bounced the ball off his knee, ready to get into his routine again. Billy stood up from the car and kicked off his flip-flops, the sand hot and familiar beneath his bare feet.

He waited until the boy lost the ball, then felt old muscle memory kick in, and the ball was on his foot and looping up against the burning sky. He nudged it with his head, let it drop to his knee, bounced it, took it with the other knee, let it fall to his foot again, then sent it back to Shawn, who stepped in and intercepted it seamlessly.

They went on like this for a couple of minutes, a perfect duet—a little ghetto ballet—ball only touching the ground when Billy faked a miskick.

Shawn laughed. "You okay for a old man."

Billy gave him a shove in the chest, and the kid laughed again. Billy leaned against the car.

"So? Who comes here?"

Shawn nodded at a busty woman who watched them from a neighboring yard. A woman born to hang on a fence and leak gossip and cigarette smoke from the side of her mouth.

"She come. Mrs. Pool."

"And?"

"The pastor." The skinny hypocrite who had spat God's name all over Clyde's grave, even while he pocketed gang money.

"Nobody else?"

The boy hesitated. The hesitation that comes from fear.

"You know I worked with your daddy?"

Shawn nodded. "Ja, I remember."

"He would want you to tell me." Feeling sick in his gut for manipulating a kid with his dead father's name.

"Manson. He come on here in his Hummer."

Billy knew now where the money had gone. Knew why Clyde's family still lived on this squalid street.

"Thanks, Shawn. Your daddy would be proud of you."

The kid shrugged and kicked the ball into the air.

Billy got into the car and drove away, watching in his rearview mirror as the boy was swallowed by the dust.

As it turned out, before the day ended, Disco was posing for the cameras.

He'd gone looking for Godwynn and the money he was owed. He found Goddy at a shebeen on Poppy Street, but instead of money he'd got a story that scared him shitless: Godwynn telling him he'd lied when he said the Benz was an order from Manson. Jacking the car was strictly a freelance deal. He was ambitious— tired of doing the hard graft, risking his ass, while Manson made the fat profits and threw him the scraps.

"Fuck that," said Goddy, all pumped up, drinking Scotch. "This time I find a buyer, and we make the big bucks."

Disco stared at the dark man.

Goddy saying, last night after he'd dropped Disco at home he'd driven over to Cape Town International and parked the Benz in the open-air parking lot, under a tent of shade cloth. Just another fancy car left in the company of the Beemers and SUVs parked there for days on end.

Saying he could hotwire cars, but he didn't know shit about finding, never mind disabling, tracking systems. So he'd leave the Benz to cool off for a day or two. Then he'd go back, and if the car was still there he could drive it away safely, without guys in black uniforms and pump-action shotguns surrounding him like Dallas SWAT on fucken TV.

Disco shook his head, the anger he felt quickly swamped by fear. "Jesus, Goddy, Manson gonna kill our asses."

Right there in the shebeen, people watching, Godwynn backhanded Disco across the face. "Shut it, you fucken rabbit. I dunno why I bother with you, s'trues God. Now fucken relax."

But Disco hadn't relaxed; he'd fled the shebeen, itching, the spiders running across his skin. Desperate to get back to the *zozo* and smoke the small stash of tik he had left.

Any other day he would've checked the unmarked car and let the wind blow him far away. But his head was full of only one thing: hitting on that tik pipe.

He didn't have a chance to run. The first cop grabbed him as he came into the backyard and threw him against the wall, Z88 9mm held to his temple. The other uniform frisked him. A plainclothes looked on, ugly little fucker with zits. Everybody knew this cop was bad luck.

"What I done now?" Disco asked as he saw a curtain twitch in the house. Fat squealing bitch would get hers.

"You know what you done, you piece of shit," the plainclothes said as they cuffed Disco and hauled him to the car. "You and your bushman buddy."

So the day ended with photographs. But Disco wasn't vibing. He was at Bellwood South cop shop, having his mug shots taken.

Held for hijacking. And murder.

ROXY WAS STANDING naked in the walk-in closet when she heard the gate buzzer. She ignored the rails of designer dresses that hung like ghosts from her past and stepped into a pair of shorts, pulling a T-shirt over her head, hair still wet from the shower.

Whoever was down at the gates kept their finger stuck to the button. Roxy crossed to the intercom phone next to the bedroom door.

"Yes?"

"It's Jane. Open up."

The moment Roxy had been dreading.

She released the gates, watching from the window as a sporty little jeep snorted into the driveway. Roxy walked down the stairs and opened the front door to Joe's daughter.

Jane Palmer, eyes invisible behind black Armanis, crossed the bricks. She had her father's jaw, which was okay on a man built like a light-heavy run to fat, but it didn't sit well on an eighteen-year-old redhead.

Roxy saw Joe as the bullet drilled into his forehead. Pushed the image away.

"I'm sorry, Jane." She lifted an arm to hug the girl but dropped it again.

Jane bumped past Roxy into the expanse of Italian tile and bleached walls, the sun turning the ocean to broken glass on the horizon.

"I didn't come here for your fucken sympathy." Her father's jaw. And his mouth.

"Then why did you come?"

"There's things I want. Stuff of my dad's. It belongs to me and my mom."

"What sort of stuff?"

"Papers."

"If you're looking for his will, you're wasting your time. It's at his lawyer."

Roxy felt a jolt of guilt when Jane removed her sunglasses, revealing swollen and bloodshot eyes.

"We're not all fucken gold diggers. I want his personal things. Old pictures, things he kept from when I was a kid." Tears were welling in her eyes.

"Help yourself." Roxy gestured toward the interior of the house.

"We're going to organize the funeral. My mom and me."

Roxy tried not to show her relief. "If there's anything I can do . . ."

"You can stay away."

She shook her head. If only she could. "He was my husband, Jane."

"Ja, right." That jaw lifted. "I just want you to know that me and my mom are going to fight you over the will. No fucken ways are you going to get all this!"

Jane's freckled hand swept the house; then she set off toward Joe's office, chunky legs emerging like tree trunks from her shorts, Birkenstocks clacking on the tiles.

Roxy went into the kitchen and took a bottle of Evian from the fridge. She hadn't killed Joe to get his money, but she wanted what was hers. She'd earned it.

The phone rang, and she picked up the kitchen extension. Spoke to a cop with an accent as thick as glue. Two suspects were being held at Bellwood South police headquarters.

She was needed at a lineup.

chapter 6

THE GOOD NEWS REACHED PIPER IN THE MORNING AS HE LAY IN THE bath, washing off the last of the blood, real tears flowing over the tattooed ones etched beneath each closed eye—one for every life he had taken—as he submerged his head in the warm water.

He would be adding a new teardrop, number nineteen, to mark his latest killing. Gutted the man like the pig that he was.

The lights had still burned the night before in the communal cell in Block B, Pollsmoor Maximum Security Prison—thirty brown men crammed into a cell built for ten. All members of the 28s prison gang.

All doing hard time for murder and worse.

Three competing stereos blasted out the East Coast gangsta rap favored by the 28s. Some of the men were watching soft-core porn on late-night TV: white women with tits like melons pretending to screw dickless men who looked like they wanted to be someplace else. The prisoners urged the women on, the rapid-fire gang patois—Afrikaans and English welded together by slang incomprehensible to an outsider—bouncing off the walls in a profane call-and-response.

Other men in the cell were fucking for real. The couples doing it half hidden by the blankets that draped the double bunks, grunts and moans mocking the TV sex.

Piper watched none of this.

He lay on his bunk smoking a tik pipe, eyes closed, in a zone of quiet, exhaling a cloud of meth that blurred his face. He was maybe thirty-five, spare and sinewy, with a prison pallor. His brown skin tinged with gray like meat gone rancid, bearing the scars of twenty years of gang warfare.

He had the stillness that comes from being on intimate terms with death.

Piper wore only a pair of briefs, every inch of skin alive with gang tattoos: hands cocked like guns in the two-fingered salute of the 28s; sickle moons; a burning candle; the words *I hate you Mom* and *Spit on my grave* rendered crudely across his chest. Stars of his rank tattooed on his shoulders. The noose dangling down his right arm showed he'd once lived in the shadow of the gallows.

Piper's eyes opened, and he looked across at Pig, a big dark man with a skin condition that left vivid pink blotches the size of a splayed hand across his face and upper body. Pig sprawled on his bunk, wearing sweatpants, watching the porn while his sex-boy, a delicate youth with dead eyes, spooned him peach halves from a can.

Piper stood and stripped off his briefs, so they wouldn't be stained by Pig's blood. The tattoo of an erect penis, black and serpentine, rose from the fuzz of his pubic hair and ended, one-eyed, above his navel. He reached under the blanket of his bunk and came out with the prison shank, a spoon with the handle sharpened to a spike.

Other men in the cell, Piper's lieutenants, knew what was coming. Two of them took up positions at the door to listen for prison guards.

Piper walked naked toward his target.

Pig's boy saw him coming and shrank away. Pig was swallowing a peach and laughing at the antics on the tube, so it took him a moment to understand what was about to happen to him.

Piper held a hand over the man's mouth and cut his throat. Then he plunged the knife into Pig's abdomen and disemboweled him. Blood sprayed across Piper's tapestry of tattoos. The blaring of the TV and the pumping stereos masked the snorts and cries of the dying Pig.

The last thing he saw were those black tears on Piper's cheeks.

Piper had killed for money, greed, lust, and power. And just for the hell of it. But this was the first time he had killed for love. Ended the life of the man who had spoken obscenely of Piper's feelings for his wife. Disco.

While Disco had been with him in prison no eyebrows were raised—a 28 of Piper's seniority was allowed his choice of young flesh. True, it was unusual that he kept Disco as long as he did, but that was no cause for concern. But after Disco was released six months ago, Piper had refused to take another wife. He lay alone in his bed. Lovesick.

The men started whispering that he had gone soft. There was talk that a new general should be elected. And that meant only one thing: Piper would have to be killed.

Piper, lovesick or not, wasn't about to let that happen. Pollsmoor Prison would be his home for the rest of his life, a life he intended to be a long one. He needed a demonstration, something that would scare the shit out of the men and encourage them to keep their traps shut. So he had ritualistically killed the leader of the whispering campaign, the man who dreamed of wearing the general's stars on his shoulders. Pig.

Piper, dripping with blood, had stepped back from the body and, with due ceremony, handed the shank to one of the young soldiers, an ambitious man who wanted to rise through the ranks of the number gang.

"The blood has saluted," Piper said, bloody right hand in the cocked gun sign of the 28s.

"Salute, General," the soldier said, his hand mirroring Piper's.

In South Africa the death penalty had disappeared with apartheid. The soldier would stand trial and see another life sentence added to the one he was already serving. He wouldn't flinch, secure in the knowledge of the rank—and attendant power—that awaited him.

Piper had risen through the 28s the same way.

In the morning the guards carried away Pig's body. They beat the soldier who bore the knife, and the blame, senseless. Cuffed and shackled him and dragged him off to solitary.

Piper walked the exercise yard in his acid-orange jumpsuit, men shrinking back from him as he passed. Word had already got around. And men feared him again. It was as it should be.

But his heart was heavy. So Piper went to the laundry room.

Each morning at this time an ancient lifer named Moonlight, a 28, prepared a bath for Piper in the industrial washer, a giant chrome vat bolted to the tiled floor of the laundry. Piper stripped off the prison jumpsuit and climbed up into the washer, lowering himself into the water inside.

He scrubbed off the last of Pig's blood.

As he lay in the warm water he wept like he never had as a baby. Wept because he knew that the only person he'd ever loved, his wife, had lied to him.

Before his release Disco had sworn he would commit a crime on the outside. Something serious enough to get arrested and returned to Pollsmoor and the arms of Piper.

But the months had passed. He'd heard nothing from Disco. No visit. No letter. No phone call. Piper didn't even know where Disco was. He had used up his phone privileges trying to find him. Sent countless messages to men on the outside to search for Disco. Information that came back was scant.

Disco was somewhere on the White City side of Paradise

Park. The turf of the 26s. Americans. An enemy stronghold. That much Piper knew. What he didn't know was how to stop the pain of being without his wife.

He heard banging on the side of the washer. "Ja, come."

A face as crumpled as an old shoe bent down close to Piper, and Moonlight whispered in his ear, the sound of rats' claws on concrete. Piper was used to stench, but even he recoiled from the decay that hung on the old man's breath. But he could have kissed that rancid mouth when he realized what Moonlight was telling him.

A 28 who had spent the night in one of the Bellwood South holding cells had been brought in to the awaiting-trial section of Pollsmoor. He had passed on a message, and that message had reached the ears of Moonlight.

Disco De Lilly had been arrested.

"Arrested for what?" Piper asked.

"Hijacking and murder, General."

Piper's heart leaped. His wife was coming home to him. Forever.

DISCO SPAT BLOOD and an incisor with it. He lay prone on the floor of the interrogation room, his vision still blurred from the last kick. He looked up in time to see the uniform's boot swinging again, and he managed to cover his head with his arm, taking the kick above the elbow.

"Talk to us, Disco." The plainclothes sat on the edge of the wooden table that was bolted to the floor. He smoked and picked at one of the zits on his neck.

"What you want me to say?" Disco got to his knees, still trying to cover up.

"Tell us who shot that whitey. You or your buddy."

"I tole you. I don't know nothing about no shooting."

"But you were in the car? The Benz?"

"I wasn't in no Benz in my fucken life. Not even by a wedding." Disco tried to fall back on his charm and flashed a grin, less appealing with the missing tooth.

The uniform wound up for another kick. The plainclothes shook his head and lowered himself down, squatting in front of Disco, right in his face. "Your buddy says it was you what shot him."

The cops were bullshitting. He and Godwynn had been kept apart, in different rooms. They had no chance to get their stories straight. But Goddy wouldn't talk. Or would he?

The plainclothes reached over and took a newspaper from the table. He opened it on page three, held it up. It took Disco a moment to make sense of what he was seeing. A color photo of a blondie. Quite hot. Felt his nut sack tighten like a pair of raisins when he recognized her. The blonde from last night, standing over a dead man.

Disco was no reader, but the words *hijack* and *murder* were within his range.

The fat white fuck was dead. Jesus. He fought panic.

The cop dropped the paper and saw the look on Disco's face.

"Talk, Disco, or we gonna throw that fucked-out ass of yours back in Pollsmoor. For life, my buddy. You'll be able to park a truck up your butt when Piper's finish with you."

The uniform laughed. The plainclothes didn't. Disco could smell Kentucky chicken on his breath. Disco saw a face coming at him, a face crying tears like black rain . . .

"I tole you. I don't know fucken nothing."

The plainclothes stared at him, then sighed and stood up. He nodded at the uniform, who stepped forward again.

"Don't fuck up his face; I want the wife to recognize the little cunt."

So the uniform worked Disco's body.

chapter 7

ROXY HAD NEVER BEEN OUT HERE BEFORE, IN THE BLUE-COLLAR sprawl northeast of the city. A buffer between Cape Town and the windswept Flats beyond. Far from the beaches and the überchic Waterfront that flaunted its Paul Smith, Jimmy Choo, and Louis Vuitton franchises.

The endless procession of strip malls, used-car lots, junk-food joints, and low-rent apartments festering under the blowtorch sun reminded her of her childhood in South Florida. Except for the cars driving on the wrong side of the road, she could be back home, living with her alcoholic mother and an endless procession of daddies. The last of those daddies had been a wannabe photographer, and by the time she was fourteen he'd taken her picture. And her virginity.

Her mother had found the photographs, slapped Roxy sideways, then smelled out a financial opportunity. She showed some of the less pornographic shots to a connection of hers at the Miami International Merchandise Mart and landed Roxy a modeling gig. At fourteen she was already five-nine, with thick blonde hair and legs that went on forever, and a local agency took her onto its books.

Roxy's first legitimate photo shoot was for a burger chain—Miss Double Cheese—but things got better in a hurry. Within months she'd been signed by Eileen Ford in New York, and then it was Milan and Paris and Chanel and Versace.

She never went home or spoke to her mother again.

Roxy sneaked a look at the woman cop who drove her. A constable. Young, mixed race—what they called *colored* out here in Cape Town—wearing a blue-gray uniform and black boots. A peaked cap obscured most of the woman's wiry hair, scraped back into a bun, but Roxy detected a hint of blusher on the high cheekbones. Roxy had tried conversation, but the woman was either intimidated or bored. Or maybe she battled with the American accent.

Roxy supposed it was a sign of sensitivity that the police had offered to send a car for her, and one driven by a woman. The phone call had rattled her. She had imagined that the two brown hijackers would just fade away into the ghettos, unaware of how they had changed her life. Then she calmed herself. The cops were in the spotlight, taking the heat for the war zone that was Cape Town.

This was a face-saving exercise for the police. A couple of random guys would have been dragged in from the Cape Flats. She'd look at them, shake her head, and the cops would make noises of regret. But there would have been a demonstration of police machinery at work. The politicians would be satisfied.

The constable turned the white Volkswagen into the yard of an ugly brick building, surrounded by palisade fencing and razor wire. Roxy opened the door, letting the cop lead her into the station house. Roxy was wearing a simple black Prada cut to the knee, low-heel sandals, and no makeup. Her widow-at-a-lineup look.

As she followed the cop through the chaos that was the charge office—men in cuffs, women in tears, hookers giving her the once-over—Roxy felt dizzy. She saw her tanned arms extended, handcuffs closing on her wrists, one of those guttural voices grinding out her rights. The woman led her into a quieter corridor, and Roxy stopped, wiped her forehead with a Kleenex. Composed herself.

The cop was looking up at her. "Are you okay, Mrs. Palmer?"

"I'm fine. Sorry."

"They won't be able to see you. It will be through a one-way."

"Sure, of course."

The constable held a door open for Roxy, tried a comforting smile. "I'll get you some water."

Roxy entered the room, and a group of men in plainclothes, standing in front of a window, turned to stare at her. Strip-searching her with their eyes. Right now it was almost reassuring. At least they weren't arresting her.

One man didn't turn, a skinny man in jeans and a creased check shirt. He stared through the glass at the empty room beyond, the wall horizontally striped, familiar from countless cop shows on TV. She caught her reflection in the glass and knew the guy in jeans was watching her.

A middle-aged man in a cheap suit introduced himself, his accent brutal to her ear. Superintendent somebody? She nodded. It was okay if she looked spaced out. That was to be expected.

Roxy took her place at the glass and sneaked a glance at the man in jeans. His face looked like a cheese grater, pitted with acne scars. A flaming outbreak of fresh pimples swelled from his collar. The guy in the suit issued instructions, and ten men filed into the room beyond the glass, standing with their backs to the wall.

They were all young and brown. And the man third from the left was the one who had pulled her from the car the night before.

The beautiful one.

chapter 8

THE SUITS WATCHED THE AMERICAN BITCH LEAVE THE ROOM, LIKE
they all wanted to gangbang her right there. Detective Ernie
Maggott stood staring at their reflections in the glass, his back to
the room, fingers probing the eruption on his neck. The pimples
seethed and burned, aggravating his already frayed temper.

The superintendent was at his side. "Release them, okay?"

"She knew Disco." Maggott watched the pretty boy and his
bushman buddy shuffling out with the rest of the lineup.

"Why you say that?"

"Because she looked at all the others but not at him."

"Ja?"

"Ja."

"And you know that how?"

"I watched her eyes."

The superintendent laughed. "Come on, Maggott. Why would
she lie?"

"Why don't you ask her?"

The stupid bastard shook his head. "Let them go, okay?"

"His landlady tell me she seen him and his buddy in a Benz."

"She'll say she saw her mother in a Benz if it put twenty bucks in her pocket."

"Gimme the rest of the day with De Lilly. I can break him."

"Jesus, I already got these human rights people halfway up my ass. Now you release those two, Detective. You hear me?"

Maggott shrugged. "You the boss, Boss."

Fucker.

BARBARA ADAMS FED cloth into the sewing machine, fingers deft, foot riding the peddle expertly. A church dress for a neighbor. Some income to keep a roof over her family's head. And work helped to calm her mind; her nerves were playing up something terrible.

Seeing Billy Afrika had opened a door she'd battled to keep closed these past two years. It'd been hard to sit with the living man and not remember the dead one. The two men inseparable. Billy like another member of the family.

But the wrong man had died.

Shawn came past the dining room table, bouncing a tennis ball.

Barbara spoke above the rattle of the machine. "You finish your homework?"

"Ja. I done it."

"Did it."

"Whatever." He slouched out of the front door, a boy who needed a father's firm hand.

She leaned back and rubbed her eyes, felt the beginning of a headache. She sat for a while, eyes closed, until she heard the percussive thump of hip hop coming from the street. Insistent. Primitive. Barbara had banned this music from her house. She didn't understand why words like *motherfucker* and *bitch* had replaced the words of love and tenderness in the songs Clyde had courted her to.

The music banged on. She went across to the window and moved the lace curtains aside.

A big black car with tinted glass, almost like a military vehicle, straddled the sidewalk, music thumping from inside. The rear passenger window was open, and she could see Manson, head of the Paradise Park Americans, slouched in the seat. This she was expecting. Knew he'd be back, demanding the money she didn't have.

Then she saw that her daughter sat beside him.

Barbara ran to the front door, her fingers fumbling the locks open. She sprinted down the pathway.

"Jodie!" The girl looked down at her like she was an irritation. "Get out of there."

Barbara pulled at the heavy car door.

Jodie, dressed in a tiny halter top and shorts that accentuated rather than hid her maturing body—clothes she was forbidden to wear out of the house—sat close to Manson, almost in his lap.

"What you doing with her?" Barbara's voice was strained, starved of breath.

Manson smiled, a good set of teeth in his light brown face. He didn't look like a gangster, more like a retired athlete in his expensive sweats. Until you saw his eyes, dark and dead as a pool of stagnant water.

"I was just giving her a lift from the store. These streets is dangerous."

One of his hands rested above Jodie's knee, slender fingers gently teasing the skin of her bare leg.

"Get out of there, Jodie." Her daughter pouted, expression shifting from woman to girl in a moment. "You heard me. Get out!"

Moving in slow motion, the girl unfolded herself from the

seat and slid out of the car, all too aware of Manson's eyes on her body. She tossed him a smile over her shoulder.

Barbara grabbed Jodie by the shoulders, shook her. "What you doing with them?"

Jodie shrugged, fighting a smirk. Barbara swung her arm back and slapped the girl across the face. Hard. The first time she had ever lifted a hand to her daughter. Jodie put fingers to her cheek, tears welling in her eyes.

"Get inside," Barbara said. "Go!"

Jodie, sobbing, ran into the house, and the front door slammed. Manson watched all of this with a smile on his face.

"Nicely built girl."

"She's a child, you filthy bastard!"

Manson held his hands up in supplication. "Easy now, sister Barbara."

"You told me you and your kind would stay away from her."

"As long as you were paying me every month. That was the deal."

"The money isn't coming no more." She stood, arms folded across her chest.

"I know, I know. I been keeping an eye on the account, don't worry. Relax a bit. Sit." She stayed standing. "I said sit." His voice sharp.

Barbara obeyed, climbing up into the high car, sitting beside him. Stiff. Hands on her knees. Two men slumped low in the front seats, jerking in time to the music. The big man behind the wheel ignored her, but the small one turned and gave her a gap-toothed grin.

Manson was watching her. "I hear he was here this morning?"

"Who?"

"Billy Afrika." She nodded. "What you tell him? About where all the cash went?"

"I said Clyde made debt."

"He won't believe that."

She stared straight ahead. Silent.

"He say why the money's not coming no more?"

She shook her head.

"I want that money." He grabbed her face and turned her to look at him. The mask of geniality had slipped. "You fucken hear me?"

"Yes. I hear."

"Find out why it stopped. And when it will start again. Understand?"

"Yes."

"Get out."

She did, and he closed the door. Leaning to talk to her through the open window: "Your girlie, she's ripe, sister Barbara. Get me that money, or I'm gonna pluck her." Manson grinned.

She tried to reach in and get her nails to his face, but he laughed and pressed a button and the window slid up. The car rumbled off. Barbara turned and saw two of her neighbors, Mrs. Pool and another woman, gossiping at the fence, staring at her.

She met their eyes. "Go look at your mothers."

They shook their heads, watched her walk into the house and lock the door. Then their heads came together again, whispers like nails on cloth.

She went to the bedroom her children shared. Knocked. No reply. The door was locked. Called her daughter's name. Heard muffled sobs. Barbara went into her bedroom and found the paper that Billy Afrika had left.

Fingers shaking, she dialed his number.

"IT WAS THE white bitch what done it." Goddy prowled the *zozo* hut, puffing on a Lucky, his ugly face furrowed in concentration.

"Talk shit, Goddy." Disco sat on the bed, preparing a tik pipe, his tongue probing the gap in his gums. He was freaking out. The hours without meth. The questions and the beatings.

"Then did you shoot the fat fuck?" Godwynn was looming over him.

Disco looked up, confused. "You know I never done that."

"And I only shot him once. In the leg. So who the fuck plugged him the second time? In his fucken head?" Goddy flicked away his smoke, and it spun to the floor, still burning.

Disco fired up the pipe and sucked on it. He sat for a moment, eyes closed, feeling the rush smack him between the eyes like a slaughterhouse hammer. Then his ears stopped ringing, and his muscles started to relax from his shoulders down. He felt that tingle around his balls, and up his butt, almost like he was gonna come.

Mother of god, that was good.

He slowly exhaled a cloud of fumes and opened his eyes. Godwynn was still staring down at him. Disco held out the pipe.

Godwynn took a hit, coughing smoke as he spoke. "Answer me, my brother. If we never done it, then who did?"

Disco, now that the spiders had scuttled off his skin and hidden back in their holes, had to admit that Goddy had a point.

"And why she say nothing, that blondie?" Goddy asked. It hadn't taken much to bribe a cop at Bellwood to tell them what had happened on the other side of the one-way glass.

Disco shrugged.

Goddy said, "Because she don't want no trouble, is why. She ID us, then there's a trial and questions and the whole fucken thing. Uh-uh. Too dangerous for her."

Disco had another hit. "Or maybe she don't recognize us."

Goddy laughed. "You stupid in your head? Me, maybe. But you? With that fucken face of yours?"

Disco stared at himself in the broken mirror. Goddy was right. There was no forgetting this face. Why couldn't he have been born looking like everybody else, taken after his father rather than his mother? Look where being beautiful had got her.

He opened his mouth, saw the gap in his teeth. Like somebody from the farms. But still gorgeous, though.

Goddy was off again, pacing. "There's something in this for us, my brother."

"Ja? What?" Disco asked, mouth to the pipe.

"Think, you dumb fuck. Think where that blonde bitch lives. There's big bucks up there, my friend."

Disco didn't like where this was heading. "Let it go, Goddy. It's too dangerous."

"Your mother's cunt's dangerous."

Disco saw his mother watching them from the wall. "Ah, ah, ah! Don't talk like that, man."

"We gonna go right now up to that fancy fucken house on the mountain and tell that blonde bitch how it gonna be. You hear?"

Disco nodded, but he couldn't take his eyes from his mother's face. Heard her voice: *You going straight to hell, my boy.*

No, Mommy, I'm there already. Honest to god.

chapter 9

ROXY RAN.

She sprinted down toward the ocean, the crucifix bouncing lightly on her collarbones. As she jogged on the spot down near Saunders Rocks, waiting for a luxury bus to pass— a tour guide mouthing mute as a goldfish behind the bulging windshield—her fingers felt for the silver cross. The bus rumbled on, leaving a trail of diesel that Roxy outran as her Reeboks hit the Sea Point beachfront, a strip of luxury apartment blocks facing the Atlantic.

Roxy wasn't a Catholic, and it said a lot about her state of mind that she'd dug the cross, tarnished after all these years, out of her closet and strung it around her neck in the primitive hope that it would protect her. But she feared it wouldn't be enough to stand up to the dark shit that she'd let into her life when she'd shot Joe.

Well, what did she want, a fetish of human bones and dried body parts skewered on rusted barbed wire? Available, she was sure, somewhere in the endless maze of shacks growing like a rash on the dunes next to the airport freeway. This was Cape Town, but it was still Africa.

The crucifix had been given to her when she was fourteen by a neighbor in Miami, a woman named Mama Esmeralda, a Marielito refugee from Cuba who read everything from tea leaves to tarot cards. Mama had told Roxy—at the time when porno stepdaddy was doing his daily shoots—that her life was about to change. That she would leave Florida and never come back.

All true.

Years later in New York, Mama Esmeralda long dead, Roxy's modeling career in free fall, and her bank account running on empty, she'd visited a Haitian woman on Fordham Road who'd practiced Santeria. Each night, at the woman's instruction, Roxy had scrawled her dreams on a page of white paper and burned a yellow candle over it, watching the wax blot her handwriting as she sipped a Stoli.

Had it worked? She'd asked for a life away from the catwalk. A life without financial care. She'd come to Cape Town and met Joe. Answered prayers.

So, here she was, reaching for superstition again. She sure as hell needed some help.

Roxy had been in shock since she'd seen the man who gun-pointed her. There was no mistaking that face. He stood in the lineup, wrapped in the aura those who are born beautiful carry with them, like he was expecting a makeup artist to appear and touch up the shine on his nose.

She'd sensed the eyes of the ugly cop, the one with the plague of zits, as she recognized the hijacker. Had she shown anything? She didn't know. She'd dragged her eyes away from Mr. Hand-some, concentrated on the other men. If the one who had shot Joe was there, she didn't recognize him. At least she didn't have to lie about that.

She'd studied all the men, carefully avoiding the beautiful

one, and shaken her head. The senior cop in the suit stood beside her. Was she sure? She nodded. Apologized. Wished she could help. She'd walked back to the car with the woman cop, anxious to escape.

Roxy told herself that the hijackers would take their lucky break and fade into the vastness of the Flats. Within a few days nobody would remember her and Joe, their story buried under a pile of newer, bloodier, more sensational crimes.

But the fear remained.

She lengthened her stride, driven by the Nirvana pumping from the pink iPod velcroed to her bicep. Music that took her back to her first year modeling in Europe, when the world felt new and anything seemed possible.

Roxy followed the walkway, the stone buffer against which the Atlantic beat itself to death, sending up plumes of spray that cooled her in the evening heat. Sea Point's small, rocky beaches were hidden below the seawall, but the stench of kelp rotting in the sun clogged the air. She dodged other runners, roller bladers, dark domestic workers and the pale kids they minded, and the homeless people—unwanted humanity washed up on the shores of Africa's most expensive real estate.

She flew past the miniature golf course and was in sight of the lighthouse, striped red and white like a bloody bandage, when she was felled by exhaustion. Roxy stopped, gasping for breath, lowered her ass to the back of a sidewalk bench and found herself looking up at the gym of a high-rise apartment block. A flabby man was framed in the window, chest heaving as he pounded a treadmill to nowhere. He looked like Joe.

She stood and walked across to the coffee shop that faced the ocean and Robben Island on the horizon. She took a table in the shade of an umbrella and ordered an Evian, gradually slowing her breath.

Her gray top was dark with sweat between her breasts, and

her ponytail dripped down her back. She kept in shape, but she'd run nearly three miles at full speed, fueled by panic.

Her drink came, and she sipped the water, feeling a breeze cooling her. Relaxing.

Somebody had left a *Cape Times* on the table. She flicked through it, happy to be distracted by a world with problems greater than hers. Then she saw herself staring up from page three.

Roxy was no stranger to seeing her photograph, but this was a first: wrapped in the paramedic's blanket, dead husband lying in a pool of blood at her feet. If she'd been naked, in a pair of stilettos, it could have been a Helmut Newton. She remembered a man shooting pictures the night before. Assumed he was a cop. Not some paparazzo.

Roxy got the irony. She'd stepped away from the cameras after more than half a lifetime, tired of those flashbulbs leeching her soul. But she hadn't escaped them.

Beneath the picture was a caption. A few bald lines. No outrage. Matter of fact. A Cape Town businessman killed in a hijacking. Joe's name was mentioned. Hers wasn't. Just a pretty face.

Sex and death sold newspapers.

The photograph unsettled Roxy, as if her guilt was somehow visible on her face for the world to see. She knew she was being crazy, irrational, but she tore the picture out, wanting it hidden. There was no pocket in her sweatpants, so she held the scrap of newsprint in her closed hand.

She became aware of the smiles of two swarthy middle-aged men, newly arrived at the table nearest hers. They wore loafers without socks, gold chains in their graying chest hair. Eurotrash looking to get lucky. She finished her water, left money on the table, and went out to the street, feeling the men's eyes—like oily kalamata olives—glued to her ass.

As Roxy started to run toward home, still holding the crumpled photograph in her hand, she was startled by a blaring horn.

A black woman, bulky as a linebacker in her layered rags, stood staring at Roxy from the middle of the road, oblivious to the traffic that swarmed around her rusted shopping cart. The wire of the cart festooned with junk: broken mirrors, feathers and bone, a headless pink doll.

Roxy heard a shout from behind her. Spun. Just a taxi driver, yelling for passengers from the open window of a red minibus pimpled with dents. The taxi rattled off toward Sea Point, leaving smoke and hip hop hanging in the thick air.

When Roxy turned back, the woman was gone. Disappeared. Roxy thought she'd imagined her—some trick of sleep deprivation and paranoia—until she saw her limping down the ramp to Three Anchor Bay.

Roxy felt a jab of primitive fear. Too much bad stuff coming down. Mr. Handsome in the lineup. Her picture in the paper. And now this woman staring at Roxy like she was scanning her soul.

This is woo-woo bullshit, Roxy told herself. *Just keep your fucking head straight.*

Still, she found the fingers of her left hand reaching for the crucifix. Her right hand was clenched into a fist. When she opened it, she saw that the newsprint had started to bleed onto her skin. She balled the scrap of newspaper and threw it into a trash can.

Roxy headed home. Time to stop running.

chapter 10

DISCO DROVE. GODDY RODE SHOTGUN, ONE HAND ON THE COLT, THE other on the door handle, waiting for the right moment to jump out and grab the blondie. She ran ahead of them, along Victoria Road, her ponytail bouncing and her tight ass doing a slow dance beneath the black spandex.

"Not too fast." Goddy was sweating, from the heat and the tension. He stank like cat piss and onions.

"I go any slower, I fucken stop."

Disco didn't like to drive, and the stolen Toyota was boiling and lurching in first gear, the clutch burning. Cars were honking at them as their slow crawl backed up the traffic. The blondie ran light and easy. Like she could go on for hours. He couldn't help it: a picture of him riding that fit body just kept on coming into Disco's mind.

An hour earlier they'd boosted the Toyota out Goodwood side and driven to the house up the mountain, same place where they jacked the Benz. Goddy had rolled over his feeble arguments, and

Disco did what he always did: he let himself be moved along by the strong of the world, passive as a straw in a stream.

They'd parked across from the house. Waiting.

"What the fuck we sitting here for?" Disco asked.

When Goddy ignored him, Disco crushed another Mandrax pill into the broken bottleneck that served as a pipe. Images of Piper oozed their way into his consciousness, and his tattoos ached and burned like they had when they were gouged into his skin. The only way to handle the fear was to whack his brain befuck with an up-down cocktail of meth and Mandrax.

Goddy glimpsed her, the blondie, walking on the upper level of the house and pointed a dirty finger. "There's the bitch. We wait for her to come out. Take her when she's away from here so the panic button don't work."

"What if she don't come out?"

"Just shut the fuck up and wait."

Disco fired up the pipe, hit it hard, and held his breath like he was going for Olympic gold, then released billowing smoke. He offered the pipe to Goddy, who shook his head, piggy eyes glued to those wooden gates. Which slid open and revealed the blondie in the tight top and stretchy pants that showed her ass and her crack.

"Follow the bitch," Goddy had said.

Disco hadn't needed a second invitation.

They shadowed her along the oceanfront, sat sweating in the Toyota while she had a drink, waiting for the right moment. Now they were right behind her, ready to take her. The chorus of horns blared, and Disco stuck a tattooed arm out the window and gestured for the cars to pass him. A white guy with a red face shot past in an SUV and almost collected a truck head-on.

Disco, made mellow by the pipe, had to catch a cackle at that.

"She's turning, fucker!" Goddy smacked him on the shoulder with the barrel of the Colt, and Disco managed, just in time, to swing the wheel and follow the blondie into the short street that died at the steps that would lead her to the road high above and home.

"Put foot!"

Disco did as he was told and the Toyota surged past her, just beating her to the steps, and Goddy was out of the car before it stopped. He shoved the Colt into the woman's face and got a handful of her ponytail, dragging her toward the car. Disco reached over and cracked the rear door in time for Goddy to throw the blondie to the floor inside, then follow her in, leading with the gun.

"You move, you cunt, I shoot you." Goddy's knee was on her chest, and she was all but blowing the Colt barrel.

Disco slammed the car into reverse, backed up, found first gear, and sent the Toyota flying back the way they had come. Disco could hear the woman's breath coming in rasps. He caught her fragrance, something sweet like flowers over the girl sweat. Then something sour and sharp.

The smell of fear.

chapter 11

BILLY AFRIKA WAS BACK IN PROTEA STREET, LATE AFTERNOON shadows lying heavy across Barbara Adams's small house. Barbara came out the front door, locking the security gate after her. Billy opened the passenger side of the Hyundai, and she sat down next to him. Closed the door. Locked it.

She told him about Manson and his threats. Speaking quickly, her fingers worrying at a small rip in her dress. She cast nervous glances down the street. Eyes darting back toward her house. Looking anywhere but at Billy.

"He's serious. He'll rape her." Barbara's voice was tight, as if a hand squeezed her throat.

"It's not going to happen," Billy said, trying to sound like he meant it.

She still didn't look at him. "Last week they got hold of a girl from Marigold Street. Twelve years old. Her mommy sent her to the store for bread, and when she came back they caught her by the park. Afternoon still. Not even dark. Six of them raped her. The people in the houses knew what was going on, closed their doors and put their TVs up loud."

A movement caught Billy's eye, and he saw Jodie at the front door, looking out at them through the bars of the security gate. Barbara saw her too. Then the girl turned and disappeared into the house.

Barbara's eyes were on Billy now. "I can't let that happen to my child."

"It won't, Barbara."

"I need to give Manson his money. You understand?"

"I understand. I'm on it," Billy said. "He get it all? The money I deposited?"

She nodded. "Every last cent."

"Why didn't you tell me, Barbara? What was happening?"

"Tell you how? I didn't even know where you were. You just disappeared. Then that money was in the bank every month."

"I'm sorry. I thought I was helping."

Shaking her head. "It was a curse."

He couldn't find any words.

"I'll keep Jodie back from school for a few days. But I can't keep her locked up forever."

"I know that. There's cash I'm owed. I'll sort this."

"You're all I've got, Billy." Like she was damned.

"I won't let anything happen to Jodie. I promise."

Barbara was about to reply. Didn't. Left the car, walking up to the house, crossing the pavement where her husband had died. She unlocked the barred gate, paused for a moment, watching Billy. Then she locked the gate and closed the door.

Two years before, Billy Afrika had stood there, over Clyde Adams's gutted body, and made another promise. Swore he'd take care of his friend's family. He'd handed in his badge and become a mercenary. No one had used the word *mercenary*, of course. You were a *contractor*, skilled in *close protection*.

Joe Palmer's company, Strategic Solutions, had provided

bodyguards and security personal to trouble spots around the world. Iraq absorbed most of these men, often doing the work that the coalition forces couldn't be seen to be doing. So Billy had been part of a deal brokered by SS, which hooked him and some other South Africans up with a U.S. company in Baghdad.

Billy had wanted out of Cape Town. To get far away from the looming mountain and the sea and windswept sprawl of the Flats. Away from Piper caged in Pollsmoor Prison and the dust devils that danced on Clyde Adams's fresh grave.

Billy hadn't cared where he was posted, as long as he was being paid in dollars. Sending the money home to Clyde's wife and children. But all he'd done was leave them vulnerable to the vultures, made them prey by laying a boatload of cash on them. He had been a fucken idiot.

Billy started the car and drove away, feeling the weight of the Glock in his waistband. Fighting the temptation to drive across to Manson's house.

He could tackle the gangster head-on, pull a High Noon on a dusty White City street. Maybe he'd get lucky and kill him. Maybe he'd die trying. Even if he took Manson out, it would solve nothing. Another tattooed punk with cloned MTV moves would pimp-roll his way up the food chain.

And Clyde's family would be even more vulnerable.

Billy had to get Barbara and her kids out of Paradise Park, away from the gangs. Take them to one of the quiet fishing villages up the coast, where they could build new lives. That would cost money.

Billy drove up Main toward the city. Cape Town was putting on one of its shows, the evening sun painting the distant mountain a pale pink.

He reached for his cell phone and dialed his cop connection. Prayed he wouldn't get voice mail again. The cop answered.

Billy said, "You got that address for me yet, for Joe Palmer?"

"I do, ja." The man laughed. "Salt River morgue."

"The fuck you saying here?" Feeling his hands tighten on the wheel.

The cop told Billy Afrika about the hijacking and the murder. Told him where he could find Joe Palmer's widow. Up in Bantry Bay, where the sun was sagging behind Lion's Head, sending up golden rays like the holy light itself.

ROXY LAY ON her back, trapped between the front and rear seats, the ugly man on top of her, forcing the gun barrel into her mouth. He stank, and a drop of sweat fell from his forehead onto her cheek, where it rolled down like a tear.

She couldn't see the driver, from where she was wedged, but she had glimpsed his face as she was grabbed and thrown into the car. Mr. Handsome from the lineup. Meaning that the troll-like man had fired the first shot at Joe.

The troll was speaking, too quickly for her to catch the words, like a rabid dog barking. When she didn't react, he twisted the gun in her mouth and she tasted blood. "I say gimme the fucken keys."

She understood him this time and unclipped the keys from the cord around her neck. He grabbed them from her and held them up. A tattooed arm hooked over the front seat, and the driver took them. There was a panic button on the keychain that worked in a half-mile radius of her house. Not that she had thought of using it.

She had no idea where they were going. Maybe they were taking her out to the Cape Flats, the sprawling ghetto she'd glimpsed from the air, and come to know from crime statistics on TV. All she could see was the darkening blue of the sky through the side window. She heard traffic around her: the hiss of airbrakes from a truck, the incessant horn tapping of a minibus taxi—the wail of the doorman: *Caaaaaape Teeeuuuuun*—and the distant scream of a siren speeding toward somebody else's emergency.

They turned into a quieter street, and for a minute she heard only the rasping breath of the man above her, and the strain of the car's engine as it fought an incline. When she saw Lion's Head in the rear window, she knew they were taking her home.

The car slowed, and the squat man was speaking again. "What color you push to open the gate?" The gun barrel slipped, wet, from her mouth.

"Green. The green button."

He pushed the barrel against her forehead, hard enough to dent the skin. "If it's the panic, I fucken kill you."

He watched out the side window, his body tense over hers. His stink almost suffocating her. She heard the rattle of the castors in their rails as the gates slid open, and the man relaxed. The car rolled through and came to a stop with a squeak of brakes.

Mr. Handsome had the rear door open, and the troll backed out. The barrel of the gun didn't move from her. His T-shirt stuck to his paunch. She could see the word *Lifeguard* lettered across his flabby chest. She pulled herself upright and slid from the car into the perfection of a Cape Town summer's evening. The beautiful man was leering at her, his eyes all over her body like hot hands.

The short one grabbed her by the ponytail and yanked her head to the side, bringing her down to his height. Jammed the gun into her neck. "There anybody in the house?"

"No."

"The alarm on?"

"Yes."

"Okay. You open the door, and you punch the code. You do anything stupid, and you dead, hear me?"

"Yes. I hear you."

He let go of her hair and shoved her toward the front door. The other man handed Roxy the keys, and they watched as she unlocked the door, her hands shaking. The alarm started to pulse a rhythmic warning tone. She had thirty seconds to enter the code into the keypad inside the door, or the alarm would activate.

She punched in the five numbers. The beeping continued. The troll was coming at her. She punched in the numbers again. Got them right this time, and the beeping stopped.

Mr. Handsome looked around. "Nice place you got here." Like he was an invited guest.

The short man was up in her face. "Where's your room?"

Roxy pointed up the stairs. He shoved her forward, and she led them up past the pink room, to her bedroom.

The troll said, "You got a girl?"

At first she thought he was asking if she had a child. Then she realized he was talking about a domestic worker. She shook her head. "She's on vacation."

The beautiful man laughed. "I can see that."

The bedroom was a mess, the bed unmade, clothes strewn across the room. She had never been much for housework.

The short man grabbed a couple of pairs of tights that hung from the back of a chair and chucked them at his buddy. "Tie up her hands and feet."

"I have to pee," she said.

"Piss in your pants."

"Please. Let me use the bathroom."

Mr. Handsome, walking over with the tights in his hand, smiled at her. "Let her take a piss, man. I watch her." Something filthy in that smile.

"I take her," said the squat man. "You start checking through the closets."

He pushed her toward the en-suite bathroom. Stood in the doorway, watching her. Roxy knew he wasn't going anywhere. She sat down on the toilet and pulled down the lycra pants. Doing her best to keep herself covered.

He looked at her with disinterest. "Hurry the fuck up."

At first she thought the pee wouldn't come, with his eyes on her, but she managed to let go. Felt the relief. She wiped herself, and they went back out.

The beautiful man had yanked open the drawers of the vanity table and found her jewelry: rings, necklaces, earrings. The spoils of having been married to Joe Palmer for five years.

"These real?" he asked, fingers dripping Cartier and Van Cleef and Arpels.

"Yes." She watched as he filled his pockets.

The troll shoved her to the carpet. "Tie her up. Come."

Mr. Handsome enjoyed doing it, his hands lingering on her body as he bound her wrists behind her back and tied her ankles together.

The ugly man sat down on the bed. He stared at her, then he smiled, showing uneven black teeth. "We know what you done."

She looked at him, shook her head.

"You kill your fucken husband and tell the cops it's us."

She stared him down. "What do you want?"

He shrugged. "Call it . . . *compensation*." He liked the taste of the word enough to repeat it. "*Compensation*." Then he laughed again. The beautiful one laughed too.

The troll stood. "Watch her. I gonna go check the place out."

As soon as they were alone, Mr. Handsome came over to Roxy, took her chin in his tattooed hand, and forced her to look up into his face. It was a terrifying face. All the elements that determined beauty were there: almond eyes, a finely shaped nose, full lips, high cheekbones. His hair was only slightly wavy and fell across his forehead. But it was a face that lacked humanity. The eyes were empty and fogged. The face of a fallen angel. She could smell the chemicals on his body.

He smiled at her. The perfect smile ruined by a missing tooth. He squatted down beside her and traced a finger along the bare skin of her arm. She felt the faint blonde down stand in revulsion and fear as his hand moved along her shoulder and followed the outline of her breast through the damp top. She could feel his stale breath on her face.

His hand dropped, caressing her inner thigh, smiling at her. Seductive. Believing she was attracted to him. He moved himself forward so she could feel his hard-on against her knee.

"You and me, we can make beautiful babies."

She twisted away from him, tried to kick out with her bound ankles and only succeeded in toppling to the side. She lay with her face against the carpet and saw the short man walk back in.

"Leave her be. Plenty time for that." He came over to her and grabbed her arm, pulling her upright. He tapped her chin with the gun barrel. "Where's the safe?"

Roxy shook her head. "There is no safe." She was telling the truth. If there had been, she would've emptied it by now.

"I said, where's the fucken safe?" Holding the barrel against her cheek.

Again she shook her head.

He grabbed her by the hair and pulled her forward so she knelt, her chin almost touching the carpet. He pushed the gun up against the base of her skull.

"Tell me, or I shoot you."

"There's no safe."

Roxy heard him cock the gun. She stared down at the carpet, wondering if this knotted woolen pile was the last thing she would see. When she closed her eyes, she knew that it wasn't. Because she saw Joe, his face warping from the impact of the bullet. She could go either way on the whole afterlife deal, but she had this premonition that Joe was out there somewhere. Waiting for her. A trigger pull away.

Then she felt the pressure from the barrel ease. She realized she was holding her breath and released it. Relaxed her locked neck muscles. The troll shoved a shoe beneath her chin, a torn

Adidas that stank of years of sweat and foot rot. Pushed her until she toppled over onto her back, staring up at him. He pointed the gun at her, held it unwavering for an eternity, then let it droop to his side.

"Okay, this is how it gonna be. You gonna get us a hunnerd thou. Cash. By tomorrow. Hear me?" She nodded, playing along. "You gonna give us your cell number, and we call you and tell you where to take the money. Okay?" She nodded again. "You not gonna go to the cops 'cause you gonna get your ass thrown in *chookie*. Big-time. I tell you something, Miss America, those bitches in the cells are gonna have fun with you. You get what I'm saying here?"

"I understand. I'll do it."

"If you don't, we come here and kill you. But first I leave him alone with you for a nice time. Get me?" she nodded, aware of the beautiful man's corrupt eyes on her, still feeling the memory of his hands. "Okay. Meanwhile we gonna take some down payments. If that's okay with you?" He laughed.

She watched as they looted the bedroom. Jewelry. Joe's camera. Designer jeans. For brown girls out on the Flats, she supposed. Roxy could hear them busy in the rest of the house. Hated the thought of those filthy bodies in the pink room. She didn't know how long she lay there, but every second was another second of life. At least her brains weren't part of the pattern on the carpet.

Mr. Handsome came in, Joe's laptop slung over his shoulder and a DVD player under one arm. "So, I see you again tomorrow, okay?"

"Yes."

"You stay beautiful, hear me?" He tipped her a wink and walked out.

The ugly man returned and stood over her with the gun. She looked up in time to see him reverse his grip, swing his arm back, and bring the butt down. The blow took her above her right ear, and she crumpled, as blood sprang vivid on the carpet beneath her.

Roxy lay stunned, bleeding.

Heard doors slamming and the car driving away.

THE LONG CAPE Town twilight slowly turned the sky to velvet as Billy Afrika parked across from the house that hung like bird shit from the cliff in Bantry Bay. He saw the high walls, the electric fence, and the wooden gates standing open onto a short brick driveway. Most of the structure was below the level of the cliff, but he'd checked out the house as he drove along the road that snaked its way along the coast, far below.

Joe Palmer had done well out of his blood money.

Billy's cop connection over at Bellwood South had come through with more than this address. Also told Billy that the widow, Roxanne Palmer, had been called in earlier that day for a lineup. Ernie Maggott had pulled in two White City punks: a 26 and a tik head. The woman hadn't made an ID, and the men were kicked loose. So she should be inside now, the grieving widow.

Billy Afrika had heard of her, Joe Palmer's trophy wife. The American model. But he'd never met her. Time to change that.

There was no sign of movement in the house, and no lights burned as darkness crept up the mountain. But the gates were open. Billy left the car and crossed the road. As he neared the gates he could see they were trying to close, humming and clicking on their tracks, making small movements toward each other, then retreating, like nervous dancers.

He walked to the front door and knocked. Knocked again. Reached out and tried the door. It opened. He stepped inside the house. He'd been a cop long enough to recognize the aftermath of a home invasion. In the fading light he saw a tangle of wires where the TV and stereo should have been. Empty shelves. Books, CDs and DVDs littering the floor.

The Glock was in his hand. "Mrs. Palmer?"

No answer. He scanned the lower level, then followed the Glock barrel up the stairs. A few closed doors. One door open at the end of the corridor. Billy paused in the doorway, saw the overturned chair, closets gaping and drawers yanked and thrown onto the floor. He saw a blonde woman lying beside the bed, hands and legs bound behind her back. There was blood in her hair and on the carpet beneath her head.

Her eyes were closed, and she wasn't moving.

Billy almost turned on his heel and got the hell out of there. Stopped himself.

He crouched down and was about to touch her neck to feel for a pulse when her eyes flickered and opened.

chapter 12

A 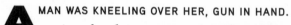 MAN WAS KNEELING OVER HER, GUN IN HAND.

Another brown man. Another gun.

"If you're here to rip me off, you're too fucking late." The tremor in her voice ruined her attempt at bravado.

The gun disappeared into the waistband of his jeans. "Take it easy. I worked for your husband."

That local accent, but watered down. And a slow delivery, unlike so many of these people who sounded like jackhammers on speed.

He untied her wrists and ankles. "You okay?"

"Hey, I'm golden."

She stood, felt faint, and sat down on the bed. The brown man stretched across and switched on the bedside lamp. She saw he had eyes the color of pale emeralds. Beautiful eyes.

"Want me to call an ambulance?"

"No."

Roxy looked into those green eyes but saw the paramedics

standing up from Joe's body, faces fixed in expressions of professional sympathy, latex snapping as they shed their bloody gloves.

She tried out something that resembled a smile. "Why don't you wait downstairs while I get cleaned up?"

"Sure." He gave her a last look, then turned for the door. A lean man in a casual cotton shirt and Levis, Havaianas on his feet. He looked like a boxer, one good enough not to have had his face messed up. Like a younger Sugar Ray Leonard.

BILLY STOOD AT the wall of glass, watching the moon rising over the ocean. A speedboat sped across the waves far below, and he could just about hear the impact on the water.

The widow, the American blonde, was upstairs getting cleaned up.

He didn't give a shit about her and her troubles. He had his own. But she was a potential solution to one of them: the money. So he had to deal with this, even though he wanted to walk out the door and drive away and forget he'd ever set eyes on her.

He turned. She came down the stairs, still wearing sweatpants, but she'd put on a fresh T-shirt. She was tall, slender but not scrawny, athletic in her tight workout gear. Barefoot. One of those women who could make a body bag look like a designer outfit.

"Feeling better?"

She nodded. "Just a bit of a sore head." That American accent.

"You should see a doctor."

"No. I'm fine. Honest."

She sat down on the sofa, tucked her legs under her. "You haven't told me your name." Looking at him with those blue eyes. There was still dried blood in her blonde hair, turning it strawberry above her right ear.

"Billy Afrika."

"Mr. Afrika . . ." She stopped. Laughed. Covered her mouth. "I'm sorry."

"What's wrong?"

"Nothing. Sounds like I'm announcing the winner of a muscle pageant, is all." She smiled one of those smiles designed to melt a man's heart. Did nothing for him. "Sorry, I guess I'm a little lightheaded. And a bit stressed out."

"You would be. Call me Billy."

"And I'm Roxy. What are you doing here, Billy?" Then she held up a hand—long elegant fingers. He noticed she wasn't wearing a wedding band. "Wait. Let me guess. Joe owed you money." He nodded. "You and the whole country. The phone has been going crazy since this morning. People pretending to sympathize but asking polite questions about who's handling his debts. I've got to tell you, I know nothing about Joe's business."

Billy shrugged. "What happened here?"

"I was out running. Two guys abducted me, got me into a car at gunpoint, and brought me home. Tied me up. Took what they wanted."

"They knew where you live?"

"No. I told them." Switched on that smile again. "I had a gun shoved in my mouth. Guess it loosened my tongue."

"These guys, they my color?"

She paused a moment before answering. "The one was. The other was much darker. Why?"

"Just getting the picture. Anything about them stick out?"

"Other than they held gun to my head, tied me up, and robbed me?" Laughing his question away.

Something wasn't adding up. Billy had enough experience of trauma to know that everybody responded differently. Tough guys shook and wept; fragile women were stoic. Maybe this attitude of Roxanne Palmer's was just a coping mechanism. But still, she should be screaming for the cops, not tossing one-liners.

Billy said, "Pretty rough. Coming after what happened last night."

"Yeah. Great city you got here, Billy." Smiling at him like a professional.

He fixed a look on her that dried up that smile. "We should get the cops."

"I don't think so. Forgive me if I've lost faith in South African law enforcement."

Who could argue with that? But there was something in the air, hovering. Something he couldn't quite get.

"The two guys, they maybe tell you they're coming back?"

She shook her head. "No."

"Try to scare you, to stop you going to the cops?"

Still shaking her head, but something clouded those eyes.

"You were at a lineup this afternoon, weren't you?"

A look of surprise. "How do you know that?"

"I used to be a cop. I'm still connected."

"Yeah. I went out to some place called Bellwood South."

"But you didn't recognize the men?'

"No. Never seen any of them before."

Now he was sure she was lying. Something turned in his head, just a little, and a couple of pieces clicked into place. Not everything. But enough for him to know what he was going to do next.

She had those blue eyes on him. "What did you do, for Joe?"

"Security contractor. In Iraq. I never got my last two months' paychecks."

"I'm sorry. Maybe after the funeral, when I've sat down with the lawyers . . ."

Sure, he thought. *You'll sit down with the lawyers, and they'll fill your head with ways to get out of paying Joe's debts. Not going to happen.*

He got to his feet. "I'll be in touch."

She unfolded those long legs from under her and stood, like

she'd rehearsed that move many times before. She probably had. In her bare feet she was almost his height.

"Thank you. For saving me."

"Oh, I didn't save you, Mrs. Palmer. Just untied you." He headed for the door.

She followed him out into the driveway. He felt her eyes on him as he walked through the open gates and crossed to the Hyundai.

Billy looked back and saw her lift the gate clicker. The gates didn't move, just buzzed and whirred like bugs caught in a bottle. She pressed the button again. This time the gates rattled closed, shutting her off from the world.

chapter 13

PIPER LAY ON HIS BUNK IN POLLSMOOR PRISON, TRYING TO FIND oblivion in a mixture of weed and Mandrax. A young 28 soldier crouched over him, skin jabbing another teardrop into Piper's face with a needle and black boot polish.

Teardrop number nineteen. In honor of the dead Pig.

The soldier lifted the needle and wiped away blood with torn newspaper. Piper took another hit on the white pipe, the bottleneck glowing red in his hand. He held the smoke in his lungs, letting it curl out through his nose and mouth, waiting for the numbness and the relief, waiting for the pain to leave his heart on the cloud of smoke. It didn't happen.

The news of Disco's release had reached him with the supper cart. Charges had been dropped. The elation he'd felt for the last day had drained slowly from him like stale piss down a backed-up urinal.

The blaring theme from *The Bold and the Beautiful* interrupted Piper's white pipe reverie. As the murderers and rapists crowded around the TV, voices were raised and opinions clashed on what this episode would bring the Forrester family. *The Bold* had been Disco's favorite. They had lain together each evening on Piper's bunk, and Disco had fed him or clipped his toenails while they watched.

That familiar music was more than Piper could stand right now. He was too raw.

Piper set the pipe aside and reached for the heavy lock that dangled from his steel trunk. In one motion he sat up and threw the lock at the TV.

The smashed tube fizzed and sparked. Then silence.

The men turned and stared, but none of them dared challenge him.

Piper tamped more weed and another white pill into the pipe and fired it up. He pulled on it while the youth set to work again on the tattoo.

After the teardrop was done, he lay on his bunk and smoked pipe after pipe, oblivious to the snores and moans around him, the stench of unwashed bodies, the sounds of men fucking like dogs. The smoke brought him no peace.

Instead it brought him images of Disco's body. His mouth. His eyes. Piper saw his own hands on the boy as he branded him. He felt that moment of surrender as he lay face-to-face with him and possessed him.

He didn't know why he loved the boy. Didn't know how that emotion had grown from the barren soil of his dark heart. But he knew that it had, and that it had changed him.

All he could think of was Disco. Alone outside.

Piper was a man of the Four Corners. Pollsmoor was his universe. The world outside was alien and terrifying.

He was first imprisoned in apartheid South Africa. At a time when the white man had made the brown man into nothing. Less than shit. The prisons were segregated, just like the rest of the country. But Piper quickly understood that in prison you could be king, ruling over brown men weaker than yourself, if you made your way up in the number gangs. Easy for a man born into brutality.

The first time he came close to parole he killed another prisoner in the yard, under the eyes of the guards. Had more time added. But brown lives were cheap, and within a few years he was up for parole again. So he killed a guard. A white one.

This got him the death sentence. Commuted to life when Nelson Mandela walked out of his cell and took over the country. Him and his darkies. Outlawed the death penalty. Only favor a darky had ever done Piper.

Left him secure in the knowledge that he would see out his days in the Four Corners.

Until two years ago.

They had come to him, the bastards in their uniforms, and told him he was free to go.

He shook his head, said they must be fucken joking. They showed him the paper. A general amnesty: selected convicts being released to cull the population in the overburdened prisons.

He saw his name on the paper and knew it was a mistake. He was proved right, later, when he discovered he'd been freed instead of a man who shared his name. A petty thief who lay dying of AIDS in the prison hospital.

But the next day they took back the orange jumpsuit, gave Piper his clothes, and left him standing outside the gates, a duffel bag in his hand and a hundred rand in his pocket.

Piper went back to Paradise Park, Dark City side, because that was all he knew.

Stepped out of the taxi in his clothes from twenty years ago, carrying a new Okapi knife. He saw the tattooed boys on the street. They had never been near Pollsmoor but called themselves 28s. One of them was stupid enough to follow Piper and speak to him in a version of the prison language that was garbled, butchered.

Piper sodomized the boy in an empty lot littered with bald tires and cinder blocks and rotting garbage, shredded plastic buzzing in the wind. Cut his throat and left him there with the trash, his jeans and boxers bunched around his ankles.

Piper knew he couldn't stay out there, in the world. He wanted to go home.

Remembered the cop who arrested him twenty years before: Clyde Adams. Set him on his course. Something about killing him appealed to Piper's sense of balance. It wasn't revenge.

He found out where Clyde lived. Married now, with kids. Over White City side. Piper was unafraid as he crossed Main Road and walked onto enemy turf, his gang tattoos making him as distinct as a leopard prowling through a herd of buck.

He went to the cop's house and waited and watched.

It was late in the day, and shadows blackened the hard white sand of the Flats. He let a shadow suck him in, stood unmoving. Felt he was invisible. He had no idea how long he stood there. A car pulled up, and Clyde climbed out. Twenty years older. Thicker around the middle, wearing civvy clothes. The black hair still grew straight and coarse as thatch from his head.

A woman and two kids—boy and girl—were in the car with the cop. They unloaded plastic shopping bags from the trunk. Piper heard the girl laugh, like a snatch of music floating to him on the wind. Clyde carried a bag, his arm around the woman as they went into the yard of the house.

Piper freed himself from the shadow and crossed the road, the Okapi knife held ready.

The cop sensed Piper and turned. Recognized him, gun hand full of shopping. Piper stepped in and sank the blade into Clyde's gut, heard him grunt. The bag fell, and pink sausage and red tomatoes spilled onto the sand. The woman screamed.

Piper gutted the cop, pulling the knife up to his sternum, felt the blade stop. Clyde sank to the ground, trying to hold himself in, his blood patterning the sand. Piper cut a smile into the cop's throat. Saw another car speeding up. And another man from the past, running at him with a gun.

Billy Afrika. A coward he should have finished twenty years ago.

Piper smiled, raised his hands, and let the knife slip from his fingers, didn't take his eyes from Billy's but caught the hard shine of the blade where it lay in the cop's blood.

Billy had the gun on him, the barrel shaking only a little. Piper could see the finger tightening on the trigger. Saw the sweat on Billy's face.

Waited.

Then the gun drooped, and Billy spun him and cuffed him, shoved him to the sand.

Piper lay and watched the last of the cop's life seep from him, his foot drumming like the hoof of a slaughterhouse sheep, kicking up dust.

The woman cradled the dead cop's head. Saying over and over again, "Clyde, Clyde, Clyde," like the words could reverse what had been done.

Piper had felt a great peace, hearing the music of the sirens. Knowing he was going home.

Agitated now, lying on his prison bunk, the white pipes doing nothing to calm him or still the craving in his heart. He knew there was no other way. If Disco wasn't coming back to him, he'd have to go out again into the world.

Bring his wife home.

chapter 14

BILLY AFRIKA DROVE THROUGH WHITE CITY AND TURNED INTO LILAC Road, the sparse streetlights weeping yellow into the cloud of dust that blanketed the Cape Flats. The wind was up, and anyone with half a brain and a house to go to was indoors. The homeless found doorways and holes in the ground and drew plastic over their faces to keep the sand out, like urban bedouins. Or they fried their brains on foil bags of rotgut wine and let the sand pepper their prone forms like buckshot.

Billy liked the wind. Liked this display of natural force, knew that when it blew itself out by morning, even the Flats would lie still and clean under a pristine blue sky.

The banging had started again, coming from the trunk, as if somebody was trying to kick his way out by dislodging the rear seat. Billy saw a deep pothole in the poorly paved road and accelerated, smacked it at speed—what the fuck, it was a rental car—and heard a metallic thump and a muffled cry. He laughed as he flicked the turn signal and slowed outside the two-story house that loomed over its squat neighbors like a guard tower. The house was surrounded by a high wall and electric fencing. A heavy iron gate barred access. Billy stayed in the car. Leaned on the horn.

He saw a face at one of the windows on the top floor of the house, caught a curse carried on the wind, and the gate blew open. Two men stood there, T-shirts and low-slung jeans billowing in the southeaster. One man, small and skinny, carried an Uzi. The other, a big piece of meat, held a .22 Smith and Wesson snubnose at his side, almost invisible in his paw. Liked to get nice and intimate when he killed, this one.

"The fuck you want?" the man with the Uzi asked, coming at him.

Billy cracked the window an inch, enough to take a blast of sand in both eyes. "I got something for Manson."

A glimmer of recognition crossed the man's face. "What?"

"Just open, man. Or he kick your ass."

The two men shouted questions at each other, then pushed against the wind, forcing the gate open far enough to allow him to drive in. The snout of the Uzi followed him. A floodlight on a motion detector kicked in as Billy parked next to a black Hummer. He stood up out of the Hyundai and felt nothing more than a breeze in the sheltered yard.

The Uzi was right up to Billy, and he lifted his hands. The man with the .22 frisked him like a pro. Billy had wedged the Glock under the driver's seat, so the man came up empty.

Manson emerged from a side door of the house, dressed in expensive white sweats and a peaked cap, as branded as a sports celebrity.

"What you want here, Barbie?"

"I got something of yours."

"Ja?"

Billy walked to the trunk. "I'm gonna open this, okay?"

Manson nodded, and the Uzi kept its black eye on him.

Billy popped the trunk, and Godwynn MacIntosh, bleeding from the nose, ears, and mouth, sprang up like a bloody jack-in-the-box.

"And what the fuck mess is this?" Manson asked.

ANOTHER CALL TO his man at Bellwood South—and the promise of more money—had got Billy the names of the two geniuses. And Disco De Lilly's address. The cop had also passed on a piece of information that gave Billy pause: Disco had been Piper's wife when he'd done time in Pollsmoor.

Snag a thread in the Cape Flats tapestry, and it unraveled all the way to Piper.

Things hadn't added up back in Bantry Bay. That blonde was into something, and Billy couldn't shake the feeling that the two fuckheads from the lineup were involved. He didn't care about Roxanne Palmer, but there was a 26 in the frame. One of Manson's crew. And Billy needed leverage with Manson.

Knew that he'd have the best chance of scaring the truth out of the sex-boy. Spending time as Piper's wife would have tenderized the toughest piece of meat.

He found Disco sitting on the step of his *zozo*, sheltering from the wind, shirtless body seething with prison ink, his head lost in a cloud of tik. Billy grabbed him by the hair, smacked the pipe from his mouth, and threw him into the hut. Kicked the door shut behind him. A naked bulb dangled from the ceiling, washing the *zozo* with piss-yellow light.

Disco was a pretty boy. A useless shit, one of life's rejects. But pretty.

He looked to be in his early twenties but was one of those men who would still be called a boy even when he was middle-aged. If he lived that long. Disco was trying to get up, trying to glue back together the pieces of his day. Billy slapped him through the face and sent him flying against the wall, where he slumped under the framed photograph of a woman who looked too much like him to be anyone other than his mother.

His body hitting the wall had set the frame askew.

"This your mommy?" Billy pointed to the picture. Disco nodded, panting. Billy approached the photograph and stuck out a hand.

"Don' break it. Please!" The voice hoarse and plaintive, fighting its way through tik smoke and fear.

"I'm not gonna break it. What you think I am?" Instead Billy carefully straightened the picture. "She passed on, your mommy?"

The pretty boy was nodding. "Fifteen years now."

Billy squatted down in front of Disco, showed him the Glock in his waistband, figured there was no need to draw it.

"Okay, this is how it's gonna go." Disco looked from the gun to Billy's face. "I'm gonna ask you a couple of questions, and, on your mommy's grave, you gonna tell me the truth. You understand?"

"Ja."

"So say it."

"Say what?"

"Jesus. Say, 'On my mommy's grave I'm gonna tell you the truth.' "

"On my mommy's grave I'm gonna tell you the truth."

"Good. Now understand me here, I'm not a cop no more, so I'm not interested in busting your dirty ass. But you try to lie to me, and I'll kill you. You hearing me?"

Disco nodded. "Ja. I hear."

"You and your buddy Godwynn jacked a car last night. Up Bantry Bay side. A Benz. That right?"

Disco hesitated. Billy pointed to the gun, then pointed to the photograph. The boy nodded.

"A man was shot. A whitey. You shoot him?"

Disco shook his head. "Not me. He try to fight, so Goddy plug him in the leg. But it's not us who kill him."

Billy took this in. "How many times Godwynn shoot him?"

"Just the once. And then we was in the car and away."

"Where's the gun?"

"He drop it there. Goddy."

Billy was staring but looking straight through this weak, pretty boy. Seeing another face, with wide blue eyes. Seeing the truth.

Meanwhile, he was scaring the tik head shitless. He refocused on Disco and saw that he had drawn his knees up, covering his face with his arms.

"I'm telling it true, I swear on my mommy."

"Relax. I believe you. You and Goddy went back to the house today. That right?" Billy could see a lie coming. "You doing very nice so far, Disco. Don't fuck it up now."

Disco shrugged. "Ja. We took some stuff."

"What you tell that blondie?"

"Tell her that we gonna come back tomorrow for money. If she don't give it, we is gonna go to the cops and tell them she shoot her husband."

Billy laughed. "And she believed you?"

Disco shrugged. "It were Goddy's idea."

"Fucken shit idea." Billy looked around the filthy hut. "Where's the stuff?"

"Goddy took it."

"Now, Goddy, he's one of Manson's boys? 26? American?"

"Ja."

"Manson know about this visit of yours to the house?" Disco shook his head. "So it was freelance, like?"

The boy nodded. "You working for Manson?"

Billy slapped Disco hard enough to snap his head back against the wall. "I ask the questions. You answer. Okay?"

Disco blinked. "Okay."

Billy stood. He grabbed the boy by his nice wavy hair and pulled him to his feet.

"Now take me to Goddy."

Disco's head was wobbling like one of those toy dogs in the back of old men's cars.

"He kill me, man."

"Not gonna happen." Billy shoved the boy toward the closet. "Come, put on a shirt. Cover up your wedding pictures."

ROXY SAT IN the looted room for a long time after Billy Afrika left. Zoned out. Blank. Wondering just what the hell she had set in motion by lifting that gun and pulling the trigger.

She forced herself to get up from the sofa. Thought of the two brown men, found herself wiping at her skin as if she could somehow slough them off. Took in the mess around her. Not only had they robbed her; they'd taken pleasure in trashing the place. And they were coming back tomorrow.

Roxy could process the assault on her, didn't care about what they'd done to the rest of the house, but knew she'd crack if they'd violated the pink room.

She had to find out. Had to open that door.

Roxy climbed the stairs. Stopped at the closed door. Put her hand out toward the doorknob. Hesitated. Finally turned it and walked in. Stood in the dark, listening to herself breathe. Then she found the wall switch, and soft light bloomed.

The pink room. Rose-colored wallpaper, butterflies dangling from the ceiling, a crib, a walking ring, and a carpet littered with infant toys. A nursery. Waiting for the daughter who had died inside her. The room untouched by the men.

She could close the door now and go downstairs and get blasted on vodka. But she knew she needed to stay here; this was the place where she could cauterize the pain and the grief.

And the tendrils of guilt tugging at her over what she had done to Joe Palmer.

Roxy sat down on the floor beside the crib and let herself remember.

She saw herself in this room a month ago. Her heavily pregnant, absurdly happy self.

Like most things in Roxy's life, getting pregnant had been an accident. A year or two into their marriage, Joe's sexual demands had cooled. She guessed he was outsourcing his needs, as he would have said. Roxy looked good on his arm, but his preferences ran to rougher trade between the sheets.

Fine with her.

She'd taken a break from the Pill, intending to have a loop fitted, which she'd never got around to doing. So a few weeks after they'd had an unexpected bout of hurried, suffocating sex—Joe drunk enough to want her—Roxy found herself peeing on a pregnancy test, watching as a thin blue line traced itself in the little window. At first it seemed a no-brainer; she'd take herself down to a smart private clinic and get this thing handled.

Then an idea snuck up on her: what if she kept it? Not an it. A baby, a child. Suddenly she understood that having a baby was everything she'd wanted. She just hadn't known it.

For the first time in her life she felt love. For herself and the child growing inside her.

The notion that Joe Palmer was a less than perfect father was washed from her mind by hormones and happiness. When she told him he she was pregnant, he looked at her and shrugged. He was hardly home as the months went by and her belly swelled. She was too happy to notice that his trademark smug expression had become haunted and he was drinking even more than usual, as if he was selling his soul along with men and weapons. Her happiness made her blind to the warning signs.

The ultrasound showed she was carrying a girl, so she created a bedroom for her daughter. A room that seemed to capture all she'd never had as a child.

A fairy tale.

A fantasy.

The pink room.

Roxy was in the room the night it happened, hanging a mobile over the crib, a butterfly with dangly feelers on springs. She heard the gates rolling open and saw the headlights of Joe's car flame against the window. Something—the time it took him to leave the car, maybe—warned her, and she tensed at the scrape of the key in the front door.

She heard his voice. "Roxanne?"

He only called her that when he was in one of his mean moods. Joe had smacked her around a little in the early years, until she'd threatened to leave him. He'd stopped with the fists, but his mouth still spewed bile when he was angry and drunk.

"Roxanne!"

She didn't answer. Heard Joe coming up the stairs, wheezing, his footfalls heavy and unsteady. Roxy left the pink room and shut the door. She didn't want him to poison the air inside. Met him on the landing. He stank of sweat and booze, his linen shirt wet against his paunch. His eyes were dark little pebbles, tongue probing his gums and cheeks like an eel feeding.

Now she knew why he had taken so long to leave the car; he'd been doing a line. She could see traces of white powder smeared on his unshaven upper lip.

She tried to brush past him, to get to her bedroom and lock herself inside.

He grabbed her arm. "The fuck you going?"

"You're hurting me, Joe."

Roxy shook her arm loose, but he shoved her back against the wall next to the stairs and kissed her, forcing his tongue into her mouth. His breath was sour, and his tongue felt rough as a cat's. His flab a mold around her hard belly.

She got out from under him, left him off balance for a moment, and almost got away. But her hair was loose, and her sudden movement swung it up toward his hand. Joe grabbed her hair and pulled her back, forcing her down onto her knees, her eyes blurring from tears of pain.

With his free hand he unzipped himself. "Blow me, baby." He was getting hard, turned on by hurting her.

She grabbed the thing, digging her nails into the shaft.

Mistake.

The pain enraged him, and as she pushed herself to her feet he punched her in the face. She had her back to the stairs and felt her feet losing their grip on the landing. In the hours that she floated backward and down, suspended outside of time, she believed everything was going to be all right, that she and her daughter would somehow be cushioned.

Until she hit.

Her belly smashed into the hard edge of a step, halfway down. She rolled the rest of the way, unable to stop herself, and landed on the tiled floor, the air crushed from her lungs. As she passed out, Roxy knew her daughter had died inside her.

When she came round, she was lying on the floor with paramedics kneeling over her. She could feel the blood between her legs. Joe had managed to clean himself up, hovering, impersonating a concerned husband. Telling the medics that she slipped on the stairs and fell.

She was too numb to think of contradicting this fiction. The next few days were a blur of hospital wards and sedatives. She came home a few days later with milk in her breasts and a still-swollen belly, but an empty womb.

A womb, the doctors told her, that would never hold a baby again.

The emptiness extended beyond her womb. She felt nothing. No pain. No grief. No anger. Just an all-consuming emptiness. Wanting to be dead.

She sat in the pink room now, hugging her knees, and let the tears come for the first time. It was only when she had lifted the gun the night before, that the wall had burst and rage and grief had swamped her, as she realized, of course, it wasn't herself she wanted dead.

It was Joe.

chapter 15

BILLY AND DISCO DROVE THROUGH PARADISE PARK, LOOKING FOR Godwynn. Disco saying Goddy didn't stay any place permanently, moved between those friends and family who would put up with him. They stopped outside a ghetto block to talk to a girl with a hairlip, who went all moist for Disco and told him that Goddy was at Five Star. A White City shebeen.

Billy parked up the block from the booze joint, beyond the tepid wash of a solitary streetlight, the Hyundai lost in a row of tired cars surrendering to rust. Five Star occupied a cramped house, surrounded by a wall of concrete wagon wheels, a sad string of colored lights dangling over the front gate. An insistent hip-hop bassline thumped from inside, like a drunk smashing his head against a wall.

There was no way Billy was going into Five Star. He would be outgunned. Things were different from back in the day, when gangsters were all about knives. Like Piper. Hard men who liked to do their killing up close and personal. Now any pimply-faced punk with a buck in his pocket scored himself a gun. The morgues were full of dead brown men sporting bullet holes.

Billy, in pre-Iraq days, had met U.S. Army doctors doing volunteer work out on the Flats, skilling up on gunshot wounds. It was the closest thing they could find to a war zone before Shock and Awe.

Disco said, "Can I ask a question?"

Billy nodded. "Ask."

"What you gonna do with me?"

"You show me Goddy, and we'll see."

Disco saw how Billy was staring at him. "What?"

"It true what I hear? You were Piper's wife?"

The boy's expression was answer enough. "I don't like to talk about it."

Billy nodded. "Okay. I can respect that."

"You know Piper?" Disco asked.

"Oh ja. Me and Piper go back a long, long ways." Billy felt his scars itching. "He still a big man in Pollsmoor?"

"Ja. A general. He fucken run the place." Disco squirmed next to him. "You got a smoke for me?"

Billy shook his head. "Don't smoke." Watched an alky stumble past the car, stop under the light, and piss on his shoes. "Tell me, why do they call you Disco?"

" 'Cause I got the dance moves, like."

"So what's your real name?"

"Ferdinand," Disco said. Saw Billy's look. "After my granddad. He were a Frenchman."

Billy laughed. "Stick with Disco."

Then the boy was sliding down in his seat as a squat, dark man in his twenties came out of the shebeen, swapped words with a couple of guys hanging in the garden, laughed, and walked down the street, away from the car. The walk of a man with booze in his blood and money in his pocket.

"That Goddy?"

Disco nodded. "Ja."

"He pack?"

"Most times. A Colt."

Billy looked at the pathetic figure at his side and took pity on him. Figured that after spending years as Piper's sex-boy he had suffered enough.

"You can go," Billy said. Disbelief made Disco hesitate. "Fucken go before I change my mind."

The door opened, and Disco let the wind blow him in the opposite direction from his friend. Billy started the car and rolled after Godwynn. A short man with an even shorter future.

MANSON LOOKED FROM Godwynn, bleeding in the trunk, to Billy. "The fuck's going on, Barbie?"

"Your boy here pulled a freelance today, Cape Town side. Home invasion, like. He's already sold the stuff."

Manson squinted down at the man in the trunk. "This true?"

Godwynn shook his bloody head vigorously. It must have hurt because he stopped pretty smartly. "He lie, this fucker."

"Why don't you check his pockets?" Billy asked.

Manson nodded, and the big man holstered his piece and stepped forward. Frisked Goddy. Found about two grand in cash and handed it to Manson. Billy could only imagine the real value of the stuff the moron had sold.

Manson slapped Goddy. "Where you get this?"

Godwynn was trying to speak faster than his swollen lips would allow. "I swear, on my life, Manson. This isn't true."

Billy gonged the lid of the trunk down on the idiot's head to shut him up. Gave Manson an outline of what had gone down up in Bantry Bay. He saw that the gangster was buying. No fool, Manson.

Billy turned as a girl, maybe thirteen or fourteen, appeared in the doorway. A hungry look on her face as she watched.

Manson said, "Go inside, baby. Daddy's working."

"I wanna see."

"Bianca, go inside." Manson waved a dismissive hand.

Reluctantly, the girl went back into the house, and the scrawny man with the Uzi shut the door.

Manson turned to Billy. "And what's your interest in this, Barbie?"

"The woman they robbed is my client. I'm bodyguarding her."

Manson laughed. "Shit bodyguard. Letting this in." Nodding at the man in the trunk.

"Got on the payroll after they pulled their move. But there's something I want from you, in exchange for this favor."

"Ja? And what's that?"

"I want you to leave Clyde Adams's girl alone."

He saw the look on Manson's face, like the moon sliding behind a cloud. This could go either way. The gunmen were like dogs sensing their master's mood shift, and all their attention was on Billy.

He pressed on. "I'm earning again, and I'll be making payments into that account. Cut her some slack until I do."

Manson was staring at him. "You got balls, Barbie. Coming here with this."

Billy shrugged. "I'm talking man to man."

Manson nodded. "Okay. Man to man, I leave her be for a week. You get your cash flow sorted."

Billy nodded. "Fine."

"Your money, Barbie, it's not as if I need it. Understand?"

"I understand."

"It's just that I wannit. I just wannit, is all." Manson laughed. Shrugged his shoulders.

"Cool. I get it."

"Ja, you better. Or . . ." He grabbed at his package, swelling beneath the sweats, and did one of those grinding dances, all hips and dick and balls, singing in a pimp's falsetto: "Oh, Jodie, Jodie, *Jo—deeeee*."

The guys were laughing. Even Goddy, still bleeding in the trunk, experimented with a smile. Sensing a shift in the mood. That ended when Manson backhanded him through the face.

"Get out, freelance."

"Please, Manson." All at once Godwynn was crying, the water dissolving the blood on his face, so he looked like he was experiencing some Cape Flats stigmata.

"Come. Out."

Godwynn hauled himself from the trunk, stumbled, tried to keep himself upright by holding on to the car. Manson kicked Goddy's legs from under him and extended a hand to the big man, who passed him the .22, butt first.

Godwynn pissed himself, a puddle appearing at his crotch and leaking from the bottoms of his trousers onto his sneakers. "Please, Manson, please . . ."

A movement on the top floor of the house caught Billy's eye: Manson's daughter, peeping through a chink in the drapes. Manson cocked the .22, put the barrel to the base of Godwynn's skull, and stepped back and sideways, so he didn't get any splashback on his outfit when he pulled the trigger.

BARBARA ADAMS WALKED down Protea Street, past the row of shabby houses identical to her own. The night was hot, and the nagging wind did nothing to cool it. She heard snatches of hip hop, a baby crying, and a man and a woman arguing—voices thick with drink and desperation. She stopped next to an empty lot, littered with garbage and builder's rubble, keeping an eye on the house where her two children slept.

She slid a box of Vogue Satin Tips from her pocket. Barbara never smoked in front of her kids. How can you tell them not to if you did? She turned her back to the wind and lit a cigarette, drew the smoke deep into her lungs. *Man, that was good.*

Barbara allowed herself two smokes a day. She lived on the Cape Flats—dying of lung cancer was the least of her worries. Sometimes she felt so helpless. If she had the money, she would take her kids away from here, to a place where children weren't raped and murdered and boys didn't consider crime an acceptable career choice.

Barbara heard a noise and tensed. Something coming at her from the open ground. It wasn't safe to walk here, a woman alone. She laughed out a puff of smoke when she saw it was just a scrawny dog, all balls and ribs, rooting through the garbage. The dog saw her and cringed away, tail curled between its legs like a comma.

Something about the dog brought Billy Afrika to mind. The way he'd looked at her when he came to the house. Beaten. She'd begged him for help because she'd had nobody else to turn to. For sure, not the police. The crooked cops had been glad to see Clyde put in the ground, and the few honest ones knew better than to go up against Manson.

All she had was the man who had let her husband's killer walk free.

Billy Afrika had called her, a half hour back. Told her he'd spoken to Manson, that things were sorted. His word. Billy hadn't elaborated, just said he had a plan for her and the kids. He'd give her the details when the time came. That was it.

God only knew she wanted to believe him. But no matter what he promised, she couldn't trust Billy Afrika. He was weak, and you didn't depend on a weak man.

Barbara took a last drag on her cigarette, ground the butt dead under her heel, and turned for home. Found a mint in the pocket of her dress and popped it into her mouth, to kill the smell of smoke.

She crossed the paving stones to her front door, tried not to remember what she always remembered. Failed. As she went inside she could hear the wind banging a loose board on the roof. The house was falling apart. She felt a rush of anger. How could Clyde have left her like this?

The anger drained, leaving loneliness and despair in its place.

Barbara opened the door to the bedroom where her two children slept, the girl too big now to share a room with her snoring brother. In the spill of light she could see Jodie sleeping, clutching one of her soft toys. Not a girl anymore, but not a woman. Not yet.

She thought of Manson and his threats. Saw Jody in the car with him, the excited look on her face, like she wanted those filthy hands on her body. An image Barbara couldn't forget.

She found herself praying as she closed the bedroom door.

BILLY AFRIKA ARRIVED back at her house unannounced, carrying a duffel bag.

Roxy's hair was freshly washed, falling to her shoulders. She wore a white spaghetti-strap top that set off her tan nicely, and a pair of blue jeans. No shoes. The crucifix around her neck added an air of virtue, she hoped. She was way more composed now, no trace of the crying jag in the pink room.

"Mr. Afrika. You're back." Keeping it light, like she always did. Trying not to show that he made her nervous. The way he looked at her as he stepped through the front door.

He said, "Those guys, from earlier. They won't hassle you no more."

She worked on a puzzled frown, but her pulse rate was up at aerobic levels. "Okay, maybe you better explain."

"I tracked them down. We had a talk."

"How did you find them?"

"Lady, I told you. I was a cop."

"And you spoke to them?"

"Ja. We speak the same language." Giving her a tight smile. "It's sorted. You don't wanna hear the details." Staring at her. Hard. "Anyways, you got other things to worry about."

"Like what?"

"Like shooting your husband."

Containing her shock, letting it play out as confusion. "I don't get what you're saying here. Joe was shot by the hijackers."

"The tik heads plugged him in the leg. Panicked. Dropped the gun and ran. You finished him." Those green eyes on her. Unblinking.

So, there it was. She'd been busted. Her hand went up to the crucifix. Hell of a lot of good it had done her. "You going to hand me over to the police?"

"No."

"Why not?"

"Because I want what I'm owed. Thirty thousand dollars. That's two hundred and ten thousand rand at today's exchange rate."

Roxy shook her head. "I don't have access to that kind of money. Everything is frozen until the estate is processed. The lawyer told me it'll take a while."

"What's a while?"

She shrugged. "A couple of weeks. At best."

"I don't have a couple of weeks," Billy said.

"It's out of my hands. If those men hadn't cleaned me out, I could've sold some jewelry, got you part of the money at least. But, hey, look around . . ." Gesturing at the looted house.

"This lawyer. He and Joe were tight?"

She shrugged. "I guess. They were in the army together, way back."

"Look, Joe had cash stashed away. Guys like that always do. For when they need to run. Bet your ass the lawyer will know how to access it, in case he needed to bail Joe out of trouble. You just need to ask nice, okay?"

She nodded. "Sure. I'll call him in the morning and schedule a meeting."

Thinking about the twenty thousand dollars Dick Richardson had promised her. No way she would give it to this man. That was her emergency fund. So *she* could run.

"Lady, I want you to understand something. I don't give a shit if you killed your husband. Knowing Joe, he had it coming. But I need that money. And if I don't get it, no guarantee I'll keep my mouth shut."

"You're blackmailing me?"

"No, lady, I'm incentivizing you."

Nerves made her laugh. "What's it going take for you to stop calling me 'lady'?" He shrugged, set his bag down on the tiles. Her eyes followed it. "And that?"

"I'm moving in."

"The hell you are!"

"Till I get my money, I'm going to take care of my asset. You."

"And what if I don't want you here?"

"Way I see it, you got no choice."

Roxy took a few moments to adjust to this change in her circumstances, wondering what the hell kind of deal she was getting into now.

Then she smiled, shrugged, laying a veneer of cool over her fear. "Do you want a mountain or an ocean view?"

"Gimme a room overlooking the gates."

"That'll be mountain."

THE BLONDE WALKED ahead of him up the stairs toward the bedrooms, giving him the benefit of another view. She was about the best-looking woman he had ever seen. Not that he'd ever let her know that. She left him alone in an antiseptic white room, the window framing Lion's Head in the moonlight. Billy shut the drapes.

As he unpacked his toothbrush and shorts from the duffel bag, Billy wondered about people who were shit magnets. Some were born like that: the Discos and Godwynns of the world. Others became that way through circumstance. Like Roxy. People called it bad luck. He didn't believe in bad luck. He believed in bad choices.

Roxanne Palmer had opened a door when she killed Joe, stepped into a world of shit. When you took a life, you lost some form of protection you didn't even know you had until it was gone. Left you in a place where bad people started tuning in to your frequency.

For sure, Roxy's shit wasn't over. And it wasn't shit that he wanted to be part of. But she needed to be managed until he got his money. Then she could take up sewage farming for all he cared.

HER SCREAMS WOKE him. The kind of screams that cut right through you, like a blade through bone. His reflexes kicked in, and the Glock was in his hand, and he was running before he was fully awake.

chapter 16

BILLY SMASHED OPEN THE BEDROOM DOOR, HIT THE LIGHT SWITCH, and went in rolling, raking the room with the Glock.

Roxy was alone, cowering in the corner where the closet met the drapes. Naked. Her eyes unfocused, her chest heaving, hair dark with sweat. Another scream was building. Then she choked it off, staring across at him.

He got to his feet, aware that he was wearing only shorts. Felt her eyes on his scars.

Billy killed the light and put the Glock down on the bedside table. The drapes were open, and enough moonlight shafted into the room for him to see Roxy as he stood over her.

"You okay?"

"Bad dream. I'm sorry." Her voice heavy with fear and broken sleep.

He could see the outline of a printed cloth, the kind of thing she would wear to the beach, lying on a chair. He lifted it and let it float down toward her. She wrapped it around herself.

When Roxy stood, he could feel the heat of her body. He retreated. She went across to the bed and sat down.

"I'm going now," he said, heading for the door.

"Sure. Thank you."

He picked up the gun and went out. The door clicked shut after him.

Roxy reached across and switched on the lamp beside the bed, the terror receding now, beyond the range of the light at least.

She had woken as if fighting her way from a depth, felt a presence in the room trying to suffocate her. The screams were dragged from her lungs, and she found herself on the floor. Hiding. Only came fully to consciousness when Billy Afrika burst in. He'd left the light on just long enough for her to glimpse the puckered, dead-white scar tissue that marbled his brown body.

Roxy walked across to the window and looked out at the fat African moon dangling over the ocean. She could hear the slap of the waves far below, followed by the hiss and suck as the water retreated. The dream that had ambushed her was like a sump being tapped: dark and clogged and dirty.

Joe had been in the room with her, looming over her bed, hands reaching for her throat. Dressed in the suit he died in, black blood streaming down his face, turning his white shirt dark.

That was when she'd screamed.

Even now his smell hung in the air, a chemical mix of booze and cigarettes and stale sweat. Like he was there watching her.

Waiting for his revenge.

chapter 17

DETECTIVE ERNIE MAGGOTT STOOD OVER THE BODY LYING LIKE trash on the edge of the dump. Dawn came early to Cape Town in the summer, and it was bright and hot by seven in the morning. Godwynn MacIntosh was already bloating and starting to stink, his shattered skull so dense with flies that it looked as if he was wearing a black ski mask.

He had been shot in the back of the head, execution style. There was no exit wound, which meant there was a slug trapped inside that thick skull of his. After what Maggott had heard from the uniformed cop leaning against the van, waving away inquisitive kids, he wished he could get the bullet dug out of this bushman's brain and sent to forensics. Christ knows, he'd be happy to stick his finger in and dig it out himself. But it would be a waste of time. Even for a high-profile crime, the waiting list at the labs was five months.

And Godwynn's profile was lower than a smear of shit on a shoe.

Maggott didn't give a fuck for Godwynn MacIntosh, but he was convinced this dark meat was connected to that hijacking and the blonde American. Screw his superintendent, Maggott still had a hard-on for that case. Knew it could be his ticket to bigger and better things.

He walked back to his Ford, toward the six-year-old boy who peered out at him from the open passenger window. His son, Roberto. Named after the Brazilian soccer star. It had been his wife's idea to call him that. She thought the chunky defender was sexy. To Maggott he looked like just another bald fucker from the Flats.

His bitch wife, living away from him these last few months, had dumped the boy on him the night before, telling him her mother was sick and she had to go to the hospital. Like hell. She was going to get laid and didn't want the kid pissing on her batteries.

So the kid had stayed the night with Maggott in the cramped room he rented on the Dark City side of Paradise Park. He'd fed him fish sticks and ice cream, and the boy had spent the early hours squirting out enough puke to get him cast in a remake of *The Exorcist.*

Maggott leaned into the window. "You okay, Robbie?"

"I wanna go to Mommy." The kid was sniveling, and there were tears on the way.

"Ja, later. Okay?"

The bitch was probably dragging her dirty ass from some guy's bed. Then she would be off to her job at the meatpacking factory in Maitland.

Maggott walked over to the uniformed cop, who was flirting with two schoolgirls in short tunics, making them giggle and squirm. He dragged the cop—thought he was a fucken Cape Flats Casanova—away from the jailbait. He was older than Maggott but still a constable. Lived off bribes and handouts.

"Tell me again," Maggott said.

"About Barbie?"

"No, about your mother." Staring the cop down. "Ja. Billy Afrika. Tell me again."

"Like I say, he phone me yesterday. Wants to know who we pulled in on the Bantry Bay hijacking."

"And you just told him?"

"Man, he could read it in the *Sun*. What's the problem?"

The *Sun*: the daily tabloid—full of lurid tales of murder, rape, and incest—that reflected the Cape Flats like a funhouse mirror.

"How much he offer you?"

"Nothing, Detective. Honest."

"Your mother's honest," Maggott said. "He ask you anything else?"

The useless bastard shook his head. Maggott didn't believe him.

He shoved a finger into the cop's chest. "Billy Afrika contact you again, I'm the first to know, okay?"

"Ja, Detective." Smiling like they were buddies.

Maggott grabbed the asshole by his shirtfront, shook him. "I fucken mean it. You speak to me, or I put you on night patrol in the squatter camps for a week."

The smile disappeared. Black cops died like bottle flies over in the darky shackland across the freeway. A colored cop wouldn't last an hour. Maggott let the uniform loose and walked back to his car. About to slide in behind the wheel, he saw the kid had puked again, all over the driver's seat.

As Maggott tried to clean up the mess with yesterday's edition of the *Sun*, he saw a trail of blood leading away from that body lying in the trash.

Leading to Roxy Palmer.

And to Billy Afrika, the coward who had let his partner's killer live.

★   ★   ★

IT WAS LIGHT when Roxy woke. She had a headache from where the squat man had whacked her with the gun. Nothing she couldn't handle. No worse than a hangover. Fragments of the night drifted back to her. The dream. How she'd exposed herself to Billy Afrika. Not just her body, though Christ knows he must have seen enough of that. But she'd let him see her fear and her vulnerability, and that made her uncomfortable.

It was time she wised up. She *was* vulnerable. There was a man moved into her house holding her to ransom. She knew nothing about him, except he wasn't like the two lowlifes who'd gunpointed her. He was way smarter. Far more in control. More dangerous.

What had he done with those two losers, anyway? Killed them? He had an air about him, an attitude, that made her believe it was possible. When he'd come into her bedroom with the gun, she'd seen the violence contained in his scarred body.

What Roxy would have liked to do was lay a little money on him, to keep him cool and make sure he didn't go talking to his cop friends. But yesterday she'd done a phone check on the one bank account that Joe had allowed her access to.

Deeply in the red.

And her credit card was maxed out.

All she could do now was wait for the money from Dick Richardson. Roxy knew she should take the twenty thousand dollars and run. Go to Europe. Do what she always did: meet a rich man. She still had what it took.

But she didn't want to get into one of those cycles again. She wanted her freedom. If she waited, she'd get enough from Joe's estate to be independent for the first time in her life. That meant she needed to manage Billy Afrika. Keep him on her side. Make him like her.

Roxy fluffed her hair in the mirror, smiled sourly at her reflection. Hell, she'd never had a problem getting a man to like her. Had more problems keeping their hands off of her.

She replaced the twisted smile with the one that had kept the camera happy for all those years. Wholesome yet seductive. And just a little vulnerable.

Better.

As she pulled on a shirt and shorts, she could smell food cooking. Bacon and eggs. She ran her fingers through her hair one more time and went down to the kitchen.

Billy stood in front of the stove, turning eggs with a spatula. Dressed in a crisp white T-shirt and sweatpants. His feet in flip-flops. No sign of those scars.

"Morning," she said. "I'm sorry about last night . . ."

He shrugged, eyes on the pan. "Forget it." Flipping the eggs before he looked up at her. "I suppose you don't want any of this?"

"Why not?"

"Dunno. You models don't eat, do you?"

"I'm not a model anymore." She opened a drawer and took out two plates, put them on the counter. "Anyway, I'll just throw up afterward."

He gave her a neutral look.

"That's a joke," she said.

Roxy grabbed knives and forks and took them to the table. She saw he had found the coffee grounds, which trickled and spat in the coffee maker. A man who knew his way around.

She poured a cup for him. "You'll have to have this black. We're out of milk."

"Black's fine."

She took an Evian from the fridge and sat down. He came across with the two plates, placed one in front of her and sat at the far end of the table. She didn't normally do bacon and eggs, but she wanted to relax him, find a way beneath that scarred shell of his. Get inside and soften him up a little.

"This is good," she said, around a mouthful of food.

He nodded, concentrating on his plate.

They ate in silence. She sneaked glances his way. A neat

eater, using both his knife and fork, wiping his mouth on a paper napkin after almost every bite. She felt like a slob eating with her fork, picking up bacon with her fingers, elbows on the table.

He finished before she did, took his plate across to the sink, and started washing up.

"Leave that; I'll do it," Roxy said.

"It's okay."

"So how does this work? You being here?" She carried her plate over to where he stood, his hands in the foamy water. Careful not to get too close to him. He didn't seem to welcome that.

"You leave the house, I go with you. You home, I'm home."

"Twenty-four seven?"

"Ja."

"What if I want to go for a run? Down by the ocean?"

"I can run." Rinsing a plate and putting it in the drying rack.

Roxy said, "So I'm your prisoner?"

"Lady, it's this, or it's real prison. You choose."

He wiped his hands on a dishtowel and walked out.

WORD TRAVELS FAST on the Flats, carried on the wind and the dust.

An hour after Godwynn's body was found, the bulk of the fat-assed landlady blocked Disco's door, the black mongrel snarling at him from between her legs. Disco still lay in bed, dragged from his drugged sleep by the yapping of the dog.

"So they shot your short-ass buddy. The dark one," the land-lady said. Disco squinted up at her. "Some kids found him over by the dump."

Disco thought he was going to hurl, fought back the bile.

Goddy was dead. Fucken knew it. Knew he'd be next.

Disco lifted himself out of the bed, fat slut staring at his ass as he pulled on a pair of jeans. He started shoving things into a plastic bag. He had no money and no idea of where to go, but he knew he had to run. Should've run last night after Billy Afrika caught up with him, but his nerves had been finished and he'd had to hit a white pipe to calm them. And then he'd passed out.

"Where you going?" the fat woman asked.

"On holiday." Disco forced the last dirty clothes into the bag.

She laughed through her missing front teeth. "On holiday? The fuck where?"

"Saldanha." The first thing that came into Disco's head. Saldanha Bay, up the West Coast. He had never been out of Cape Town, but there was always a first time.

"So you can afford to go on holiday, but you don't pay your fucken rent?"

"I have it for you before I go, Auntie. I promise."

Now he had to pack his most treasured possession. As he headed across to his mommy's picture, the fat slut blocked him. She reached for the photo, lifting it off the nail.

"Uh-uh, sonny. You think I'm fucked in my head? I keep this until you come with the money, okay?"

Disco grabbed at the frame, tried to wrestle it away from her. She smacked him across the side of his head. The bitch hit like a heavyweight, and he went down on one knee, ears ringing. The dog danced on its tiny paws, barking and snapping at Disco's face, eyes bulging.

"Come, Zuma. Come my lovey." The fat woman shook the *zozo* as she stomped to the door.

By the time Disco got to his feet, she was waddling across the yard, holding his mommy in her fat hand, the stinking little dog scuttling after her.

MAGGOTT DROVE ACROSS Paradise Park, heading back toward the dump. He had the windows open wide, even though the wind pumped in dust and grit, but the car still stank of Robbie's puke. Fish sticks and ice cream coming back strong.

People called Detective Ernie Maggott a cunt, a bastard, a bad-luck motherfucker. But nobody called him crooked. He was an honest cop. A rare beast out on the Flats, where the pay was low, the job was dangerous, and the temptations were plentiful. It was easy to turn a blind eye for a couple of bucks. Or get in deeper: wear a badge but work for the gangs.

Christ knows, there were enough bad role models out there. The police commissioner, the country's top cop—still head of Interpol when he was arrested—was in court for racketeering. Taking bribes from gangsters and hit men.

Maggott's bitch wife had never understood. Why did they have to live in a crap rented house when the others cops' wives wore new clothes and bragged about their custom kitchens? What the fuck was his problem? But Maggott refused to be bought. Thought himself better than the bent cops around him. Knew all he needed was one big case, something high profile that would get him in the papers and get him promoted.

That's why he was all hot and sticky for this American blonde. And Billy Afrika, who was tied into this somehow. Problem was, he had no idea where to find Barbie's burned ass.

He'd known Billy Afrika back when he was still a cop, as close to Clyde Adams as a butt boil. Maggott had respected Captain Clyde Adams. Hoped that the older man would recognize him as a kindred spirit, take him under his wing. But instead Clyde groomed Barbie, putting the right words in the right ears, fast-tracking Billy Afrika from uniform to detective branch in record time.

And what thanks had he got?

The person Maggot really wanted to talk to—no, fuck talking, wanted to shove his Z88 down his throat until he got the truth—was Manson. Find out if Billy Afrika was connected to the death of the 26, Godwynn MacIntosh, and where the American blonde fit into all of this.

But Manson was protected. You couldn't touch him. He was

part of a pipeline that pumped tik money straight into the pockets of police chiefs and local politicians.

So Maggott had to work with what was available to him.

He'd made a turn by Disco's place. The piece of shit wasn't in his *zozo*, and the fat landlady, who smelled like the fish sticks, said the tik head had been busy packing his things. Like he wanted to run.

Maggott looked through the grimy window of the *zozo* and saw a plastic bag lying on the floor, crammed with clothes. Told the fat bitch to call him when Disco came back.

"And what's in it for me?" she asked.

"The usual. Fifty bucks," he said.

"Make it a hundred, lovey. Airtime's expensive."

Maggott cursed under his breath as he handed over a banknote. There went his cigarette money for the week. He heard a laugh and looked across at Robbie, who sat in the dirt playing with the fat woman's skinny little mongrel.

Maggott still hadn't been able to get hold of his bitch wife. He couldn't afford a babysitter. He was an orphan, and he'd cut all contact with the human wreckage his wife called family. So he had to keep the boy with him, sitting at his side as he drove down Main Road.

Maggot sneaked a look at the kid and wondered, as he always did, how he could have fathered something like this. Saw nothing of himself in the child. The way his wife put her plumbing around Paradise Park, this was probably some other fucker's handiwork.

"I wanna doggy," Robbie said.

"Ja? What kinda dog?"

"Like that one now."

"That's not a dog. That's a rat."

The boy was shaking his head vigorously. "No. It were a dog."

"How you know?"

"I seen his balls."

Maggott snorted. "And a rat don't have no balls?"

"Not big ones."

"I'll tell your mommy, and she can get you a fucken dog."

The boy looked at him suspiciously, used to promises that weren't kept. "Ja?"

"Ja. You just be good today. Okay?"

The kid nodded. They pulled up at Doc's. The hovel looking as if it was being slowly claimed by the dump looming behind. The place stank worse than ten tik whores in a shithouse.

"Wait here, I won't be long," Maggott said as he left the car. The kid started to moan, but Maggott was already walking away.

He banged on the door, finally got the old boozer to open up.

"What's wrong now?" Doc said, bloodshot eye peering through the crack.

Maggott walked him backward into the pigsty. As always, the big-screen TV flickered with images of men in white, endlessly smacking a red ball to nowhere.

"What did Billy Afrika want here yesterday?"

"He popped in to say hullo. What of it?"

"I'm asking again: what the fuck did he want?"

"Nothing. Just a visit, for old time sake, like. Watched some cricket."

Doc's gaze was drawn to the screen, where a bowler was jumping in the air, being hugged by his teammates. Then his eyes flicked across to Robbie, who came walking in the front door, staring around at the squalor with interest.

"What's that?" Doc asked.

"My boy. Don't worry with him." He saw Doc's questioning look. "His bitch mother dumped him on me. You wanna babysit?"

"Not me. Closest I ever got to one of those was with a coat hanger." Doc laughed.

Maggott didn't. "Barbie, he score a gun by you?"

Doc shook his head. "No ways."

Maggott pointed a finger at Robbie. "You sit your ass down and watch the cricket, hear me?"

The kid nodded, and Maggott took off toward the kitchen, Doc limping after him.

"Where you going now?"

The kitchen was as filthy as the rest of the house. Stove full of dirty pans, sink overflowing with scummy dishes. The room was dominated by the huge box freezer Doc had bought cheap from a fishmonger who went bust. There was still a peeling sticker on the side: SOMETHING FISHY.

Described Maggott's morning.

He lifted the lid of the freezer and leaned inside. A putrid smell washed the room, competing with the stink from the dump. Doc was plucking at Maggott's shirt with soft, palsied fingers.

"Hey, what you doing?"

Maggott lifted out a black garbage bag. He took it across to the table, untied the knot at the top, and shook out a human arm, severed above the elbow. A black man's arm. Frozen. It clanged when it hit the tabletop.

"Tell me what Billy Afrika wanted, or I phone the *Sun*. You know how they love shit like this."

For sure it would make the front page—six-inch headlines and lurid color photographs—and send Doc's body parts suppliers running.

The drunk shook his fuzzy head, wheezing.

Maggott caught a movement and saw Robbie standing in the doorway, staring at the arm. Fascinated.

"Don't you got ears? I told you to fucken watch the cricket. Now go!"

Robbie took one last look, then fled. Maggott had his cell phone out, scrolling for a number.

Doc held up a shaking hand. "Okay, okay. Slow down to a panic. Ja, listen, I gave Barbie a Glock 17."

"He say why he wanted it?"

"No."

Maggott pocketed his phone. "You know where he's staying at?"

"No. Never said nothing."

Maggott stared Doc down, saw he'd squeezed all he could out of the old boozer.

"You see Billy Afrika again, you tell him I'm looking for him."

Maggott headed toward the front door, grabbing a handful of his son's T-shirt on the way out. The kid was stroking the fur growing on a long-forgotten plate of food like it was a pussycat.

chapter 18

As Billy ran, the Glock at his hip rubbed up against his scar tissue, and he knew he would have a blister by the time they got back to the house in Bantry Bay. Doc's service hadn't run to holsters, so Billy had to improvise. Took the money belt he used in Iraq and tied it tight around his waist, hidden by his sweatpants and T-shirt. Shoved the Glock underneath the belt, against his skin. Not ideal, but the best he could do. No way he was going out into the world without a gun.

Roxy spoke without breaking stride. "You okay?"

"I'm fine." Fucked if he was going to let her know he was suffering.

"Tell me if I'm pushing you too hard." Her voice was easy, no strain. A trace of amusement.

Billy's reply was to accelerate, trying to run his way through the pain. She cruised up next to him, matching him stride for stride.

He'd expected a short jog, the kind of thing these women did to con themselves into believing they were working out, but she'd surprised him. She hit the bricks hard, wearing her sweat-stained clothes the way she must have worn designer outfits on the ramp. No denying it, she was good-looking. Beautiful, even. And he'd seen too much of her body in the night. Pushed the image away.

Jesus, she was his asset. A piece of meat he needed to keep alive until he got his money. That's all. Switched his thoughts from her body to his own.

As a kid Billy had been a pretty useful sprinter—needed to be where he'd grown up—but these days he worked out in private. So he wasn't running fit, and by the time they reached the ocean-front his leg muscles were tight, and a stitch stabbed him beneath the rib cage.

He tried to breathe his way through it.

Billy heard the music first, the frenetic, banjo-driven sound of the Cape Flats. Then he saw a group of men in bright satin costumes, face paint, boaters and top hats, playing to a small crowd on the sidewalk beside the ocean. They finished the song to halfhearted applause. One man removed his boater and used it to collect small change, before they struck up another tune.

"What are these guys all about?" Roxy stopped, not even breathing hard.

"It's a big thing this time of year. Minstrels," Billy said. "There are thousands of them out on the Flats, and they have competitions, parades. Used to be called the Coon Carnival, but that's not PC no more."

"They look like Uncle Toms in blackface."

"Ja. There's a connection. Listen to what they're singing." Playing out the moment, giving himself time to breathe the pain away.

She tried to catch the words. "Something about Ali Baba?"

He laughed. "Close. *Allie—bama*. Alabama."

"As in the state?"

Shook his head. "No, some American warship docked here hundred and something years ago. During your Civil War. There were black minstrels on board, so people say. And the whole look, the costumes and all, kind of became a big tradition."

The banjos were at one another like fighting cocks, and Billy caught the dust in his throat as he ran next to the minstrels in a Paradise Park street, ten years old, letting the music and bright colors and dancing men transport him away from the ghetto apartment that stank of white pipes and his mother's juices.

He came back to the now with Roxy staring at him, jogging on the spot, blonde ponytail swinging. "Guess you grew up with this stuff?"

He nodded. "Ja. Some of my mother's clients were minstrels."

"What did your mother do?"

"She was a whore." Trying to shock her.

Roxy stopped jogging and gave him a cool look. "At least she got paid for it. Mine gave it away for free."

She laughed. So did he.

"Where's she now, your mother?" Roxy asked.

"Dead."

"Sorry."

"Don't be. I'm not. And yours? Dead too?"

"No, worse. Living in Daytona Beach, Florida, with a taxidermist, last I heard."

She started running again, waited for him to catch up, and increased her speed. They ran on past the swimming pool, heading toward the lighthouse. The pain under his rib was like a hot blade, and his calf muscles were starting to scream. He saw her sneaking a look his way, amusement in her blue eyes. He pushed himself harder, deep into the pain. Pain he could understand. Pain he could trust.

They were nearing Rocklands Beach. A crowd of people stood up at the railing, staring down at the sand. The beach was enclosed by crime scene tape, buzzing in the breeze, cops keeping the suntanned rubberneckers back.

Billy slowed. "Stay here," he said. "I'll go find out what's the story."

Glad for the chance to suck air.

ROXY WATCHED HIM walk toward the uniformed cops. She knew he'd been struggling. That scar tissue must itch and burn like hell, and she'd seen him adjusting the pistol at his hip. Roxy had taken pleasure in his discomfort. Knowing she was pushing him. Wanting to pierce that bubble of cool. The certainty that he could invade her world and she had to keep her mouth shut.

Billy Afrika was different from most men she'd met. Men who saw her and immediately wanted her. Or what their limited imaginations told them she was. A beautiful canvas for them to project their fantasies onto. For nearly twenty years she'd populated her life with the Joe Palmers and Dick Richardsons of the world. Men with money, always older, using the lure of their wealth to have her on their arms and in their beds.

But Billy Afrika hadn't given a damn. He hadn't come on to her; no reflex calculation of her *fuckability*—as Joe used to say—appeared in his eyes when he looked at her. All he wanted was his money. When he'd told her he knew she'd killed Joe, he hadn't blinked. The needle hadn't moved. He'd stayed cool, detached.

She saw him over there, talking to a couple of brown cops. The three of them laughing as they looked over the railing at the beach below.

Roxy felt a sudden primitive dread, the fine down on the back of her neck rising like antennae. She turned to see the homeless black woman from the day before, standing with her shopping cart under a stick of a tree, watching her. Roxy tried to stare her down, but the woman's eyes didn't shift.

She's just a crazy woman with a pimped cart, Roxy told herself. But it was creepy the way those eyes seemed to skewer her.

"There's been a murder."

Roxy turned, relieved to see Billy walking back toward her.

"What happened?"

He shrugged, half laughed. "Listen, I know this is gonna sound like one of those jokes, but there's a blonde down there. Without a head."

chapter 19

As Maggott drove through Paradise Park he saw Godwynn MacIntosh's pulped skull. Saw Billy Afrika with a Glock 17. Had to be a connection. Cursed not having access to forensics. *Fucken banana republic run by jungle bunnies.*

Meant Maggott had to go primitive himself, grab on to trees and shake the hell out of them. See what fell out. He stopped at a house on Hippo Street, Dark City side. Nothing flashy, but set apart from its neighbors by the new Beemer parked in the driveway and the satellite dish on the roof. The paintwork on the house was fresh, and the wire fence didn't sag like an old pair of tits.

Manson was protected from the law, but his 28 enemy, Shorty Andrews, wasn't. His senior, a Muslim with a sprawling house in Constantia—vineyards and horses and money so old that it stank—had finally been sold out by an ambitious underling. The Muslim sat in Pollsmoor awaiting trial, and a new protection deal hadn't yet been struck with his successor. So Maggott had a gap.

He cracked the car door and shoved a finger into Robbie's face. "You wait here. And I fucken mean it."

Robbie nodded, but he was watching a kid his age wearing yellow swimming trunks, jumping around in a small inflatable pool in the cramped front yard. Maggott went through the gate and walked up to the front door. The door opened before he had a chance to knock. Got the eyeball from a punk in his early twenties, wearing a tank top and a pair of baggy jeans held up by the swell of his balls. His scrawny arms boasted fresh 28 tattoos. Street, not prison. He hadn't graduated yet.

They called him Teeth. Because he didn't have none.

Teeth knew who Maggott was, slid tik-glazed eyes over him. "Ja?"

"Tell Shorty I'm here."

"Says who?"

Maggott was one of those skinny guys who punched above their weight. You learned that young on the Flats. So when he sank his fist into Teeth's abdomen, he did it with conviction. The punk sagged, and Maggott shoved him aside and stepped into the house.

Shorty Andrews and two other guys were slouched in front of an LCD TV the size of a billboard, watching reruns of English soccer. A cloud of smoke hung over the room. Shorty sat with a toddler on his lap, tamping a bottleneck of weed and Mandrax. The toddler held a pretend pipe in his closed little fist, mimicking his father.

Shorty looked up from his prep. "The fuck you want, Maggott?"

"Step out and talk to me."

Maggott went back outside. He saw that the passenger door of his Ford stood open, and the car was empty. He looked across at the pool, and it took him a moment before he started running. The kid in the trunks had hold of Robbie's head, pushing him under the water, Robbie's feet kicking like crazy.

Maggott shoved the kid aside and hauled his boy out of the pool. Robbie was coughing and spluttering, fighting for air. Maggott raised his hand to give the little fucker in the trunks a clip across the ear hole.

"You touch my kid, and I kill you." Shorty was coming across the yard, all six-foot plus of him.

Maggott dropped his hand. He gave Robbie a shove. "Go wait in the car." Coughing and crying, the boy dripped his way across the patchy lawn.

Shorty picked up his son, held him in one arm. Gave the little thug a kiss on the forehead. "Talk quick, Maggott, then get your ass off my yard."

"You seen Billy Afrika since yesterday?"

Shorty shook his head. "The fuck would I?"

Maggott said, "He was round White City with a Glock, looking for a 26 and the wife of your man Piper."

"Piper's not my man. And what do I care about a 26?"

"You don't need to. He's dead meat."

"And the wife?"

"Hiding his stretched ass."

Shorty shrugged.

Maggott looked up at the big man. "The ceasefire you got with Manson . . ."

"Ja?"

"Think, Shorty. How long's it going to last with a 26 wearing his brains on the outside and fucken Barbie running around with a gun, stirring up shit from the past?"

Shorty was looking at him, impassive as a buddha. But taking it in. Maggott used his thumb and pinky to mime "call me" and went across to the car. Robbie sat in the passenger seat, sobbing, snot drooping from his nose like stalactites.

Maggott started the car. "Ah, shut the fuck up. It was just a bit of water."

As he drove away he saw Shorty in the rearview, holding his bastard son, staring after the Ford.

Maggott was stirring things up. Him and the wind in the dust.

PIPER WORE CUFFS and leg irons, the chains trailing after him and whispering against the concrete like a legion of the dead.

Two guards in brown uniforms flanked him; another walked behind. The guards' heavy shoes drummed as they moved Piper through the massive prison, built to house four thousand inmates, home to twice that number. Each time they came to a gate, the man on his left would unlock it with one of the keys on his ring, let the procession pass through, then lock it again.

It was after 4:00 p.m., past lockdown, so the corridors were empty. But sound and stink seeped from beneath the solid steel doors of the communal cells. Rap. East Coast if they were in 28 territory. West Coast if they were passing by the cells of the 26s. Cries and moans and laughter. TVs tuned to Oprah. The stench of bad food and unwashed bodies. The sweet-sour smell of Mandrax and tik and weed. These guards didn't worry with men smoking drugs. By the time they unlocked the cells, the drugs would be stashed. Under mattresses, in rolled-up clothes. Inside the bodies of the men themselves.

They left the maximum security wing behind and entered a corridor of offices. One of the guards knocked on a door and opened it, gestured for Piper to enter.

A man sat behind a desk in the faceless room, empty of decoration except for a calendar showing a variety of Cape wild flowers. The man wore the same uniform as the men who had escorted Piper. But he was older and had some seniority.

He looked up at Piper. "Johnson."

Rashied Johnson. Piper's almost forgotten name. Piper said

nothing, stared at the dung-colored man in his dung-colored uniform.

"It is my duty to inform you that you have been subpoenaed to appear in court tomorrow. To testify in the Bruinders case."

Bruinders: a trainee guard who got stabbed dead in the exercise yard. Piper had played no direct role, but he'd acted in a supervisory capacity. A youngster was being blooded into the 28s, and Piper ordered him to stab the guard. It wasn't meant to be fatal, just a wound to draw the blood needed to initiate the soldier. But the youth had lost control, and he'd killed the guard. Now he was up for murder.

"I seen nothing," Piper said.

"Tell that to the court."

"I tell them nothing."

The senior guard shrugged and waved Piper away, and the other men opened the door and he started the long walk back. Back along the dim, echoing corridors, high windows like gun turrets offering slices of the mountain beyond, brilliant in the hot sun.

Piper knew these men felt fuck all if the cops dragged him, chained like an animal, to the court in Cape Town only to have him stand mute in the dock. It had happened before. Only this time he wouldn't get as far as the courtroom.

Piper had just been given his ticket out.

chapter 20

ROXY STOOD OUT ON THE DECK, THE HOT WIND CATCHING THE ENDS of her hair. Bantry Bay was sheltered, but the southeaster still came through in gusts. She stared down at the pool, which had turned swamp-green, the line between the water and the blue sky no longer ambiguous. All it needed was a couple of gators sunning themselves on the steps. The pool man who usually came in once a week hadn't shown up, and there was no more Joe to walk his gut around in the evenings, tossing chemicals into the water.

Roxy looked up to see Billy appear through the sliding doors.

"There's a Dick here to see you," he said. Deadpan.

Billy turned and went back into the house. Roxy followed him and found Dick Richardson standing in the sitting room, looking at the mess that Roxy hadn't got around to cleaning up.

"Redecorating?" He flashed a smile, but his face looked drawn. There was a food stain on his Armani tie.

Roxy had called him earlier, putting pressure on him about

the money. He'd assured her it was his number one priority, sounding distracted as he said it. But here he was.

"This is a surprise, Dick," she said, giving him her best smile. If he was bringing her money, he deserved it.

Billy was on the stairs, walking up toward his room. Dick's eyes followed him.

"Who's that guy?"

"One of Joe's people. A bodyguard. He's staying here."

"Good idea." He shot a cuff and looked at his Rolex. "Want to grab a bite down in Camps Bay?" Same old Dick, never stopped trying. But his heart wasn't in it.

"Thanks, but I'm tired," Roxy said.

"Sure." He hesitated, tugged at his collar. "Rox, wanted to ask you something . . ."

"What?"

"Joe's laptop . . . Think I could have it for a day or two? There's some info relating to the estate that I need to capture."

Roxy shook her head. "Sorry. It was stolen."

That jolted him. "When?"

She gave him an edited version of the home invasion. He stared at her.

"Jesus, Roxanne. What a couple of days."

"Hey, what do they say about keep on keeping on?" She put a little folksy twist on this, some trash in her drawl. She took his arm and edged him toward the front door, got a whiff of the killer aftershave.

When they were outside, walking over to his Range Rover, she leaned in close to him, keeping her voice soft. "Dick, how are we doing with the money?"

"I haven't forgotten, Rox. Give me a day or two, okay?" He smiled. A smile that didn't touch his eyes. She had a bad feeling.

"I've got to run." Jangling loose change in his pocket. "So I'll catch you at the funeral tomorrow?" He saw her face. "You didn't know?"

She shook her head. "Nobody told me."

Dick looked embarrassed. "Well, it's at Claremont Catholic Church. Three bells."

"Thanks."

He looked like he was about to duck in and kiss her cheek, so she stepped back. Dick climbed up into the car and drove away. She waited until the gates finally rolled closed, after a few false starts, and went through the house, back out to the deck. She heard Billy behind her.

"Know anything about pools?" she asked, turning, trying a smile.

"Lady, I grew up out on the Flats. Our idea of a pool was a hole in the ground filled with ditchwater."

It was "lady" again.

"Stop calling me 'lady,' for Chrissakes. Makes me feel like a dog. Call me Roxy."

"Okay." A pause. "But I like Roxanne better."

"Whatever grinds your crankshaft." Irritated as the wind blew her hair into her eyes, reaching up to smooth it away. "What's wrong with Roxy, anyway?"

"It sounds . . . I dunno. Cheap."

"Thanks." Despite herself she was amused. "Well, since we're getting all formal here, maybe I'll call you William."

"You can call me that. But it's not my name."

"Billy's not short for William?"

He shook his head. "Not on my birth certificate, anyways. It says Billy Afrika. End of story."

She shrugged, turning away. His voice stopped her.

"That suit, he say anything about the money?"

"Joe may have had some cash stashed away. I'll know in a day or two."

He was watching her carefully. "I wouldn't like to think you're bullshitting me, Roxanne."

"I'm not. Okay?" Walking away from him, so those green

eyes couldn't X-ray her. "Dick told me that it's Joe's funeral to-morrow. I don't know that I can go. Given the circumstances."

"You're going." Following Roxy, staring her down. "When a man dies, his wife goes to the funeral. She doesn't go, people start asking questions. We don't need no questions. Understand?"

"Yes. I understand."

Billy turned and walked back into the house.

The wind died suddenly, and in the lull Roxy heard the fading rumble of jet engines. She saw a vapor trail drawn on the darkening sky, slowly starting to smudge and blur as the plane disappeared north. Roxy wished she was on it.

DISCO WAS STRESSING big-time. He was so freaked out that feeding the meth into the pipe was turning into a major mission. His hands shook, not only from a craving for the drug, but from mind-fucking fear. He was in his *zozo,* in the dark, door locked, lights out. He crouched on the floor, under the empty spot where his mommy's picture used to hang, and forced his fingers to obey him, trying to feed the powder into the pipe, working blind.

He'd been out on the streets, managed to scrounge thirty bucks to buy a straw from the tik dealer down on Sunflower Street. The dealer, Popeye, operated from a rusted trailer lying on its axles in the dust of a vacant lot. Peeling paintwork scarred by gang graffiti, like tattoos on an old man's skin.

Popeye had a taste for his own product, and he was as scrawny as a Brazilian supermodel, his cheekbones sunken in on smacking gums, his teeth long ago lost to tik. A radio inside the trailer was tuned to a hip-hop station, and Popeye moved his skinny ass as he took Disco's money and handed him the meth-filled drinking straw, plastic melted closed at both ends.

"I hear Manson looking for you, my brother." Popeye, like so many people this side of Paradise Park, had sold his soul to the Americans.

"Ja? He know where to find me." Disco trying for attitude and coming up short.

Popeye laughed. "My advice, you don't wait for him to come to you. Otherwise he kiss you bye, bye like he kiss your buddy Godwynn." Popeye made a wet smacking sound with his toothless mouth. He laughed again, then coughed up a greenie and spat it next to Disco's Chuck Taylors. "Show respect. Go talk to the man."

Disco had taken his straw and hurried home in the dusk, grateful that most of the streetlights in White City were dead, the innards of the lampposts gutted for copper wire. The lights of each passing car like gun sights on his back.

But he was safe now, in his *zozo*. Once he'd had a smoke, his mind would be nice and sharp and he'd know how to deal with this Manson situation. And figure out how to get back his mommy's photo. At last he fed the meth into the pipe. Had to risk a quick match, guiding the flame toward the powder, already feeling the rush that was to come.

When the door smashed open, Disco dropped the pipe and the match died. He saw a shape coming in at him, and a heavy shoe caught him in the abdomen. He was down flat, face squeezed against the rough wooden floor, bile in his mouth. The naked bulb hanging from the ceiling flared into life, and he saw the shoe that had kicked him: a scuffed black wingtip. Not what Manson or his crew would be sporting.

Disco lifted his head, a tendril of drool connecting his mouth to the floor. The cop, the ugly one with the zits, swam into view. He was holding up the pipe.

"The fuck's this?" Out on the Flats this was definitely a rhetorical question.

Disco felt his hands being pulled roughly behind his back and then the cold steel on his wrists as the cuffs were locked.

chapter 21

MAGGOTT TOOK ROBBIE TO McD'S FOR A BURGER, LATE FOR A kid to be awake. They sat at a window table, and Maggott watched the tik whores out on Voortrekker, stumbling like the undead through the night. Robbie had his face deep in his double cheese.

Maggott was hanging for a smoke, but you couldn't take kids into the smoking section these days. Fucken laws against everything in this so-called new South Africa. Petty laws that punished a guy who wanted a smoke while the murderers and pedophiles walked free.

"Where's my mommy?" Robbie asked, face smeared with barbecue sauce the color of congealed blood.

Maggott leaned across and wiped the boy's cheek with a paper napkin. "She's sick. So you gonna stay with me a few more days, okay?"

The kid looked uncertain, but he nodded and crammed a handful of fries into his already bulging mouth.

Maggott's wife had called him earlier. She was up in Atlantis with her new fuck. Maggott had to laugh: the Man from Atlantis. If the Flats were bad, then Atlantis was hell. A cluster of shacks and nasty houses, rotting up on the West Coast. The bitch knew how to pick them. When he'd asked her when she was coming home, she'd said she was getting engaged. She'd hung up before he could tell her you needed to get divorced before you could get fucken engaged.

When he called her back, he'd got her voice mail. If there was anything worse than his wife's voice live, it was the recorded version. She affected an Americanized drawl that was about as sophisticated as two dogs fucking in the dirt.

Shit thing was, he still loved the bitch.

Robbie was tugging at his sleeve. "Daddy, I wanna choc shake."

"Fuck that. You just gonna puke it up again. Come; we gotta go." He stood and walked out, Robbie scrambling to catch up with him.

As they crossed Voortrekker toward the blockhouse shape of Bellwood South, Robbie forced his sticky hand into Maggott's. A tik whore clinging to a lamppost gave them a leer.

"Father's Day special."

Maggott strangled a laugh.

He left Robbie with the grumbling woman constable at the front desk and hauled Disco De Lilly into an interview room. Time to see if he was ready to talk.

THE SHAKES WERE bad enough to rattle the cuffs that the pimply cop left on him. Disco sat at the table in the interview room, trying to force himself to stay calm and keep his fucken trap shut. He told himself the cop couldn't hold him for more than a night on the pathetic bit of tik he'd busted him with. He just had to stay nice and cool.

The cop sat smoking a Camel, looking at him like he was dogshit. "Disco, my buddy, talk to me."

" 'Bout what?"

"Tell me what really happened up there on the mountain the night you jacked that Benz."

"What Benz?"

The slap rocked him back in his chair. But he hardly felt it. His whole body was itching, feverish, his joints aching for a pipe.

"And tell me why your bushman buddy ended up with a bullet in his head."

Disco licked his dry lips. "I dunno. I swear."

The cop dug in his pocket and came out with Disco's pipe. Set it down on the table. Then he fished around in his jacket and came up with—honest to God—a straw of tik.

"Okay, Disco, listen. You talk to me, and you can have this." The cop held the straw so close Disco swore he could taste the bitter powder on his tongue. "Serious. You can make it right here and get nice and *zooked*. I won't say a fucken word. What you reckon?"

Disco stared at the meth. The cuffs rattled on the tabletop, and the spiders crawled out of his ears and ran into his eyes. Every nerve end in his body was being blowtorched. He was ready to spill, the magic word *yes* already forming on his coated tongue when the cop was no longer sitting in front of him.

Piper was.

Rotten teeth smiling at him, the tattooed teardrops dripping down his cheeks.

Disco squeezed his eyes shut so tight he thought his eyeballs would pop like zits. When he opened his eyes the cop was back, checking him out. Waiting for him to speak.

"Your mother's cunt" was what Disco said.

*   *   *

A HEAVY DOOR slammed shut behind Disco. The lock fell, and he heard the cop walking away. He was alone in a cell at Bellwood South, kept away from the men in the other holding pens. Heard their catcalls and whistles as the uniformed cop walked him down the corridor. He lay on the filthy mattress, shaking so badly from tik craving that he didn't even feel the bedbugs and the lice as they swarmed his body. He was in the system again. Knew where he was going to end up if he didn't keep his mouth shut.

Same place he'd ended up two years ago.

Another heavy door had slammed behind him as he'd stood in a crowded communal cell in Pollsmoor Prison. Sentenced to three years for housebreaking and meth dealing. He was in D section, the 28s' turf.

Disco was greeted by sibilant sucking sounds. Through a haze of tik smoke he saw men crouched on the floor. Men lying on bunks. Staring at him. Making the smooching noises. Knew what that meant. The sucking got louder. And the mocking laughter followed. He was surrounded, and the men ripped off his clothes, rough hands on his naked body.

A body as yet unmarked by a tattoo.

A man thrust a dirty towel at him. "Wear it."

He wrapped it around his middle like a miniskirt. It didn't cover his balls.

"Pretty bitch."

A skinny man, small as a monkey, hopped up onto a bunk and grabbed Disco's face. The monkey man had a chunk of cooked beetroot in his hand, the juice staining his palm like blood. He pressed the beetroot against Disco's lips, painting him to look like a whore.

"Pretty, pretty bitch." The monkey man cackled and skipped away.

Hands forced Disco down. When he screamed, a rag was shoved in his mouth. He writhed, fought, but the prisoners held him. Seventeen men had their turn with him on the floor, against one of the double bunks. The pain was beyond anything he could have imagined. A nylon rope, an improvised washing line, reached from the barred window to the upright of the bunks, and the dangling orange jumpsuits danced like empty men in time to the thrusts.

The next day Disco limped along the corridor, coming back from the showers, where he had tried to wash away what was done to him, knowing it would all be repeated after 4:00 p.m. lockdown.

Disco saw a man watching him, standing dead still, the others prisoners flowing past him like muddy ditch water around a rock. Tattoos circled his arms and climbed from the neck of his jumpsuit. Most unsettling of all were the black teardrops falling from each eye as the man stared, transfixed by the curse that was Disco's beauty.

Piper followed Disco to his bunk. The 28s nodded obediently when Piper told them to pack Disco's belongings and bring them to his cell, where he evicted the man in the bed beside his own. Piper lay with his tattooed face close to Disco's and raped him that night and every night for the next year and a half until Disco got paroled.

When he wasn't raping him, Piper spent endless hours of agonizing, obsessive worship—tearing into Disco's flesh with the blade and the needle, mopping the blood with a cloth, concentrating fiercely as he branded him. An excruciatingly painful, intricate filigree of black tattoos. Culminating in the name Piper curling down Disco's back, disappearing into the curve of his buttocks.

At the end of each session Piper had smiled, revealing the two false front teeth with a 2 inlaid in gold on one and an 8 on the other.

"Beautiful," he had said as he surveyed his handiwork.

chapter 22

ROXY WENT TO THE FREEZER AND POURED HERSELF A STOLI. NEAT. Felt the burn of the chilled alcohol as it slid down to her gut. She took the bottle and the glass and walked through to the sitting room where an early Chet Baker vocal was playing. After the gangbangers' visit, all she had for music was a portable CD player—shitty speakers—but she needed something to fill the silence in the house.

She lay down on the sofa and looked out at the night, the vodka and Chet Baker's "Old Devil Moon" going some way toward relaxing her. The young Chet, when his voice was still high and girlish, long before the smack had turned him gruff and wrinkled as a hobo.

She saw Billy Afrika reflected in the glass of the sliding doors as he came down the stairs, dressed in one of his crisp shirts and a pair of Levi's. His scars invisible. He'd been quiet all night, his door closed.

"Hey," she said.

"Hey." He walked past her to the kitchen. She heard the fridge door open and slap shut. He came back out carrying a plastic bottle of water.

She sat up, lifted the liter of Stoli, glass cold on her fingers. "Want a drink?"

He tapped the water bottle. "I'm sorted."

"Want to sit down?"

Billy hesitated, then surprised her by shrugging and sitting opposite her, still holding the water. He nodded toward the CD player. "Who's she?"

Roxy laughed. "Not a she. That's Chet Baker." He shook his head, and she said, "Before your time."

"You like this old-school crooner stuff?"

"I did a shoot years ago with a photographer who knew Chet from way back. He was playing it in the studio. Saw I liked it, so he gave me the CD."

"You miss it?"

"The modeling? No. It was good to me, I guess, but it was time to move on. All that air-kissing and ass-kissing. Not exactly a deep and meaningful existence."

Giving him a smile, getting nothing back.

Roxy poured herself another vodka. "Okay, I've had a couple of these"—she held up her glass—"and I've had a seriously weird couple of days, so that's going to be my excuse."

"For what?"

"For crossing some line and asking what happened to you. Where you got those scars."

His face closed, and Roxy regretted speaking. She held up a hand. "I'm sorry. I'm being a bonehead. Forget it."

Billy looked at her as if he was weighing something up. Then he surprised her for the second time. "No, I can talk about it. But it isn't no bedtime story. Sure you wanna hear it?"

"I'm sure."

He took a drink from the water bottle, screwed the cap back

on, staring out into the dark. "Okay. Happened when I was a kid. Sixteen. I'm in a gang out on the Flats. Little punks really, stealing stuff. Mugging people. Causing shit. Then the gang leader has some issue with a girl; she disses him or whatever. So he wants us to punish her. Gang-rape her, then kill her."

He looked at Roxy now. She tried to stay cool, sipped her drink.

"But I don't want no part of it." Almost a smile when he saw her relieved expression. "Relax, not 'cause I'm some good guy. I'm just chicken. Her father owns a liquor store, middle-class. Kinda people who piss perfume. His money will make the cops take notice. I don't wanna go to jail. So I fade. Try to disappear." Shaking his head. "You can't."

"And what happened to the girl?"

"They rape her. Cut her throat. Piper does. That's the leader. Piper. Dump her outside her daddy's store. The cops are after them, and Piper decides that it's me that talked. I didn't, but that don't make no difference. They get hold of me and beat me up, stab me, set me on fire, and put me in a hole and bury me. Leave me for dead."

She was staring at him, her drink forgotten halfway to her lips. "Jesus." She took a swallow, set it down on the table.

He shrugged. "I got lucky. Some little kid saw what happened and called a cop who lived nearby. Young guy. He dug me out, did some CPR, took me to hospital. I was in the burn unit for a few months."

"And the gang?"

"They got caught. Went to juvie. Juvenile prison. They all turned on the leader, Piper."

"Where is he now?"

"He pulled a whole lot more shit later, so he's in Pollsmoor. For life. No option of parole."

"Piper. Sounds so sweet."

"Not his real name. Gang name. Means 'to stab' in gang talk."

"Not so sweet," Roxy said.

"No." Looking at her before he spoke. "Wanna hear something weird?"

"Sure." Not so sure.

"Those two guys who came at you, the pretty one, they call him Disco . . ."

"Yeah?"

"He was Piper's what-you-call . . . wife in prison."

"You're kidding me, right?"

"No. S'trues God."

"That's seriously spooky."

"You're in Africa, lady. This is a spooky place."

She laughed but found her fingers on the crucifix at her neck. "And you? What happened after the hospital?"

"The cop took me under his wing, you could say. These days I would be called a 'youth at risk.' Then I was just a little punk going one way. He came and saw me in the hospital, brought me Cokes and comics and stuff. Kept up the visits when I went home. When I was better, he took me to a gym where he taught Flats' kids to box. I got my strength back, and I found out I was pretty good. Fast, strong for my size. Good enough to turn pro, he said."

"Did you?"

"Roxanne, no matter how good you are, nobody gonna put you in the ring when you look like a leper." He grinned. "It was cool, though. When I hit eighteen, he helped me get into police college. Years later, when I became a detective, we were partners. I was best man at his wedding, godfather to his firstborn kid."

She smiled. "So, kind of a happy ending."

"Ja. Kind of." She saw something soften in his green eyes.

He stood and walked over to the glass doors, looking out into the night. Chet was singing about his funny valentine. The trumpet swelled and faded, sad sweetness hanging in the air. Maybe it was the vodka, or just the last few days knocking her off center, but she was finding Billy Afrika weirdly attractive. Not whiz-bang-with-the-cheese-on-top hot, something more subtle. There was that quiet, self-contained thing he had going. Or was it just emotional autism? But now, after he told her the story, she saw a little vulnerability.

Roxy stood, walked across to him. Knew what she had to do to get back some control in the game. She'd hoped Joe's death had ended a cycle. But here she was again, getting ready to use her body as a weapon.

Billy turned, looking at her with those green eyes.

"That fire. It never touched your face," she said. Standing close to him, closer than she had ever come, and she could see he was uncomfortable.

"I told you I was lucky," he said.

She moved even closer. He stepped away.

"What's going on?" Picking up the water bottle from the table.

"Do I need to draw you a map?" Fighting hard to keep her smile alive. Knowing she'd screwed up. Too much vodka.

He shook his head. "You don't seem like the sympathy-fuck type to me. So, must mean you wanna soften me up. Take my mind off my business." Heading toward the staircase. "Not gonna happen."

"What if I'm just scared and lonely?"

Billy stopped on the stairs, turned to face her. "Lady, we're all scared. And a woman looks like you don't stay lonely for long."

He was gone.

The CD ended, and Roxy could hear the moan of the foghorn, prodded awake by the fingers of mist reaching in from the ocean.

chapter 23

THE FOGHORN WOKE BILLY AT SIX FIFTEEN. LYING IN BED, HE RE-
membered the night before and cursed himself for talking
so much. Opening up to her. *Fucken idiot.* By telling Roxanne
his story, he'd encouraged her to put the moves on him. And,
fuck, he had wanted her to. When she came up close, he'd nearly
responded. *Jesus.* A man like him had no room for that shit.

The scars on his body had made relationships difficult, so paying for sex had become the easy option. Over the last few years
even that had stopped. Stopped when he shut down. After Piper
killed Clyde.

Billy had once believed that only the rich had the luxury of
regretting the past or worrying about the future. Growing up
poor had a way of focusing the mind. Yesterday couldn't fill your
empty belly, and knives and guns and starvation and disease
stood between you and tomorrow. Booze stores and tik merchants offered a cure if living in the present was too painful
to bear.

When Billy was a boy in the streets of Paradise Park, everybody around him had lived that way. And so had he until Piper had set him alight and thrown him into that hole. Then the past took on a form. Became an engine that drove him forward. An engine fueled by revenge. He had waited nearly twenty years for the day when he could make Piper pay.

When the day came, Billy had even more reason to waste the bastard—Piper smiling at him with Clyde's blood still dripping from his hands.

But when Billy felt his finger curling on the trigger of his Z88, a voice told him: *Do that, and you're the same as him.* Told him the law was more than a line drawn in the sand of a windswept ghetto street. So he had lowered the gun and cuffed Piper and handed him into the patrol vehicle while Barbara and her children and the people of Protea Street looked on.

Billy turned as the cop van drove Piper away, saw their faces. Saw they'd wanted him to kill Piper. Execute him right there next to the body of his dead partner. Despised him for not doing it.

Billy carried Clyde's coffin the day they buried him out on the Flats, his skin burning from sweat beneath the black suit, unable to meet the accusing eyes of Barbara Adams and his cop colleagues. For them, sending Piper back to Pollsmoor could never be forgiven. Pollsmoor was home to Piper. He wanted to be there. Sending him back was a favor. A reward.

They had never spoken the word, but Billy Afrika knew what they were thinking: *coward.*

Billy rolled off the bed and hit the floor for his push-ups. Took his body into agony and beyond, until he was a sodden heap on the carpet. He lay awhile, listening to the bawl of the foghorn, then hauled himself to the shower to wash off his sweat and the memories that pressed down on him with the weight of the dead.

*   *   *

WHEN HE GOT down to the kitchen she was already making breakfast.

"You've turned me on to this whole bacon-and-eggs thing," Roxy said as she worked at the stove. She gave him a neutral smile. No sign of hurt feelings or embarrassment. No reference to the night before. Just the smile.

He sat at the table. The TV was on, the flat screen on the wall mount. Morning news. The Zulu anchorman had an accent that took off in Soweto and crashed somewhere over the mid-Atlantic.

"They've found another decapitated woman down in Sea Point," Roxy said, scrambling eggs. "Also a blonde. They're calling this guy the Barbie Doll killer."

Billy smiled inwardly. One Barbie to another.

"How do they know it's a *him*?"

Roxy saying, "Only men are screwed up enough to do shit like that," but smiling at Billy as she scraped eggs out of the pan.

"Body in the same place?"

"Pretty much. On the oceanfront."

The anchorman gave an update. The latest victim had been taking a late-night stroll by the ocean, her fiancé a minute or two behind her. The fiancé had heard her scream, followed a trail of blood and found her headless body. He hadn't seen her killer.

They were having a fight, Billy thought, *and she went off into the fog. That fiancé is one guilty bastard this morning.* The news anchor was replaced by photographs of the two dead blondes taken in happier times, smiling.

Roxy set down plates on the table, looking up at the TV. "They look like headshots."

"What're headshots?"

"What modeling agencies put out to show their range of models. Head and shoulders portraits, I guess. Used to be posters or catalogs; now you just go online."

"They look like you," he said.

"Come on, the one on the right's ten years younger than me."

"Five years, maybe. Still. The look. It's similar."

She shrugged. "Because they're blonde."

"Ja, but not only that. There's a resemblance. Admit it."

She walked back to the stove, laughing it off.

Billy said, "Don't go running on your own, is all I'm saying."

"It's getting old, Billy, give it a break." Scraping bacon into a serving dish, picking a piece up with her fingers and crunching on it as she came back to the table. "God, this bacon is good. I love it. Dunno why I haven't eaten it all these years."

Dishing food onto his plate.

On the screen a police profiler, an Afrikaans woman with shoulders and hair straight out of the WWF, said with deadpan certainty that the killer was most likely a white man in his thirties. A loner. Sexually repressed.

"Bullshit," Billy said. He reached for the remote and killed the audio as the news moved on to a suicide bomb in Karachi. "This is *muti*, man."

"Witchcraft?" Talking around a mouthful of food.

"Ja. They kill people for their body parts. I worked on a couple of cases when I was a cop. Kids with their heads and hands and balls cut off." He saw her face. "I'm sorry. You're eating."

"No. Go on, I'm interested." She put down her fork. Her eyes held his, encouraging him to continue.

"They, the darkies—Africans—believe that if you harvest the body parts while the victim is still alive, it makes for stronger *muti*. And a white, especially blonde, woman equals seriously powerful *muti*. People will pay plenty for it. To get rich. To get love. To get cured of AIDS. Or impotence. Win a fucken soccer match. You name it."

"So why are the cops putting out that profile?"

"Because its all PC bullshit. Firstly, you hear they actually said a 'white man'?"

"Yeah, so?"

"Okay, this place is so PC befuck, that if the perp—perpetrator—is colored or black, you're not allowed to say it. Not even allowed to use the words *dark complexion*."

"But you can say *white*?"

"Ja. That don't count. They don't want the bleeding hearts shouting that the cops are down on darkies. Better to have a whitey as a suspect."

She stared at him. "Let me get this straight. You're calling people who are black *darkies*?"

"Ja."

"But aren't you black?"

He laughed. "Okay, this is how it works. I'm mixed race. In other words, *colored*. I'm fine with that. But it has become a term that people are embarrassed to use. You hear people, these days, saying 'so-called colored.'" He shook his head, chewing. "After apartheid ended, anybody who wasn't white was called black, officially, on forms and documents and so on. Except now that's changed, and you have black and you have black Africans. Or ethnic black. Makes a difference when it comes to affirmative action points."

"So black Africans are . . . ?"

"Darkies."

She shook her head. "This place is fucked up."

"You're a bloody foreigner. What do you know?" He laughed around his scrambled eggs.

PIPER SAT IN the back of the police van dressed in an acid orange jumpsuit, staring out the barred window opposite. He was handcuffed and manacled.

It was more than two years since he'd seen the outside world, driving in the opposite direction on this same freeway, heading to Pollsmoor to start his life sentence for gutting the cop, Clyde Adams. This world of mountains and vineyards and big houses lost in the trees meant nothing to him. It was an illusion, like something you saw on the TV.

It wasn't real.

Pollsmoor was real. Life fading from dying men's eyes was real.

And his love for Disco was real.

There were three other men in the van, awaiting-trial prisoners on their way to court. Two of them were *franse*, unaffiliated nothings. Terrified, they kept their mouths shut and their rabbit eyes averted. The third, sitting opposite him, was a cocky punk in his early twenties, with tattoos he'd got on the street, not in prison: 28 tattoos. Or so the fucker thought.

He bobbed like a fish in a barrel, trying to get Piper's eye. "Salute, General."

Piper stared through him. Saw that they were approaching the freeway bridge at Ladies Mile Road. It was time.

Piper sat forward. "Come closer, brother."

The man leaned in, eager, smiling. Piper sprang, and in a moment he had the chain of the handcuffs wrapped tight around the piece of shit's throat, throttling him. The man was clawing at Piper's hands with his own, the cuffs getting in the way of his grip, his manacled feet doing a dead man's tap dance on the metal floor of the van.

One of the *franse* started to shout, banging on the glass that separated them from the cops in the cab.

Piper dropped the dead fucker, found the sharpened spoon in the folds of his orange jumpsuit and jammed it in the eye of the *frans*, who stopped banging and slumped against the man beside him.

Piper withdrew the spoon with a wet, smacking sound. The last man looked up at him and pleaded, lips moving soundlessly. Piper jammed the spoon into the man's throat like he was performing a backyard tracheotomy, blood geysering onto his jumpsuit.

The van had skidded to a stop under the Ladies Mile bridge, and the two cops were out of the cab and coming at him, pistols drawn.

This was as it should be. They had been paid to play their parts.

The day before, Piper had consulted with a member of the Air Force, the gang that organized prison escapes. Cash—the proceeds of Piper's cellblock drug sales—had changed hands. Some of the money had ended up in the pockets of these two cops. All Piper had to do was make it look good. He did that.

And more.

The first cop, a chubby darky, unlocked the back door of the van and pointed his weapon at Piper, bracing himself for the kick that he'd been told to expect. When Piper delivered the kick, the black cop stumbled back into his buddy, who dropped his gun. All according to plan.

These two should be on TV, Piper thought.

Then he rewrote the script.

As he landed on the blacktop he reached down for the darky's weapon. He hated guns, preferred the intimacy and control a knife gave him. But it was time to be practical. He leveled the Z88 at the cop, who looked at him in astonishment when Piper shot him in the face. The other cop, a skinny white man, realizing that things had taken a very bad turn, tried to get up and run. Piper dropped him with two shots to the back.

Passing motorists were honking and braking. Those brave enough stopped on the shoulder. Piper fired at them, starring windshields. Two cars collided, spun out onto the median strip in a spray of glass and dust.

Piper found the keys to the cuffs and manacles in the pocket of the chubby cop. Just where he'd been told they would be. He freed himself. Then he dodged cars and ran across the freeway and scrambled up the embankment beside the bridge, into a stand of trees where a bag of clothes waited for him.

chapter 24

MAGGOTT DROVE SOUTH ON THE N2 TOWARD THE MOUNTAIN AND the city. He drove fast, tailgating slower drivers until they gave way, venting his anger on the gearbox of the Ford and the civilians who slowed his passage.

Robbie, strapped in beside him, held a huge, fluffy, pink bear. The boy seemed to enjoy the speed, miming driving gestures with his dirty little hands, making *vroom vroom* noises into the bear's ear. The child needed a bath and a change of clothes, but he looked really happy.

Who knew with fucken kids?

Maggott had finally heard back from his bitch wife that morning. A text message, saying that it was Robbie's birthday. Jesus. Nothing about when she was coming home. He had a feeling she'd dumped the kid on him and made a run for it. Forever.

On his way to Bellwood South HQ, Maggott had stopped at a toy shop on Voortrekker. He'd wanted to get the kid something manly, like an action figure or a rugby ball. But no, the boy had seen this pink bear, and he wouldn't leave without it. Maggott hoped he wasn't going to grow up to be a bloody queer.

He'd endured another uncomfortable night, sleeping with his son on the single bed in his cramped and airless room. The kid had been restless, cried out in his sleep, and demanded that Maggott take him to the bathroom every hour.

So Maggott had felt like shit when he'd finally got into Bellwood. But he'd been banking on Disco De Lilly feeling even worse. A long night, and part of the morning, without tik would have the little sex-boy laid out like a piece of meat on a chopping block.

Maggott left the kid sitting in the charge office with his bear and a Coke, and went off to find Disco.

He was blocked by the superintendent. "Maggott."

"Supe."

Maggott's boss beckoned him into his office and closed the door. "You've had De Lilly in here again?"

"Got him on possession."

"Jesus Christ, Maggott, less than a bloody straw. It's still about that hijacking, isn't it?"

Maggott shrugged. "Something's up with that American woman. I know it."

"You know what? You psychic now?" Maggott said nothing, stared his superior down. The superintendent, spineless jerk-off cracked first. "You hear there's been another one of those Barbie Doll killings, Sea Point side?"

"Another blondie?"

"Ja. There's panic over there. A task force has been set up, and they're requesting manpower. Detectives in particular. You're going to go across to Sea Point and help."

"Help with what?"

"Door to doors. Interviews. Whatever they need you for. They media are crawling all over this thing like cockroaches."

"And the Flats just look after themselves?"

"Detective, I'm following orders. Just like you."

Maggott edged toward the door. "Can I at least have one more talk with De Lilly?"

The superintendent shook his head. "Too late. I chucked his ass out an hour ago."

Maggott wanted to slap the fucken pencil pusher. But he held on to himself and left the office, went to collect his son, who sat with the bear on his lap, staring in fascination at a tik whore who had passed out on a bench in the charge office, her skirt hiked up around her waist. At least he was looking at a woman. That had to be a good sign.

Maggott grabbed the boy by the hand and yanked him and the fucken bear out to the car. They wanted him to go Sea Point side, he'd go Sea Point side. But not to worry with dead blondes. There was a live one he wanted to see.

BILLY WAS SITTING downstairs flicking through a women's magazine—seven steamy sex tips to keep your man happy and your butt trim—when he heard the gate buzzer. Roxy's sandals slapped the tiles as she walked toward the door, but he overtook her, the Glock snug at his hip.

He stared at the small monochrome monitor beside the phone. Then he burst out laughing. Maggott and a kid holding a giant furry toy were standing outside the gate.

Billy pressed the button that disengaged the gate lock and hung the phone back on its cradle. Roxy was looking at him, fear clouding her blue eyes.

He shook his head. "Don't hassle. I'll deal with this."

He went to the front door and opened it. Saw Ernie Maggott walking across the pavement, trying to look all cool and authoritative, the kid clutching at his hand, wrestling a pink bear along with him.

"What's this?" Billy said. "Starsky and Hutch?"

Maggott looked ready to explode, like the zits that bloomed like berries on his sallow skin. "I need to speak to the lady." Maggott was looking over Billy's shoulder at Roxy, who had come up behind him in the doorway.

"Mrs. Palmer isn't answering any questions today."

Maggott scratched at his neck. "I'm sorry, Mrs. Palmer. But this won't take long."

"Does your superintendent know you harassing Mrs. Palmer on the day of her husband's funeral?" Billy saw he'd scored a hit. Same old Maggott, always trying to fly solo. And always crashing and burning. "Go back to Paradise Park, Maggott. You making a fool of yourself."

Billy was about to close the door when Maggott looked embarrassed. "Um, my boy, he needs the toilet."

The child said, "I got to *po po*."

Billy laughed.

Roxy stepped forward, reached out a hand to the kid. "Come, I'll take you to the bathroom."

The kid looked up at his father, who nodded. "Ja. Go with the lady."

Robbie, still clutching the bear, took hold of Roxy's hand.

"What's your name?" Roxy asked as she led the kid down the corridor.

"Robbie," the boy said. "And it's my *birfday*."

"Oh, well happy birthday, Robbie."

Then they were out of earshot.

Billy leaned against the doorjamb, relaxed, eyeing the cop. "The fuck you want here, Maggott? This isn't your turf."

"And, what, it's yours?"

"Just doing my job." Billy gave him a bland smile.

"Ja? Bodyguard?"

"Asset protection."

Maggott tugged a pack of Camels from his jeans, shook out a cigarette and lit it. "Hear you were looking for a 26 over White City side?"

"Who told you that?"

"Heard it in the wind. Found the American's dead ass in the dump this morning."

"Occupational hazard." Billy shrugged. "Only American I care about is the lady inside."

Maggott was nodding, exhaling. "Ja? Where were you, Barbie, night her husband was wasted?"

"On a plane from Dubai to Jo'burg. Emirates. Wanna see my ticket?"

Maggott shook his head. "It's okay." Scratched at a zit. Smirking. "So, seen Barbara and the kids yet?"

Billy kept it cool. "Why don't you wait in your car? I'll bring your brat out when he's done stinking up the house. And don't you come back here again without a warrant, okay?"

He closed the door in Maggott's face.

THE BROWN CHILD'S grubby clothes looked slept in, and the hand she took to lead him to the bathroom was sticky. He was joined at the hip to the huge pink bear, like a fun fur Siamese twin, rattling off in that singsong accent about it being his *birfday*. She didn't need to know too much about his circumstances to understand that it wasn't going to be a joyous occasion.

She showed the boy into the downstairs toilet—left the door slightly ajar—and stood at the window in the corridor, looking up at Lion's Head, watching a paraglider circling the summit like a giant moth. The toilet flushed, and the kid emerged, pulling up his jeans.

She took him into the adjacent bathroom, managed to separate him from the bear and washed his hands and face. He tried to wriggle from her grasp, as if he was afraid of water.

As they walked back to the front door the boy's eyes snagged on a small porcelain figurine on a table at his eye level. A Malay slave girl in Victorian dress, carrying a bundle of washing, her bodice open to reveal dusky breasts. It was in the house when Roxy moved in; something Joe's gay interior designer would have found amusing. Roxy hated the thing but had never got around to chucking it out.

"You like that, Robbie?" she asked, lifting the figure.

"Ja. It look like my mommy." He peered up at Roxy with huge dark eyes, beautiful and without guile.

"Then your mommy is very pretty." She handed the figure to the boy, who took it in his free hand.

Robbie stared down at the slave girl, then looked up at Roxy. "My mommy gone. With another uncle. What hit me."

Roxy had read some poetry in her time, even tried to write some years ago, but she couldn't recall anything as gut-wrenching as these three brief lines.

She found a smile for the child. "You keep it then, Robbie. As a birthday present."

He stared at her. "S'trues God?"

"Yes."

The boy took the figurine and hurried off as if Roxy might change her mind, went to find his father, who had been banished to his car by Billy Afrika.

Billy walked the kid out. When he came back he saw the look on Roxy's face.

"Don't stress about that guy. He's an asshole."

"What was he doing here?"

"Think about it: he's stuck out on the Flats investigating gangs and domestic assaults. Highlight of his month is arresting some tik head who raped and strangled his own toddler girl. Hid her body in the roof till it stank too much for the mother to pretend no more."

"Jesus, Billy . . ."

He shrugged. "Sorry. But that's the life out there. Then he comes across you"—he waved a hand around—"and all this. He has a dream of cracking a big case that'll get him posted to this side of town. Problem is, half his brain is missing, and the other half's gone looking for it. Get what I'm saying?"

"I get it. He's dumb as dirt. But dumb people are dangerous."

"Relax. I know his commanding officer. Any more crap from Maggott, and I'll go over his stupid head. Okay?"

She nodded. Then she went to dress for the funeral.

chapter 25

PIPER SAT AT THE BACK OF THE MINIBUS TAXI, TRYING TO KEEP HIS face in shadow so the light didn't catch the tattooed teardrops. But they were still visible, even though he'd pulled the cap low, and the other passengers avoided him like a disease.

Two dark women, squeezed into the seat ahead of his, were talking about this Barbie Doll killer who was all over the *Sun*.

"He chop the head off. Only blondes, they say."

"My daughter—the fair one—she work in Sea Point by the hair salon. She got the light streaks in her hair. Natural. I'm gonna tell her to dye it."

"Better you do. It's too terrible."

Piper tuned them out. He wore the blue jeans and brown shirt he'd found in the bag under the trees, left there by the Air Force's connections. It was as hot as a crematorium in the packed taxi, but he kept the sleeves of the shirt rolled down to hide his tattoos.

Under the trees he'd stripped off the orange jumpsuit. Then

he'd squatted with his briefs around his ankles and retrieved the condom containing a fifty-buck note he'd sent up his rectum for safekeeping before he left his cell that morning. It was slick with Vaseline and slid out easily. Over the years Piper had kept money, drugs, and even a cell phone in this God-given safety deposit box. A fifty-buck note was nothing.

He'd hidden the jumpsuit and the cop's gun under a bush and changed his clothes. But he'd kept his Grasshoppers, the shoe of choice of old-school gangsters: leather lace-up moccasins with hand stitching around the blunt-toed uppers, and wedge-shaped crepe soles. Soles that let you creep up nicely on somebody. Over the years the original tan leather had disappeared under layers of oxblood polish.

At Retreat a colored woman was forced to squeeze in next to Piper, a toddler on her lap. From the way she sat—rigid, head turned away from him—the woman knew very well what the tattooed tears signified.

The child, a girl in a T-shirt with *tweet me wight* written across the chest in pink letters, stared up at Piper's face, fascinated. Children unnerved Piper. They were bad luck, the way they could look in your eyes and see your soul like it was a flipping TV.

Another advantage of prison: no kids. Except on visiting day when the families arrived. But nobody ever came to visit Piper, and he'd spend the day in his cell, never having to clap eyes on the dwarves.

The child was still staring, unblinking, a bubble of drool forming in the corner of her mouth. Piper reached out a hand and turned the child's face away. She opened her mouth and howled.

The mother risked a glance at Piper.

"It look at me again, I break its neck," he said.

The woman didn't doubt him, just scooped up the child and fought her way to the front of the minibus, calling for the driver to stop. As the taxi jerked back into the traffic, Piper saw them standing on the sidewalk outside a loan agency. The child still crying, the mother smacking its ass like the whole thing was its fault.

A cop van cruised up beside the taxi, and Piper pulled his cap lower and stared down at his shoes. Out the corner of his eye he saw the cops turning into a side street.

As he flexed his toes, an image of Disco came to Piper. Sitting on a bunk, that beautiful face concentrating as he used a rag over his index finger—stained the color of blood—to dip into the shoe polish before he rubbed it into the leather of these Grasshoppers.

Not long now. Piper felt himself harden inside his jeans.

THE SPIDERS CRAWLED from Disco's eyes, scuttled down his face, disappeared beneath his T-shirt, losing themselves in Piper's brutal artwork. He lay on his stinking mattress and begged the spiders to stay away. Acrid sweat ran from him like he'd sprung a leak, and his joints joined in a chorus, singing along with his nerves and his cramping gut, pleading for the sweet relief that only tik could give him. He tore off the T-shirt and dabbed it at his body. It was soaked through within seconds. Then he put the sodden thing in his mouth and bit into it to stop himself from screaming.

Ice. Choef. Crystals. Tik-tik. Globes. Meth.

The names danced in front of his eyes like they were written in neon.

It was going on for a day since he'd caught a tiny hit of that straw he'd scored from Popeye. Barely got half a chesty into his lungs before that cop kicked it out of him. After the interrogation and the hellish night in the cell, he needed something to calm him. But he didn't have no money. Not one fucken cent.

He knew he was stupid to come home to the *zozo*, that Manson could have been waiting, but he wanted a dark hole to crawl into and hide. But what he really needed was to score. He lay shivering, staring at the wall where the picture of his mother used to hang. Even though it was gone, inside with the fat woman, he could still see his mother's face. That beautiful face, so much like his.

Then he was hearing disco music, his mother's favorite song . . .

First I was afraid . . .

No. He couldn't handle that. Not Gloria Gaynor. Not now.

But the words were coming. He couldn't stop them, even though he wrapped the rancid pillow around his head. He couldn't stop the music and the memory that rode in on the back of it like the devil on a dark horse.

I was petrified . . .

Three-year-old Disco dancing to "I Will Survive," dancing the dance that gave him the nickname that stuck to him like glue. A hot sweaty night in that apartment on Hippo Street, Dark City side, airless now the wind had died. Disco swirling around in the cramped sitting room, between the torn sofa and the old black-and-white TV, a ghetto blaster banging out the music on a tape stretched from overplaying. The music loud in the Cape Flats night.

But not loud enough to drown the words of Disco's mother, Evangeline De Lilly—Vangie—and her boyfriend, Pedro. They were at the kitchen table, and Pedro was making another white pipe, the apartment already hanging with smoke like smog on a still day. Disco spun, dizzy, head swirling, a feeling he would seek to reproduce the rest of his life. Snatches of conversation reached him, but he forced himself not to hear.

"He go, or I go," Pedro said.

"But it's my son."

"I'm telling you, Vangie. I fucken mean it. Do it, or I go."

Then his mommy, beautiful and forever young, came toward Disco, drying tears on her face, reaching her arms out to him. Disco smiled up at her, swaying his tiny hips, ready to dance with her the way he always did. His mommy was on her knees in front of him, and she wrapped her arms around him, trapping him, stopping his scrawny body from moving to the beat. She released him, took his face in her hands, and kissed him.

Then his mommy's hands were at his throat, squeezing, until he was choking and gasping. Little fists trying to fight her off.

His mommy's face like he had never seen it before. Made mad by drugs and lust.

Disco went into a place darker even than his mommy's eyes.

Blackness. No air. A heat like none he had ever known. And a noise, a mechanical bellowing, crashing. He reached out his hands in the dark and felt something. Something slick. His fingers scrambled for purchase and he grabbed and tore, and a chink of light burned through the blackness. Tore deeper, and he saw a mound of trash and beyond it the landfill stretching to infinity.

Disco fought his way out of the black bag, a tiny figure on the wasteland of junk, seagulls screaming as they dived out of the hot white sky. The noise he heard was a bulldozer, balanced high above him on a mountain of garbage, its front end lifting, about to send a heap tumbling down on him. Disco ran, pumping his little legs, sliding, falling, making no progress in the quicksand of slop.

The bulldozer tipped its load.

Disco was smashed, rolled, flattened by the flood of trash. It clogged his eyes and his nose and his ears. The weight of the world's waste burying him. His breath smashed from his lungs. Once again all was black. Silence.

Then an arm, a thin reed waving in the ocean of offal. And a head, like a newborn fighting itself way out of a womb of shit. He pulled his way to the surface, stinking, exhausted. Dragged himself upward, lay for a minute, coughing sludge and slime.

Disco walked forever through the filth. Saw people in the distance, black scribbles on the horizon, scavengers looking for

food and empty bottles, same as him and his mommy did sometimes. Saw the ghetto apartments built right up to the edge of
the dump, like rusted trawlers becalmed on a sea of trash.

Home.

Reeking, body covered in slime and rotting food, he dragged
himself up to the third floor and banged on his door. No reply. He
banged again, crying. Sobbing. Loud enough for the old woman in
the next apartment to peer down at him and cluck before she
slammed her front door.

He banged and banged until at last the door opened and his
mommy stood there, wrapped in a towel. She screamed and
jumped back, hands to her face, the towel falling away from her
bare body. Disco walked in and saw Pedro filling the doorway
to the bedroom, naked, scratching at the fat, wet thing that jutted from the wiry hair at the base of his tattooed belly.

"Fucken useless cunt," Pedro said as he walked back into
the bedroom and slammed the door.

Pedro beat his mother, beat Disco, and drove away in a '73
Beetle, never to be seen again. And two days later Disco found
his mommy lying in her own blood in the bathtub, Gloria Gaynor
on a loop in the background.

I will survive.

Not this time.

Disco screamed, screamed himself all the way back to the
here and now.

Him lying on his bed, sweating, hanging for tik more than
he had ever hung for anything in his whole fucken life. Disco
lifted himself off the bed and dragged his branded ass across to
where his clothes were still shoved in the plastic bag. He found
a pair of Diesels, the ones that sat nice and low-slung on his
hips. Sexy like. Bought after one of him and Goddy's more suc-
cessful scores.

Godwynn.

Disco's fevered imagination—on a roll now—served him up

an image of Goddy lying in that same dump, his brains oozing out of his mouth, a living carpet of flies buzzing like dentists' drills as they clung to him, making him even blacker. Disco spewed. He couldn't stop it. Yellow bile onto the Diesels. Fuck it. He wanted to trade them for a straw. Knew that Popeye had a hard-on for these jeans.

He edged to the window and peeped out, terrified he'd see Manson and his crew. The cramped yard was empty. He needed to get to the faucet next to the fat woman's kitchen. The only place he could rinse these jeans before he went down to Popeye to beg him to trade for tik. Got to his feet and opened the door an inch. Put a weeping eye to the crack. Saw a slice of blue sky and white sand. Empty.

Disco left the *zozo* and scuttled across to the faucet, bent double as the cramps took him again. He was washing his kotch off the jeans when a shadow fell across him. His nerves were so befuck he swore he felt the weight of it.

He waited for the cold mouth of a gun to kiss the back of his neck. Resigned himself.

What the fuck . . . ?

The smell clued him in even before the voice. "What's up with you?"

The fat woman stood over him, in the fluffy nightdress that seemed to grow on her like the mold on rotting meat.

"I'm sick, Auntie," he said.

She laughed. "Sick for a pipe, ja. You not careful, you'll be dead, too."

He squinted up at her, the massive breasts sheltering him from the sun that burned his skin like flames.

"Ja, they was here. Last night and this morning," the fat bitch said.

"Who?"

"Manson's people. They wake me and Zuma up."

The little black mongrel hid behind her and yapped at Disco, dancing on three paws in the dust, fourth leg jiggling in the air like it was on a spring.

"What they say?"

"What you think they say? They gonna kill your fucken ass dead."

She bent down and picked up the dog, clutched it to her, almost losing it in her breasts, kissing its head. "Come, come, little Zuma boy. Let Mommy give you some nice fish cakes." She waddled off into the house.

Disco scrubbed like crazy.

chapter 26

THEY LEFT THE SUN BEHIND AS THEY ROUNDED HOSPITAL BEND, driving into a low cloud draped like damp cotton wool over the mountain and the heavily treed suburbs. Leaving behind what remained of Roxy's good mood, too.

A perfect day for a funeral.

Roxy sat beside Billy in the Hyundai, traveling deeper into the cloud. Billy drove fast but well, seemed to sense gaps in the traffic before they opened, avoiding the minibus taxis that hurtled like scuds toward the Flats. He wore a pair of dark jeans and a white shirt under a black leather jacket. No tie. Wearing shoes, too, a pair of black lace-ups that looked freshly polished.

Light rain splattered the windshield of the car, and Billy flicked the wipers into a slow moan. The rhythm of a funeral dirge. After five years the mysteries of Cape Town weather were no clearer to Roxy. The locals said, being on a peninsula, you got four seasons in a day. Not only the weather changed on this side of the mountain, away from the ocean. Her part of town, still marinating in rich sunlight, had something Mediterranean about it, the feel of the Riviera. But this looked more like England. Houses that wouldn't be out of place in a prosperous London suburb, sheltering behind oaks.

Roxy dropped the visor on the passenger side and looked at herself in the mirror. No makeup, except for a smear of lipstick. She decided that should go and dabbed at her lips with a Kleenex until they were bare.

She wore a simple black dress. No jewelry except for the crucifix and her wedding band. She'd nearly left the house without the ring, having removed it the day after Joe died. An unconscious act of self-liberation.

She'd felt strangely upbeat over breakfast. After her clumsy attempt at seduction the night before, she'd expected Billy to retreat into silence. But he'd seemed eager to talk, even if it was that macabre conversation about the Sea Point killer. Conversations with Billy Afrika were the weirdest she'd ever heard. Fascinating, though. Sometimes the best stories were the back stories.

Then that cop with the skin like last week's pizza had arrived with his kid. The interlude with the boy had left her feeling off course and depressed.

Roxy saw a row of cars and a black hearse, parked outside a small Catholic chapel in a quiet, tree-lined street. Had Joe ever been a practicing Catholic? She'd never known. They'd married at a registry office before flying off to Mauritius for their honeymoon. She knew, though, that Joe had wanted to be cremated, so at least she wouldn't have to endure the graveside rituals.

Billy parked, came around to her side, and opened the door.

"I'll catch you afterward, okay?" Closing the door after her.

"You're not coming in?"

"I am. But I'll hang near the back."

She nodded and walked toward the chapel. The Hyundai chirped behind her as Billy used the clicker to lock it.

People were drifting into the church. Men in suits, women

wrestling down the waistlines of dark dresses they hadn't worn in a while. They sized Roxy up and held tighter to their men. She scanned the faces, mostly white, mostly middle-aged. Nobody she knew.

An undertaker, a gaunt man in a shiny black suit, materialized from around the side of the chapel, cigarette smoke seeping from his nostrils like his head was on fire. She felt his eyes on her butt as she walked up the stairs. "Abide With Me" warbled out of speakers inside the church, the high notes distorted. She paused at the top of the stairs and looked back. Billy was standing on the sidewalk, watching. He nodded at her. She turned and went inside.

Joe's coffin, covered in wreaths, rested on a silver bier.

The reality of what she had done hit Roxy and nailed her to the aisle, like the nails in the hands and feet of the wooden Christ that hung over the pulpit, staring down at her in anguish. She felt as if the crucifix dangling from her neck was burning into her flesh.

She forced herself forward.

Jane and her mother sat in the prime mourner's seats, in the front-row pew. Roxy had never met Joe's first wife, but she'd glimpsed the woman once at the Waterfront, battling heels too high and too young for her, face fixed in the permanently startled smile that comes with cosmetic surgery. Or maybe she was still shocked that all the nipping and tucking hadn't stopped Joe from trading up.

Roxy found a seat on the aisle, halfway down. She slid a hymnbook out of the rack in front of her. Flipped though it to distract herself. People around her were standing, and a man wearing vestments and a dog collar took to the pulpit. He had a comb-over, and layers of flesh sagged from his chin, like the bellows of a church organ.

He'd worked hard to achieve what he reckoned was an informal manner, as if that would make the words he spoke about a man he'd never met seem more sincere. It didn't. He waffled on fulsomely about a man Roxy never knew either: a dutiful husband and father. A businessman.

Off-key hymns were sung. Roxy went into a quiet place within herself, like she was in a floatation tank. Not awake exactly, but not asleep. Blank.

Until she heard the unmistakable moan of Bob Dylan singing "Death Is Not the End." Jane's idea of a send-off for her father. It sounded like a threat to Roxy, and she remembered the dream of the undead Joe that had left her screaming. Jane came to stand next to the coffin, mulish jaw raised as if to defy the tears that streamed down her face, pink knees showing under a badly hemmed dress.

Dylan came to an abrupt halt, left standing at the crossroads he could not comprehend.

Jane was sniffing, talking through the tears, about Joe. Was Roxy imagining it, or were the girl's eyes fixed on her?

Roxy needed air. She left the pew and walked toward the door. Told herself not to run.

It was still drizzling outside, but Roxy was out in the open, breathing gratefully, smelling the ozone. As she walked toward the road, a thin wire of lightning strobed on the horizon.

PIPER LEFT THE taxi at the Mowbray stop, near the station. He was on his way to catch a train through to Paradise Park—it would be emptier and more anonymous than another taxi at this time of day. But first he needed to do a bit of shopping.

As Piper approached Ebrahim's Superette, a dingy corner store in a sagging Edwardian building, two Muslim men in knitted kufi caps stepped out. One was young, in jeans and Nikes, a patchy beard like a fungus straggling across his face. The other was much older, in a pantsuit and sandals, his full white beard touching his chest.

The young man took off down the sidewalk. The old one was busy closing the door, hanging the hand-lettered sign that said the store was shut for Friday lunchtime prayers.

He barely looked at Piper when he approached. "We closed."

Piper held out the fifty-buck note. "I just need me some soap."

The Muslim was about to lock the security gate; then he squinted at the money.

"Okay, but you have to make quick."

He opened the door and went inside. Piper followed and closed the door, heard the click of the lock as it engaged. The store was typical of those found in the low-rent neighborhoods of the inner city and out on the Flats. Everything from bicycles to clothes, candles, primus stoves and grocery items. Incense and the rich smell of curried meat hung in the air. The small windows were jammed with faded shirts and bolts of fabric, the glass dirty enough to keep out prying eyes.

Piper saw what he was looking for, in a finger-smeared display cabinet beneath the cash register: a range of Okapi knives. This ring-lock folding pocket knife, with a four-inch carbon steel blade, curved wooden handle inlaid with metal crescents and stars, had sent generations of brown men to their graves. Or the emergency room if they were lucky and the knifeman was shoddy in his work.

Piper had first held one of these knives in his hand when he was ten years old. And had killed his first man with one a year later. That was one thing he missed in prison: the curve of that wooden handle in his palm. He'd killed men with sharpened spoons or slivers of plastic torn from buckets, but there was nothing like flicking the Okapi open on the seam of his trousers, seeing the gleam on the blade, and putting it to work.

"Gimme one of those." He pointed into the cabinet, to his preferred model.

The man looked hard at Piper and didn't seem to like what he saw. "That going to set you back more than a soap."

"Don't worry, old man. I got it."

The Muslim wheezed and coughed as he unlocked the cabinet. He lifted out the knife and handed it to Piper, who weighed it in his palm and smiled his 28 smile. *Perfect.*

He opened the blade and tested a finger against it. It needed to be honed, but it would do. The next part was pure instinct. He reached across the counter with his left hand and grabbed a handful of the Muslim's shirt, pulling the man toward him. At the same time he raised the blade so that it hung for a moment at ninety degrees to his body; then he brought his arm down and felt the knife pierce the old man's chest. Pulled the knife out and plunged it down three more times.

He let go of the Muslim, who slumped across the cabinet, then slid back and fell behind the counter, a smear of blood on the glass top.

Piper wiped the blade clean on a dishtowel that hung on display and slid the Okapi into the pocket of his jeans. He reached over and took the twin of the knife he'd just used and pocketed it, too.

He opened the cash register and grabbed the notes inside. Probably not more than five hundred rand, but enough for his needs. He didn't intend to be out for long.

Piper helped himself to a pair of dusty sunglasses from the rack on the counter. Cheap plastic knockoffs, chunky black things from the *Super Fly* days of the seventies. They would cover at least part of his tattooed face. Then he pocketed a bar of Caress bath soap. A gift.

Piper left the store. Now he was going to do what any man getting out of prison does: he was going to see his wife.

chapter 27

ROXY WAS STARTING TO FEEL MORE COMPOSED, WANDERING ALONG A lane of oaks that cut through the old graveyard facing the chapel. Crumbling headstones, dismembered angels reaching up to heaven through long grass.

She heard the tap of high heels behind her and turned to see the African cannibal and the Ukrainian whore approaching through the drizzle. It took Roxy a moment to place them. Not that they weren't memorable, but a lot had happened since that dinner in Camps Bay, the night it all began.

The whore held an umbrella over her man, keeping his silk suit dry, the rain turning her yellow hair to string. The hair was no longer braided but hung loose, split ends brushing the dandruff on her dark coat.

The cannibal reached out and enfolded Roxy's hand in both of his.

"Mrs. Palmer. So tragic." *Tragique.* The limpid eyes brimmed with sympathy. "All my condolences."

His hands felt like a cane toad Roxy had found nestling near a scummy swimming pool in Hialeah when she was a kid. She'd made the mistake of picking it up, and it had squirted a toxic goo on her hands, leaving the skin inflamed for days.

She took her hand back.

"Thank you for being here."

"And to think that we were together. For the last supper." A shake of the noble head.

Roxy was feeling out of whack anyway, and the last-supper reference nearly had her giggling. But she bit back the laughter. "Yes. Who would have thought?"

The bottle blonde T-boned the conversation. "Your dress, it is a Nina Ricci?"

Roxy nodded. "Yes, it is."

The whore looked like she was about to rip the dress off Roxy's back and make a run for the main road. The African elbowed her aside.

"Mrs. Palmer, of course it is difficult to discuss these matters at such a time. But . . ."

Roxy was staring at him, shaking her head, confused. She looked over his shoulder and saw Billy Afrika standing on the sidewalk outside the church, watching them.

The cannibal pressed on. "That night, I left Mr. Palmer with an attaché case. You remember, perhaps?"

Roxy nodded. She did vaguely recall Joe carrying a case as they walked back to the car. Saw him sling it into the trunk of the Mercedes after opening the door for her.

"It was a deposit on some equipment your husband was going to supply. Equipment my country very desperately needs, Mrs. Palmer."

Billy was walking toward them. Roxy looked at the African. "I'm not sure I get what you're saying here . . ."

"That money, that down payment, was a substantial amount

of dollars." *Dollairs.* "Money, Mrs. Palmer, that is like the blood of my people. You understand?"

"No. I don't."

"I, we, our country needs it back, Mrs. Palmer. At all costs."

She laughed. Understood why they were here. "Get in line, buddy. And speak to my husband's lawyer."

She tried to walk past him, but he put out a hand to stop her. Billy was there, and very suddenly the African had pulled his hand away and was rubbing his arm. She hadn't seen what Billy did; he'd moved too fast. But it had hurt.

The cannibal was breathing heavily, saying something in French that she was sure wasn't another expression of sympathy.

Billy took Roxy gently by the arm and walked her away.

"What did they want?"

"Same as you." He looked at her. "Blood money."

She stepped away from his hand and headed toward the car, wanting to get out of there before the mourners left the chapel.

MANSON SAT IN the rear of the Hummer, parked outside the high school in Paradise Park. A grim-looking place with more razor wire surrounding it than Pollsmoor. He was waiting for his daughter, Bianca.

Manson had offspring littered across the Flats. But he had a soft spot for this kid, always had. She'd been born a tiger. Just like him. Bianca's mother had been a good-time girl, who was all sex at sixteen, a used-up tik head at eighteen, and a corpse at twenty.

He'd put the child with his sister, Charneze, over by the tik house. Had Bianca at his place sometimes, on the weekends.

The girl was in the shit again. His sister phoned him and told him to go get her at school. Charneze was too busy cooking—big weekend coming up. So Manson got Arafat and Boogie to drive him over. Didn't have time for this mess, he had a business to run, but what could a father do?

While he waited, he thought about sorting out that little rabbit, Disco, who was hiding his punk ass away. Couldn't hide forever. Didn't think he'd kill him, just carve his initials in Disco's pretty face, let him walk around reminding everybody not to fuck with Manson.

He looked out the window, saw Clyde's kid. Jodie. In her netball outfit, close by the fence. Tight little ass in that tiny pleated skirt, didn't cover none of her goods. She saw him and waved—fucken begging for it—then skipped up to take a shot at the hoop, skirt lifting to show her panties.

He could get any girl he wanted, by choice or force. And he didn't need the money her mommy was giving him. But it was all about power. Power over the dead cop's family.

Captain Clyde Adams had been a hard-assed bastard. Proud that he couldn't be bought. Spat in your face when you tried to bribe him. Made life tough for the Paradise Park gangsters. There had been a number of attempts on his life before Piper got it right.

He wasn't missed.

And the wife, Barbara, refused to greet Manson on Sundays over at the New Apostolic Church. She always held herself better than everybody else. As if the holy light shone right out her crack.

Manson remembered laughing when some little piece of ass he was screwing—worked at Standard Bank near Bellwood South—came and told him about the dollars going into Barbara Adams's account every month. All it had taken was a visit or two, Protea Street side, to persuade Barbara to hand that cash over to him.

Manson had enjoyed making her squirm and beg. And fuck his promise to Billy Afrika; he was going to enjoy this little Jodie, too.

Manson's eyes moved from the girl playing netball to his

daughter crossing the dusty yard toward the Hummer, hips swaying under her short school skirt, tits pushing at her blouse.
Way too developed for her age. She had grown up wild and beautiful. So much like her mother he had to squint sometimes to
see who he was looking at.

Bianca slid into the car next to him, blowing a pink bubble
of gum the size of a balloon. She popped it with a wet smack
and started chewing again as Arafat got the Hummer rumbling
down the street.

"The fuck's up with you, Bianca?" Manson asked, trying for
a parental tone. Failing.

"Nothing's up with me."

"It true about you pulling a blade on some girly?"

"Of course, yes. Any bitch gimme shit, I gonna cut her."

"What happened?"

"She say my mommy were a bushman. That's why my hair
is like so." She fingered her wild tangle of curls.

"Okay, that's a lie, first. And it's a shit thing to say, second.
But you can't go round killing people, understand?

"Why? You do."

"That's different," Manson said, sensing thin ice ahead.

"Why so?"

" 'Cause, it's my fucken job is why."

"Okay. But you had to start somewheres."

"Bianca, you fucken thirteen."

"So?"

"So, these things can wait a few years."

"You saying I can only kill some bitch when I'm a grown-up?"

"Ja. That's what I'm saying."

"Fuck that. I want me a gun. Shoot the cunts." She popped
the gum. Smacked like a gunshot.

Manson shook his head, saw himself when he was her age.
Didn't understand life sometimes. Why the hell couldn't she
have been born a boy?

* * *

BY THE TIME they passed the Waterfront they were back in the sun, and the air had turned thick and hot. The other side of the mountain like a foreign country.

Roxy had been silent since they reached the car, and Billy let her be. Still, he wondered who the darky—so black he was blue—and the bottle blonde were. Needed to know if they were going to come between him and his money.

They were winding up toward Lion's Head when Roxy spoke. "You kill people, don't you?"

"Not if I can help it."

"But you have? In the past?"

He nodded. "To defend myself."

She hesitated, as if searching for the right words, gazing out at the last clouds burning off the flat blue sky. "How are you meant to feel, when you've done something like that?"

He shrugged. "Every time it's different."

"I don't feel any remorse, or guilt, for what I did. I'm just totally terrified I'll be caught. Is that bad?" Her eyes were on him now. Like she wanted some kind of absolution.

"Roxanne, I told you already, I don't give a fuck you shot Joe. He's dust. Nothing more to say. You need to talk about it, see a priest or a shrink."

Billy looked across at her.

Saw her blink. Nod.

ROXY DIDN'T SPEAK the rest of the way home.

She felt spaced out, like when she was fourteen and taking cheap drugs to smear and soften the hard edges of her life. Ten years later, in Europe, the drugs were expensive and she chased them with French champagne, but they'd still left her hollow and fragmented, her life a blur, like images glimpsed from a speeding train.

Roxy closed her eyes. She hadn't told Billy the whole story. She was afraid, of course, of getting caught for what she did. Doing jail time. But back there in the chapel, with the ghoulish Christ staring down at her, she'd felt another kind of fear: that she was going to have to pay for what she did to Joe. In whatever way.

"Fuck."

Billy's voice startled her. She opened her eyes.

He was slowing outside the house. Gates standing wide-open. Police vehicles and an occupying army of uniformed and plainclothes cops cluttering the driveway. Billy smashed the Hyundai into reverse, looking back over his shoulder, accelerating.

She looked back, too, in time to see a police van slide in behind them, blocking their exit.

chapter 28

ROXY STEPPED OUT OF THE CAR. SAW THE FRONT DOOR OF THE house standing open, blue uniforms in the hallway merging with the ocean beyond.

Billy was around to her, speaking in low tones before the cops reached them: "Don't say anything to these guys until you speak to your lawyer, okay?"

A man in a suit, too expensive for a cop, approached her. "Are you Mrs. Roxanne Palmer?"

"Yes, I am."

"My name's Ronald Barker. I'm the *curator bonis*, executing the warrant to seize property under a preservation and forfeiture order." He was flapping something official-looking under her nose.

"Want to run that by me in English?"

"I am working with the Asset Forfeiture Unit. We have been granted a high court order to seize all assets belonging to Mr. Joseph Palmer."

"But he's dead."

"Exactly. In these cases we have to move promptly to prevent the estate absorbing the disputed items. Mr. Palmer was under investigation on various charges, including tax fraud and the recruitment of mercenaries for foreign countries. As such, all his assets are to be seized and all bank accounts frozen."

Roxy stared at Billy, still not getting this.

He took her arm and walked her away, her eyes still on the man in the suit.

"Roxanne," he said, voice low. "Look at me." She looked at him. "This isn't about you killing Joe. You understand?"

"Yes. Kind of."

"So say nothing. This is a whole other deal. Joe was in deep shit. That's why I wasn't being paid. Why his business fucked up. He didn't mention this to you?"

She shook her head. "No. He was just drinking more. Angrier."

Angry enough to smack her down the stairs and kill her baby.

"Good news is, you're not being busted for murder."

"And the bad news is, I'm out on my ass with nothing?"

He nodded. "Ja. That's about it." A tight smile. "At least you got your ass, though."

"That's hilarious." Not smiling. "And there's not going to be any money? Ever?"

He shook his head. "No. If these vultures are here, it's gone."

She was taking this in. Adjusting. "What are you going to do?"

"Whatever I need to do," he said.

"I'm sorry."

He shrugged. "Don't be. Worry about yourself."

Roxy nodded, then walked over to the man in the suit. "Mr. . . . ?"

"Barker."

"I need to speak to my lawyer."

"Would that be Mr. Richardson?"

"Yes."

"You'll need to find another attorney. Mr. Richardson is in custody. Let's just say he was giving your late husband pretty bad legal advice." He looked smug. A man who enjoyed his job.

It made sense now, the way Dick had looked when he'd come by the day before. Wanting Joe's laptop. The bastard had known the shit was about to hit, and he hadn't even warned her.

Roxy tried to keep her voice level. "What can I take from the house?"

"You'll be allowed to take a limited amount of personal effects, toiletries, and so on. Some clothes. No jewelry or household items. One of the female officers will accompany you."

A woman cop had appeared at her side. Roxy looked across at Billy. He shrugged.

She turned and entered the house, the cop walking a step behind her.

BILLY, A YOUNG white uniform dogging his heels, went up to the spare room. All of his things were already in his duffel bag: razor, toothbrush, the lot. An old habit. He was always ready to roll. The cop scratched around in the bag. Nodded. Billy zipped the bag, slung it over his shoulder, and walked.

In the corridor he passed a room he'd never seen open before. A pink room, like a kid's nursery. Roxy stood inside the room, the woman cop hovering in the doorway. Roxy looked up at Billy. He saw an expression of pure pain on her face. It almost made him stop, go to her, and comfort her.

Then he turned and walked away, toward the stairs.

She had her problems. But that's all they were: her problems.

He had a family to protect. And he had to find the money to protect them with.

*   *   *

MAGGOTT WAS LATE for the strategy briefing.

He opened the door at the end of a dim corridor on the top floor of the Sea Point cop shop, saw some darky in a flashy suit running the show—brought in from regional HQ, pretending he knew what he was talking about.

Maggott found a seat, sensing an air of embarrassment in the room. He almost laughed. When you looked past the suit, you saw straight out onto Three Anchor Bay and Rocklands Beach. Where the two blondes had lost their heads.

No wonder these guys felt small.

The room was full of the cops you got everywhere: good, bad, bored. The darky was saying they had "developed a profile." Passed around the Identikit of a suspect who had allegedly been seen in the area around the time of the murders. White guy with a face flat as a shovel. Maggott could smell the bullshit. This was for the media. End of story.

Maggott had his hand up.

The suit raised his eyebrows. "Yes?"

"Detective Maggott. Bellwood South."

"What's on your mind, Detective?"

"These women, no signs of sexual assault?"

"We covered that before you arrived. Answer's no."

"So just their heads taken? You not thinking *muti* here?"

Mutters around the table, nobody wanting to meet his eye except the suit who looked like his pants had suddenly grown too tight.

"Jesus, not again. What is it, this obsession with witchcraft? Soon as you get a body part missing, it has to be an African indulging in some primitive ritual."

Maggott pressed on. "Just, I've worked some *muti* cases out in the"—he almost said "squatter camps," caught himself in time— "the informal settlements. Always have the missing bits."

The suit shut him down. "Thanks for sharing your expertise, Detective. We've got a serial killer here. Different ball game.

And serial killers prey on their own ethnic groups. Fact. Our perpetrator is white. Apartheid is alive and well among the psychos
and bipolars." A couple of chuckles. "In fact it always was."

Laughter at this, leaving Maggott's face red and zits ready for
liftoff.

The darky held up the Identikit. "This is our suspect. Okay?"

The briefing wound down with the suit assigning tasks. Maggott could have predicted it: he was from the Flats, so he was
sent out to walk the oceanfront with a bunch of trainee cops in
uniform. Hand out xeroxes and talk to the pensioners and the
homeless and the lunatics the state could no longer afford to
keep locked up.

Fuck.

Maggott grabbed a handful of the Identikits and went down
to his car. Robbie, for once, had obeyed him and stayed inside.
Looking tearful and as pink-faced as the bear he clutched. Maggott took the boy across to the strip of grass next to the ocean. He
sat Robbie under a tree, while he walked the beachfront, stewing
with rage. Sun beating down on him. Sweating in his lace-up
shoes, jeans, and shirt. The people strolling around him were
in shorts and swimwear, and the smell of coconut oil fought the
stink of rotting kelp.

He wasted his time handing out the flyers and speaking to the
derelicts, lying on the lawn like junk washed up by the ocean.
Maggott had ambitions to work this side of town, but they didn't
include speaking to people who stank worse than those out on
the Flats.

He approached an elderly white woman who crabbed across
the grass, clutching a plastic bag. Maggott thought she was wearing baggy tights, until he saw that her sun-damaged skin sagged
in furrows around her ankles, legs bare beneath tiny shorts. The
old woman cringed back from him as if he was going to mug her.
He flashed his badge and showed her the Identikit. She stared at
it, blank.

Shook her head as she took a stale crust of bread from the bag and broke it apart with shaking fingers, throwing bits onto the grass. Within seconds she was lost in a boiling cloud of screaming seagulls, fighting each other for crumbs.

Maggott walked off, cursing in Cape Flats Afrikaans.

He couldn't keep his mind off that house up on the mountain, sure that if he craned his neck past a drunk digging in a trash can, he could see its glass front catching the sun. He was obsessing, and he knew it.

Maggott stood by the railing, looking out over the ocean. He lit a cigarette and ran his theory: the blonde gets those two lowlifes from Paradise Park to take out her husband, make it look like a hijacking. She does it for the money, what else? Then something goes down, maybe Disco and Godwynn try to blackmail her. So she pays Billy Afrika—guy who works for Joe Palmer—to sort them out, and he kills Godwynn.

It could fly, he thought as he drew on the Camel and trickled smoke from his nostrils. But there were holes, he had to admit. Like, why was Disco still walking his punk ass around White City? And Billy Afrika—Barbie—was fucken chickenshit. Couldn't even plug the guy who killed his partner, so was he up for a hit, point-blank, execution style? If Maggott could run ballistics on the slug in Godwynn MacIntosh's head, he'd be able to answer that. But some brown life meant dick.

Kill a white bitch or two, and you had a media circus.

Maggott finished his smoke, thinking of the lip Barbie gave him, while that American blonde stayed all cool and untouchable in the background. Thinking of the two of them getting away with murder. What he needed was to get Billy Afrika out of the way and do the Cape Flats version of social networking: Facebook without the Internet. Put Disco and Roxanne Palmer in a room together, in each other's faces. Bet that one of them would crack.

Maggott flicked his cigarette butt onto the grass and looked around for Robbie. The fucken kid wasn't under the tree any-more. He saw him standing next to a homeless woman who sat on the grass beside a supermarket cart. A darky, dressed in rags, with one of her legs—a weird red color—stuck out in front of her.

"Robbie!" He shouted, but the kid didn't hear him. Maggott walked toward the boy, who was staring at the cart, which had all sorts of shit on it, mirrors and feathers, and what looked like a doll tied on with rusted wire.

And the stink. *Fuck. What did she keep in there under that rancid blanket?*

The woman was muttering to herself, gazing into a piece of broken mirror hanging from the cart. He saw something leak-ing from her swollen leg, and the flies were enjoying it.

"The fuck you doing here?" Maggott grabbed the boy by the arm. "Thought I tole you to stay by the tree?"

Before he could stop himself he whacked the kid on his butt with an open palm. Harder than he meant to, and Robbie opened his mouth and leaned back like one of the Three Tenors and let rip with a scream.

Maggott waited until the boy had to pause to catch air, panting.

"You shut the fuck up, and I'll take you to the Spur tonight. Okay?"

Robbie looked up at him, all snot and quivering lips. But the Spur, a steakhouse chain where the waiters sang to kids on their birthdays, was irresistible.

"You swear?"

"Yes, Jesus. I swear."

Without warning, the darky woman growled, like she had some animal in her throat, and reached over and grabbed Mag-gott by the cuffs of his jeans. Her eyes were dipped right back, white as bone fragments in her black face. He tried to pull loose, but Christ, her hands were like steel claws. She opened her mouth, made a gargling sound, and spewed all over his shoes.

Maggot kicked free of her hands, cursing, the sour smell filling his nostrils. He could feel the tacky wetness on his socks.
The woman slumped forward like she was boneless, face almost
touching that oozing leg, something that sounded like a jungle
song coming from deep inside her.

Cursing, Maggott grabbed Robbie's hand and dragged him
over to the line of sprinkler heads spraying a mist of water onto
the grass. He sat down, loosened the laces of his shoes and took
them off, trying to keep his fingers out of the sticky puke. He
removed his socks, too, rinsed them in the water. Then washed
the slime off his wingtips.

He stood, holding his shoes and dripping socks. Sweating,
his zits seething. Rage cooking his blood.

His fucking nympho wife.

The asshole superintendent.

Billy Afrika and the blonde.

Maggott reached his tipping point.

He dumped the Identikits in a trash can, and, carrying his
shoes and socks, he headed for his car. Robbie running to keep
up with him.

chapter 29

DISCO WAS THE KING OF PARADISE PARK.
Living the dream, driving the Benz convertible and listening to West Coast rap on the radio, still buzzing nicely from
the pipe he'd made before he went to the airport. *Fucken amaz-
ing how things can change in an hour or two,* he thought, filled
with tik-fueled optimism. Now all he had to do was to figure
out which button to press to send the Benz's roof back.

Disco had washed the puke off the Diesels, pulled on a
hoodie to cover him nicely—despite the heat—and made quick
down to Popeye, looking over his shoulder for the men with guns
he knew were coming. He found the dealer in his trailer, lying on
a stained mattress with a couple of girls in school uniform, tik
smoke curling from their mouths, their legs flopped open like
rubber chickens.

Popeye had mocked Disco, being the Man in front of the
jailbait, but he'd craved those Diesels a long time now. Disco
swapped them for two straws—fucken rip-off—and made a pipe

right there in the trailer, his hands shaking so much he battled to feed the tube. His teeth tapped against the glass like dead men's fingers when he brought the pipe to his mouth. The girls laughed at him, but their skirts rode higher on their puppy fat thighs, and he could have screwed them both for the price of a couple of puffs.

The last thing on his mind, as he set fire to the tik.

Then the smoke was in his lungs, and the spiders were a memory. Even Gloria Gaynor had shut her trap.

Disco took it careful, watching his ass as he hurried across White City. He had to travel six blocks to get to the apartment Goddy was living in when he died. Crashing with his auntie and his cousins.

The girl with the harelip opened the door to him, mouth pulled nearly to her nostril, exposing her teeth in a permanent snarl. She was alone in the apartment, which was good. And he knew she had the hots for him. So he played her a bit, nice and relaxed after the pipe, making her laugh behind the hand she used to cover her deformity.

She wasn't so bad-looking when you couldn't see that mouth, and she had nice little titties jiggling under her T-shirt. He felt the tik sending that warm glow to his balls, and for a moment he considered giving her one, doggy-style, so he wouldn't have to see her face.

Definitely no blow job, though.

But then he remembered Manson, and a flash of Goddy's bloody head came to him.

He was here for a reason, and it wasn't this snarling girl's snatch.

Disco got her to show him Goddy's stuff: a bag lying next to the torn sofa he had slept on. The cousins had already helped themselves to anything of value. All the bag contained were a few pairs of dirty briefs and Goddy's *Lifeguard* T-shirt, stinking of his sweat. Nothing else.

Despite the tik, Disco felt terror gnawing like drain rats at his innards.

Then the girl, still scheming she might get lucky, took him to a bedroom, a narrow piss-stinky cell, and showed him a Checker's plastic bag she had hidden under the mattress of the bed she shared with her brother and sister. Said she'd seen Goddy stuffing it behind the wall unit that held the TV and the stereo in the sitting room.

Disco opened the plastic and found a bank baggie of the weed Goddy liked to smoke and—*thank you, sweet baby Jesus*—the keys to the Benz they'd jacked and the ticket from an automated parking machine. Disco saw CAPE TOWN INTERNATIONAL printed on the front. He flipped the ticket and could just make out Goddy's scrawl in red ballpoint: T30. The bay number. Goddy knowing he couldn't trust his tik-fried memory.

Better than a winning Lotto ticket right now.

The girl was lying back on the bed, ready for her reward, but he was out of there—not even thanking her. She stared after him, seeing her afternoon of nice times disappearing with Disco.

He cut through the dump to get to the airport. Stink didn't bother him. Smelled like home. Disco had grown up with jets screaming low overhead, shaking his mother's apartment like aftershocks.

Half hour later he was walking across the open-air parking lot at the airport: endless rows of cars crouched under little tents of shade cloth. Plenty of luxury models, some of them left there for days while their owners flew off to places Disco would never go. He found bay T30. And there it was: the Benz.

Disco checked around to see that he wasn't being watched. A whitey in a suit wheeled his case away from an Audi higher up in the row, all his attention on the phone in his hand as he scrolled for text messages.

Disco saw the turn signals flash and heard the familiar tweet as he used the button on the key to open the Benz. He slid inside, settled back on the cool leather, and started the car, feeling that nice, low rumble of the V8. Then he remembered he first had to take the parking ticket to one of the auto-pay stations outside the airport building. He killed the engine.

Fuck it. He had no cash. Not a cent.

He opened the glove box and rooted inside. Got lucky. His fingers found a few hundred bucks in notes shoved under a pile of CDs and a packet of Stuyvesant. For once, things were going Disco's way. With this cash he could pay for the parking, score some more tik, and even get his mommy's picture back from the fat bitch.

He walked over and fed cash into the machine, and it spat back the stamped ticket. As he drove the Benz through the exit boom, Disco switched on the radio, quickly moved from a news bulletin—a second blondie had lost her head in Sea Point—and got tuned to Bush Radio. Nice pumping hip hop taking him out onto the road back to White City.

While he was trying to figure out how to open the Benz's top, he caught the smell of that other blondie, the American one, a trace of her perfume still hanging in the car. The same scent he'd caught the day he and Goddy had gunpointed her. Maybe he'd still see her sometime. He knew she wanted him.

But first he had to see Manson. Take him this Benz and swap it for his life.

ROXY WALKED DOWN the stairs carrying a small Louis Vuitton suitcase. The house was full of people tagging furniture and the trash Joe had thought was art. A flabby man in low-slung jeans that showed his butt crack wandered around with a clipboard, taking notes. He lifted a bronze figure of a many-armed Hindu god, one of Roxy's few additions to the interior of the house.

"What would you call this?" Speaking to a woman with a mustache.

"I'd call it fucken ugly."

They both laughed. The butch woman looked up at Roxy, unembarrassed. Like she enjoyed putting this fancy American bitch in her place.

If ever there was a time to practice detachment, it was now.

The tough part had been leaving the pink room. The idea of a child, the dream of something good—something positive—had somehow remained in the air of that room.

Time to move on.

Roxy walked out the front door into the sun, too hot in her black dress. She saw Billy Afrika's white car was gone, and she felt about as alone as she ever had. Had to stop for a second and work with her breath, consciously calming herself, facing down the wave of panic that threatened to engulf her, willing it to drain slowly away.

She had no friends in Cape Town. When she first arrived she'd hung out with other models, but they'd bored her. The endless talk of diets and designer labels and Brazilian waxes. After she married Joe and stopped working, she'd lost touch with them. Joe had a few friends, men in their fifties with wives who were beating back middle-age with Botox and scalpels. The women had closed ranks against the trophy wife—their greatest fear made flesh.

So, nobody to turn to for a bed and a DVD chick flick and a glass of white wine.

Roxy's credit card was useless, but she had a little cash in her purse, enough for a cab and night at a cheap hotel. Her wedding band had to be worth something. She'd take it down to the Waterfront tomorrow and sell it for what she could get.

And then? Who knew?

She set the case down and extended the handle that allowed her to wheel it out to the street, past the police vans, castors clacking over the bricks still stained with Joe Palmer's blood. She felt a sense of lightness after the panic. Realized how much she hated this ridiculous house perched on the cliff, defying gravity and good taste. It was pure Joe, and she was glad to see the back of it.

She walked toward the cab she'd called, a small blue car idling at the curb.

Then she saw the pink bear staring at her through the side window. The driver's door opened, and the pimply-faced cop stood up out of the car. She was about to wheel her suitcase past him, when he put a hand on her arm.

"I need to ask you a few questions, Mrs. Palmer."

"This isn't a good time."

"Where's Billy Afrika?"

"Gone."

"Where?"

"Beats me. Gone where people like him go, doing what people like him do."

She was wheeling again, but he still had her by the arm, holding on. Tight.

"Take your hand off me."

"I need to talk to you."

She shook free. "I've just buried my husband, and you people have grabbed everything I own. So, much as I'd love to hang out and chat, I think we should reschedule, okay?"

Roxy saw his face redden, the acne in violent bloom. A quick-tempered man running hot. He boiled.

"Roxanne Palmer, I'm arresting you for the murder of Joseph James Palmer."

She almost laughed. This couldn't be happening, could it? But it was. The zit-ridden little man was reading Roxy her rights. And those handcuffs she'd imagined the day of the lineup became real as he took her wrists and clicked the cold steel closed.

chapter 30

DISCO CRUISED THE BENZ THROUGH DARK CITY, THEN CROSSED Main Road into White City, heard the whistles of the punks who propped up the graffiti-scarred walls and junction boxes, some selling tik, others selling their sisters. Or their daughters. Heard that wet sucking sound, the mating call of the street girls on the Flats, tongues bulging through missing front teeth.

Teeth that were pulled to give better head.

Disco didn't look right or left, just rode low at the wheel of the Benz, his tattooed arm lying on the top of the door like a painted snake, leaving a V8 growl and some Ludacris hanging on the thick air as he passed.

He was about to turn onto Lilac Road and drive up to Manson's place, but at the last second he put foot and headed for his *zozo*. He wanted his mommy's picture back, all of the morning's nightmare memories washed clean away by the tik. Then he wanted to score another straw from Popeye, so by the time he reached Manson he was surfing a wave of cool, calm, and fucken collected.

He eased the Benz past the rusted gates that hung crooked on their posts outside the fat woman's house. Couldn't wait to see the look on that ugly face when she cracked the drapes and saw him in these wheels. But the drapes stayed shut.

Disco vaulted out of the Benz and headed toward the backyard, ready to hammer hard on the bitch's kitchen door.

An image stopped him. A flashback through the tik haze. The fat white guy locking a small silver case into the trunk of the Benz the night of the hijack. Goddy wouldn't have seen, he'd been under the dash, hot-wiring the car. So the case would still be there. In the trunk. And who knew what was inside? Maybe his run of good luck was going to continue.

Disco was about to turn back to the Benz when he saw something else: his landlady's skinny dog, lying sleeping on its side, a black silhouette on the white sand beneath the sagging washing line. But it wasn't sleeping. Not with its insides trailing red and wet and glistening away from its body.

As the wind blew hot air onto the damp shirt that clung to Disco's back, he heard a muffled smack. Turned and saw the kitchen door creak open on the breeze, then swing closed as a draft from inside the house caught it. It stopped against the thick brown leg that jutted out of the kitchen doorway, the sole of the bare foot smeared with blood. Blood that was still bright and fresh. The door yawned lazily open, revealing the fat woman lying on her back, with her guts spilling out onto the linoleum floor.

Then Disco heard the door of his *zozo* open.

Manson's guys. They'd come for him.

Disco turned toward his hut, hands in the air, shit-eating smile in place. Ready to say, "Hey, it's cool, my brothers. We can sort this, okay?"

But he stopped. Mouth gaping.

And it was Piper, leaning against the doorjamb—Okapi knife dangling nice and casual from his bloody right hand—who spoke.

"I come to take you home."

Driving.

Through the endless smear of poverty. Desperation seemed to drag the phone wires lower and soak the flaking walls of the small houses. Roxy in the back of the car, feeling pretty sad herself, watching the Cape Flats pass her by. A beautiful blonde murderess in a black Nina Ricci and handcuffs. A long way from the catwalks of Milan and Paris on spring evenings.

Even South Florida seemed like a fond memory now.

The cop drove, puffing on endless cigarettes. The boy sat beside him, keeping up a constant, unanswered, babble of chatter. Incomprehensible to Roxy.

When they had driven away from Bantry Bay, she'd felt stupid and numb. Then it occurred to her to ask Maggott where he was taking her. He'd looked at her in the rearview and asked a question by way of reply: "Hear you were a model?"

"Yes. A long time ago."

"A person can see it. You look very pretty in that dress. Pity you done such a ugly thing, hey?"

He'd fallen silent, driving onto the freeway and then into this windswept maze of small houses and open lots, littered with the carcasses of wrecked cars. Roxy found herself staring at the back of his neck, at the ripe pimples between his collar and the tight curl of his hair. Remembered her old model's trick—used many a panicky night before a fashion shoot—of smearing a dab of toothpaste onto a zit to dry it out.

Jesus, this guy would need a couple of tubes . . .

The kid was looking at her through the gap between the front seats. "Are you gonna come with us to the Spur?"

She shook her head. "No, Robbie. I don't think so."

"But it's my *birfday*. And they give you a cake and sing 'Happy *Birfday*' and *everyfing*."

The cop took the boy's head in his hand and swiveled it so he faced forward. "Leave the lady alone, Robbie. She got other plans for tonight."

She saw Maggott's dark eyes in the mirror, pinning her. Roxy had to grab the front seat to steady herself as he sped into a turn. Something clattered at her feet, and she looked down and saw the porcelain head of the figurine she'd given the child. No sign of the body, just the head rolling as the car cornered.

Roxy trapped the head under her shoe. The Malay girl smiled up at her.

PAIN. ALL TOO familiar. Pain that tore deep into Disco's innards, making him feel as if the next thrust would split him open like a peach.

Piper above him, eyes closed, the dripping black teardrops so close that he inhaled his rapist's sour breath, felt the rasp of his beard. Disco watched as a drop of sweat swelled from Piper's nose, dangling for a moment before it splashed hot and wet onto his cheek.

Mixed with his own, real, tears.

It was always face-to-face with Piper. The way a man made love to his wife. None of this rear-entry stuff. That was for rabbits, *moffies*. Call Piper a *moffie*, and you were dead.

Dead like Disco would have been if he had refused Piper.

Disco looked past Piper's thrusting torso at the empty nail where his mommy's picture had hung. Glad she wasn't here to see what her son had become.

Piper's eyes were still closed in ecstasy as he rammed himself into Disco, repeatedly, endlessly. Like back in Pollsmoor when Piper had ridden him for hours at a stretch, staying hard and ready from the tik.

Then the eyes flicked open. Black eyes, flecked with reddish brown streaks, like blood clotting on an oil-stained rag.

Terrifying eyes. Made even more terrifying by the mad love Disco saw shining from them.

BILLY AFRIKA STOPPED the rental Hyundai outside Popeye's trailer.

He sat in the car for a while, getting focused, the Glock in his hand.

It was as quiet as this corner of Paradise Park, White City side, ever got. Friday afternoon, before the schools released those kids who'd bothered to attend. The housewives had taken their gossip inside, away from the dry heat that burned your lungs worse than smoke.

Even the jobless men who usually draped the street corners, swapping hard-luck stories and cigarette butts, were absent. The disabled ones—missing limbs, or eyes, or lungs, or reason—went to collect their handouts this time Friday, ready to drink the money dry by Sunday.

It was as if Paradise Park was pausing.

Once the sun slumped behind the thick layer of khaki smog that strangled the Flats, the boomboxes would crank out hip hop, and the cars without mufflers—chopped low enough to spark on the pavement—would own the streets. Gunshots would roll like thunder, the emergency rooms running red with Friday-night blood. But now it was quiet.

Billy sat for a while, getting his head straight. Finding the zone. He knew what he was about to do was crazy. But crazy was all he had.

He left the car, climbed two steps and filled the open doorway of the merchant's rusted trailer. Popeye lay on his back on the filthy mattress, wearing only a pair of stained boxers. He was alone, and he was asleep, ribs like the pleats of an accordion jutting from his fleshless chest as he snored.

A tik pipe sat on the floor beside the coffee mug that served as an ashtray. A used condom, trailing slime like a slug, lay curled where it had been tossed. Popeye had been entertaining.

Billy stepped forward and stood over the dealer. A meat fly nibbled on a tik sore at the corner of Popeye's mouth. Billy knelt and waved the fly away with the barrel of the Glock. It rose slowly, fat and reluctant, and droned its way over to the condom.

Popeye's mouth sagged open in his sleep, tendrils of slime joining his lips like sutures in a badly stitched wound. Billy slid the Glock barrel between the lips. One of the dealer's eyes flicked open. The other eye, infected and weeping pus, was glued closed.

But that one eye saw enough and threatened to bulge out of its socket.

Popeye hadn't got his name from eating spinach.

As he turned onto Protea Street, Ernie Maggott's eyes moved to the mirror, taking another look at the blonde in the rear. What was it with some people that no matter how much shit they were in, they still looked cool and composed? And fucken beautiful, he had to admit.

Like something out of one of those shiny magazines his bitch wife used to waste his money on. Paging through them while she lay on the bed smoking Rothmans Special Mild and eating fatcakes, licking her greasy fingers, reading out loud about Britney and J.Lo and Paris like they were her buddies from the meat factory.

His wife had her charms—he still found himself dreaming of her on the long, parched nights—but this woman was from another universe.

Maggott knew he had done a crazy thing, arresting the blonde. Even though his intuition told him she was guilty as hell. He'd lost it, back there on the mountain. Acted on impulse, had her in the car with the cuffs on before he knew what he was doing. He had nothing. All he could hope to do was scare a confession out of her.

But, Christ, this wasn't some tik monster from Dark City who he could smack around until she cracked. She was an American citizen. The fucken papers would swarm all over this like tapeworms on shit. If he fucked this up, he'd be pulling the graveyard shift over in the squatter camps until he got his pension.

If the darkies didn't kill him for his sidearm first.

His only lifeline was the missed call he'd seen on his phone when he got back into the car after cuffing the blonde. From Disco's fat landlady. No message, just her number. He'd called a few times as he drove, but she hadn't answered. He had to believe that Disco was home. The tattooed punk was his last hope. Pick him up, put him in the car with the blonde. Scare one of them into talking.

Approaching the fat woman's house, Maggott found himself doing something he hadn't done since he was Robbie's age: he was praying. And his prayers were answered.

As he pulled up outside the house, he had to laugh. It was a sign, by God, that he'd been right: the jacked Benz—as out of place in White City as the blonde in the rear—was parked in the driveway.

Maggot went around to the back of the Ford and unlocked the cuff from the American woman's right wrist. Then he looped it around the handgrip above the rear window and locked it again. He cracked the window an inch to give her some air.

"Just got me an errand to run, Mrs. Palmer. Won't be long."

Robbie was opening his door, wrestling himself and the stupid fucken pink bear out. Maggott shoved both of them back in and closed the door.

"You wait here, Robbie."

"I wanna come *wiff*. See the doggie."

Maggott leaned into the window and prodded the kid in the chest. "Any more shit from you, and no Spur tonight, understand?"

The boy's bottom lip was wobbling and tears weren't far away, but he nodded his head and sniffed.

Maggott hitched up his jeans and walked up the driveway. He edged past the Benz, running a finger across the hood. Warm. Checked out the interior of the car. No wires dangling from the steering column. Meant Disco had the keys. Nice and neat.

Maggott walked around to the backyard.

He saw the dead dog first. Heard the soft thud of the kitchen door behind him.

When he saw the gutted woman he reached for his Z88. First he had to unclip the strap on the police-issue holster at his hip. By the time he had the weapon in his hand, Piper had already severed the left ventricle of Maggott's heart and was raising the blade for the next strike.

Maggott got off one shot that flew over the roof of Disco's *zozo*; then he took the knife in the chest again. The ground beneath his feet tilted, and he fell back onto the white sand, pistol bouncing out of his hand.

The last thing he saw were those black teardrops as Piper came in, slicing him open from pubes to sternum, saving the pathologist the trouble.

Roxy HAD TRIED, over the years, to meditate.

Her roommate in Milan, a towering Australian—all diphthongs and bushfire hair—had folded herself into lotus every morning, closed her eyes, and stared at her third eye for an hour.

She'd shown Roxy the basics. Roxy was naturally supple, so lotus came easy. The tough part was stilling her mind, keeping her thoughts from magpieying from one thing to another. The Aussie girl had taught her to count her breaths, to help keep her mind quiet. And that had made it a little easier. But still a battle.

"That's the challenge, Rox," the Aussie had said. "Finding the calm in your storm."

Through the years she'd tried to build a meditation practice. But it had never taken. Now, handcuffed to a cop car out in the middle of an African ghetto, she may just have got it right.

As soon as the cop walked away, some children who were playing nearby—kids a little older than Robbie—were attracted by Roxy's blonde hair. They came up to her window.

One of them laughed. "Hey, she in a handcuff."

Another pressed a snot-caked nose to the glass. "Hey, missus, what you done?"

The third, a girl with the face of an old woman, shook her head. "No, man. It got to be a movie."

A boy shoved the girl aside. "And where's then the fucken camera?"

The kids interrogated Robbie in Afrikaans, and Roxy closed her eyes and started breathing. Counting her breaths until she got to five. Then starting again. Tuning out the heat and the gabbling kids. Tuning out the handcuffs and the rising cramp in her cuffed arm. Slowly starting to detach herself from the nightmare.

Or maybe she was just calling denial by a fancy name. Shutting down, pulling back, the way she'd done as a kid when the bad things happened. Like she was looking down at herself.

That was okay, too.

She'd completed two sets of breath cycles when she heard the pistol firing.

Knew it was close by. Roxy opened her eyes, felt the calm and serenity leaking from her. The kids scattered like pigeons from birdshot, disappearing down the street.

Robbie was staring at her between the seats, hugging his bear.

Roxy saw drapes twitch in the house opposite. Nobody came out. A movement on the sidewalk to her left. She turned. Screamed.

A man, tattoos swarming across his naked torso, tore the car door open. Grabbed her by the hair and pulled her toward a knife blade aflame with sunlight.

She saw black teardrops etched into his face. And she felt the blade pierce the skin of her throat.

chapter 31

***T**HUMP. THUMP. THUMP. THUMP.*
  Popeye's shaved head drummed against the bottom of the glove box as another spasm of terror shook him. The dealer was folded into the hollow beneath the dash of the Hyundai, skinny arms wrapping his legs, leaking nose squashed up against his knees.

Billy sat behind the wheel, watching the tik house, feeling salt sweat tracing the landscape of puckered scar tissue on his chest and back. Burning like a bastard.

A chopped Beemer, sporting fat tires and mags, bodywork sprayed a backyard shade of blue, was parked outside the house. As he'd slowed the rental car half a block back, Billy had seen two guys—probably still in their teens—leave the BMW and slope into the house. The designer wear that hung from their scrawny asses could feed this street for a week.

Merchants. Dealers. Higher on the food chain than the

pathetic fucker who shivered beside Billy. Or maybe less in love with what they sold. Give them time.

Money was changing hands in the tik house. Friday was a busy day, and the cookers would have been working a twenty-four-hour shift, supplying the dealers ahead of the weekend rush.

Thump. Thump. Thump.

Another tremor rocked Popeye.

"Keep still, or I'll shoot you," Billy said, feeling the heat and the adrenaline starting to cook in his gut.

"You fucken crazy, Barbie. You gonna get both our asses dead."

Billy lifted his left foot—still in the shoe he'd worn to the funeral—and kicked Popeye in the head. Just hard enough for the heel to draw a crimson crescent on the dealer's skull.

Popeye put a finger to his scalp and took it away bloody. "The fuck you do that?"

Billy lifted his foot to kick him again, and the dealer folded in on himself and hugged his knees tighter. Billy brought his leg back and rested his foot on the clutch pedal.

Billy Afrika had arrested Popeye more than once back when he was a cop. But Popeye was small-time. He'd go into Pollsmoor, get another 26 tattoo and be back on the street in a couple of months, dealing again. Growing prematurely old from the tik, and more rancid by the day. Selling the brand of poison that had become the drug of choice out on the Cape Flats.

Easy to manufacture.

Cheap.

Deadly.

While Billy had waited for Popeye to pull on his stinking clothes, two kids had arrived at the trailer. A boy and a girl, in the uniform of the school Billy had attended twenty years before. They couldn't have been older than twelve.

They stuck their heads into the trailer and asked for "lolli-pops." The straws of tik that Popeye sold for thirty bucks a hit. Billy Afrika had thrown a scare into them, told them he was a cop and that he'd lock up their asses. They took off. Only as far as the next merchant, he guessed.

Billy watched as the two men emerged from the tik house. They each carried a backpack, loaded with product, ready for the weekend ahead. The men slung the packs into the rear of the Beemer, and the driver cranked the engine. Hip hop thudded, bass bins banging out the electronic beat that punched you low near your balls. Billy could feel his fingertips vibrating on the steering wheel.

The Beemer took off in a spray of gravel as the driver threw it into a U-turn and sped down toward Main Road, leaving dust and a last smash of percussion.

Billy started the Hyundai and drove the half block until he was outside the house. Just another squat White City bunga-low. Only difference was, it had a high fence and a security gate with a buzzer.

He had busted this place a couple of times in years gone by. The security was there to give the tik cookers inside enough time to flush merchandise before they let the cops in.

They were always a joke, though, those raids. The tik house was owned by Manson and run by his sister, Charneze. The gangster had enough cops with their hands deep in his pockets to get advance warning. So the detectives would leave with a couple of bags of drain cleaner, radiator fluid, and head-cold medicine. The raw materials for cooking tik, available over the counter. And all legal.

Billy got out of the Hyundai and walked around to the pas-senger door, opened it to reveal the mess inside.

"Come, Popeye. We going to score."

The merchant tried to burrow his head deeper into his folded legs, stinking up the car with his fear. Billy racked the slide on the Glock. He saw a gummy eye peering from between the knees. The eye closed.

"Get out. Or I'll shoot your knee fucked up."

The eye stretched open again. Popeye knew that he meant it. The skeletal man unfolded himself like a mantis and stood up. Billy closed the car door, grabbed a handful of Popeye's shirt, and got him moving toward the security gate.

"Now you do what I said, okay?"

The dealer nodded. They reached the gate, and Popeye stuck out an index finger—stained yellow from pipe smoking—directed it toward the buzzer, then stopped it in midair. Leaving it shaking, a hair away from the smeared red button fastened to the gate with rusted wire.

Billy prodded him with the barrel of the Glock.

Popeye pressed the button.

After a few seconds the drapes next to the door shifted, then fell back into place, and the gate buzzed and clicked open like a set of dentures in a wet mouth.

Another prod of the Glock sent Popeye forward.

To begin with it was as easy as Billy had hoped.

The front door opened, and Billy and Popeye walked in, welcomed by the sound of West Coast rap. A guy in his early twenties checked them out. Billy vaguely remembered him from a lineup, way back. He had sallow skin and a livid scar that traveled from the left corner of his mouth in a straight line toward his ear. He'd said something, sometime, that hadn't been appreciated.

"What the fuck you want here, Barbie?" Smiley asked.

Hadn't learned his lesson.

Billy arced his right foot in a low scythe and took Smiley's legs from under him, sending him to the linoleum. He rested the Glock on Smiley's flat nose.

"How many of you in the house?"

"Just me and Manny."

"Where's Manny?"

"In the kitchen. Cooking."

Billy looked toward a closed door leading off the sitting room. He caught a telltale whiff of chemicals.

"And Charneze?"

"Gone shopping."

Sounded so domestic.

Billy frisked Smiley. No gun. But there'd be weapons in the house. "Where's the cash?"

Smiley shook his head. "Manson already collect."

That earned him a smack on the nose with the barrel of the Glock. "I know he'll only collect in the morning. Come. Get it for me."

Smiley was looking at him through tears. "You a dead man, fucker."

"Ja, but I'm a dead man with a gun. So, get your ass up."

Smiley walked across the dingy sitting room, opened the cabinet beneath the TV. Billy was there with him and saw the .38 on the shelf before Smiley could reach it. Billy kicked him in the balls and took the .38 and shoved it into the waistband of his jeans. Stepped back, covering Smiley, who was cupping his nuts and sucking.

A bulging paper shopping bag was shoved into the cabinet.

"Take out the bag, Popeye."

The merchant scuttled forward and grabbed the bag by its string handles and ducked away from Smiley.

"Show me what's in it," Billy said.

Popeye tilted the bag so that Billy could see the banknotes crammed inside.

Smiley was still holding himself when Billy brought the butt of the Glock down behind his ear. The scarred man fell to the floor like some switch inside him had been clicked off. He didn't move.

The kitchen door opened, and a man in a surgical mask stepped out, followed by a trail of smoke and a chemical odor.

The Jamie Oliver of Paradise Park.

The cooker ducked back into the kitchen and reappeared with a sawed-off shotgun. Let go with both barrels leveled at where Billy had stood.

But stood no longer.

Popeye took the blast, raining a spray of blood and bone and brain over Billy as he came out of a roll and shot the cooker in the head. He heard the shotgun clatter to the floor.

The silence after the firefight was broken by Smiley groaning and puking.

Billy lifted the Glock, took a bead on his head. The man lay still and stared up at him. It would be a clean ending to all this if he shot Smiley. Stop that scarred mouth from leaking his identity to Manson. Buy him a whole lot more time.

He felt the trigger under his finger. Smiley's eyes widened, his brain desperately trying to signal his muscles to move. Best he could do was scratch at the linoleum with his fingernails. But Billy couldn't pull the trigger.

He lowered the Glock, and Smiley fainted, breath leaking from his nose like the hiss of airbrakes. Billy grabbed the bag of money and headed for the door.

The bullet took him in the meat of the left shoulder, and he dropped the bag. The second round clipped the wall where his head had been before he spun, dropped, and fired.

Saw a body fall back into the open bedroom doorway, a pair of bare feet left jutting out into the sitting room. Bare feet with toenails painted pale peach.

Billy followed the Glock barrel toward the doorway.

A girl, maybe thirteen or fourteen, lay dying, blood in dark gouts pumping from her mouth as she coughed out the last of her life. Limp fingers still curled around a .44 Smith and Wesson, chrome plated. It would have kicked at her wrist like she was trying to drive a jackhammer one-handed. That kick had saved Billy's life.

Panting, bleeding, he saw who she was. Who she had been.

Manson's daughter.

chapter 32

MEAT FLIES BLACKENED THE HUT'S SINGLE WINDOW, BEATING their wings against the glass as they fought to get to the feast within. The sun sliced through this seething mass, throwing a shifting shadow across the three bodies on the floor of the hut.

The cop.

The cop's son.

And Roxy.

The cop lay sprawled on his back, his guts spilling from him. The boy pressed up against his father, motionless. Roxy lying barefoot, her funeral dress riding high on her legs, blonde hair spread like a fan beneath her.

Her hands were cuffed behind her back, ankles tied with a length of cord that the terrifying man had torn from a bedside lamp, the wire cutting into her flesh. A soiled pair of briefs had been shoved into her mouth and taped in place. She gagged from the ammonia on her tongue, battled not to vomit in case she choked. Drew air in through her nostrils.

The hut stank of the dead cop's blood and innards and shit, and the flies that forced their way in through the gaps in the wood buzzed as they banqueted.

Roxy was tied up again, but this time there was no Billy Afrika to rescue her.

Why she was alive she didn't know.

At the car the tattooed man had been about to cut her throat. Even before she heard the beautiful one use his name, she knew this was the man who had burned Billy.

Piper.

Then Disco had spoken a few words, a machine-gun burst in the local language. She had no idea what was said, but the knife had left her throat and Disco had run off, come back with the keys to her handcuffs.

The men dragged her and the boy from the car. When they walked her into the backyard, Roxy was numbed by the horror that confronted her.

The disemboweled cop.

A small black dog, lying dead a few feet away.

And a massively fat woman's body a doorstop in the kitchen.

Piper threw Roxy to the floor of the hut. Disco came in carrying the sobbing child. He'd lost his bear.

Roxy tried to get to her knees, and Piper kicked her in the ribs. She lay on the floor, winded, staring up at this demonic vision, his entire body crawling with tattoos. He grabbed hold of her crucifix and yanked at it, snapping the chain.

He stood over her, the silver cross dangling from his bloody hand. Then he called the other one over and gave it to him, watched while he put it in his pocket.

Roxy waited for the inevitable, the rape and the torture that she knew must follow. When the man loomed over her again, knife drawn, she closed her eyes. But he reached across to the lamp and sliced off a length of cord. They bound her and the boy, and Disco dragged the cop's body into the hut.

The acrid smell of burning chemicals reached her nostrils, and she saw the men crouched beside the mattress, sucking on a small glass pipe held over a lighter flame. The smoke adding another layer to the foulness of the hut. After a muttered exchange in guttural patois, they had left, closing the window and locking the door after them. The heat and the stench bore down on Roxy, suffocating her.

Roxy knew she couldn't wait for neighbors to sound the alarm. She didn't know if anybody other than the kids had seen her and the boy taken into the yard. And even if they had been seen, her sense of this street was that the people here lived in fear of both the gangsters and the law.

Roxy was lying facing the boy. She tried to attract his attention, but his eyes were closed and his breath was ragged. She moved herself like a worm, inching in segments until she got closer to him, oblivious to the splinters from the unsanded floor that stabbed the flesh of her arms and legs.

She battled to flip herself, so she had her back to the boy. She was going to try and free his hands. Get him to untie her ankles. She'd be cuffed, but she could smash the glass of the window and run. It was their only chance.

But first she had to get herself close to Robbie, which meant that she had to squeeze her body between him and his dead father. She felt the dead cop's viscera sticky and slick against her bare arms and legs as she pushed herself upward.

She tasted the vomit rising again. Breathed. Gagged. Breathed again.

Forced herself deeper between the man and the boy. Used her legs to push the dead cop away. Felt something soft and wet bulge beneath her knees. Breathed, the stench almost overwhelming her.

Found herself close enough to the dead man's face to kiss

him. His mouth open in a snarl of disbelief, blood staining his lips like berry juice. His milky eyes stared at her, unblinking as the flies crawled over him.

Roxy closed her eyes. Touched her fingers to the boy's hands.

And felt his small fingers respond, moving against her palms like sticky worms.

BARBARA ADAMS STOOD in her bedroom blow-drying her daughter's hair. Even though it was past eight in the evening, the tin roof of the house sucked heat from the late sun like a solar panel, and the small room was airless and ovenlike. Made hotter by the hair dryer that howled in her hand as she brushed the natural curl out of Jodie's hair.

Out on the Flats the straighter your hair, the paler your skin, and the lighter your eyes, the more desirable you are. Tonight Jodie had a social at the New Apostolic Church and refused to set foot out the door with a kink in her hair.

That morning before school, when a few low clouds had drifted overhead—broken loose from the mass that produced the unseasonal rain far away in the southern suburbs—Jodie had stared up at the sky in anguish.

"It's gonna rain, and my hair's gonna mince." Meaning that the moisture in the air would cause her hair to tighten into corkscrew curls. Curls that would keep her away from the social.

Barbara had told her the clouds would burn away. But her daughter wasn't happy until she returned from school and the sun blazed, a layer of pollution replacing the clouds in the hot blue sky.

Barbara hadn't wanted Jodie to go to the social. Wanted her at home where she could watch her. But Billy Afrika's words had calmed her a little, and she knew she couldn't keep the girl locked up like a prisoner. Anyway, these church events were patrolled by the deacons, who stood for no nonsense.

Still, she'd fret until the child was dropped home safe.

Jodie, sitting on the bed, wore a robe after a shower. Her white blouse and jeans—the decent ones that didn't look as if they were sprayed onto her body—were draped over a chair next to the vanity table.

Barbara shook her head as a trio of orbiting flies tried to settle on her. She'd never known flies like this. There had always been flies in Paradise Park, drawn by the dump. But the last few days had been chronic. People said it was the slaughterhouse, across the veld. Or the squatter camp near the freeway, with holes in the ground for toilets.

Flypaper strips hung throughout the small house, black with insects. But still more came. Flies made her think of disease. And death.

The doorbell pierced the scream of the hair dryer.

"Shawnie!" Barbara yelled for her son, slumped in front of the TV in the sitting room, playing a video game. Even though he was right by the front door, it would be an effort for him to get up and answer it.

"Shawn!"

"Ja?" Mumbling over the noise of the game.

"See who's there!"

It was probably that bloody Mrs. Pool from next door, come to bum a tomato or some cooking oil. The woman came around at least twice a week on the scrounge, her little monkey eyes flicking around the house for anything she could trade as gossip with the other wives in the street.

Mrs. Pool had witnessed Clyde's murder, and it had turned her into a local celebrity for a couple of days. She'd even appeared on TV news, not bothering to remove her hair rollers before she went on camera to deliver her sensational report:

"He did gut him like a fish, the *Keptin*! Oooooh, it was too terrible!"

As Barbara smoothed the last wave from her daughter's shining black hair, she closed her eyes a moment, trying to dissolve away the image of Clyde sinking to the sand.

Shawn pushed the door open and stepped into the bedroom.

Jodie, in a display of outraged modesty, pulled her robe closed. "Hey, don't you even knock?"

For a moment Barbara stood staring at Shawn, convinced that some trick of memory had caused her to project the image of her dying husband onto her son. It wasn't possible that he could be clutching at the white T-shirt that was turning crimson, looking at her with the light fading from his eyes.

Jodie screamed and jumped up from the bed as Shawn sagged to the floor.

Piper filled the doorway, with his knotted muscles and his tattoos. The bloody knife in his hand. The stink of death reaching out from him.

chapter 33

BILLY AFRIKA KNEW HE'D CROSSED A LINE. HE'D KILLED A KID. A KID with a gun.

But still a kid.

He steered with his knees and stretched across his body with his right arm to get to the stick shift. His left arm hung bloody and useless. He checked his mirrors, expecting Manson's Hummer to bear down on him or a white patrol van driven by crooked cops to block his path.

But he saw no sign of pursuit. Just the shadows lengthening across the trash and the sand and the gang graffiti.

Before he'd left the tik house he'd hammered Smiley one more time with the butt of the Glock. Not sure if it was snot or cerebrospinal fluid dripping from the man's nose.

He'd locked the front door of the house and pulled the security gate closed. Even if the neighbors had heard the shots, they knew better than to interfere. He had a gap until Charneze walked in on the carnage, her arms full of tik ingredients.

Until Manson saw his daughter lying dead.

Once Manson got Smiley to talk, he'd mobilize every last foot soldier to track Billy down. But the scarfaced fucker wouldn't be talking for a while, and Manson's first thought would be that Shorty Andrews and the 28s had broken the truce.

Billy Afrika wasn't a praying man but heard himself asking something, somewhere, to give him the time to get Barbara and her children to safety.

Billy had been shot before. Knew what was ahead. The impact—like a heavy blow from a hammer—had been followed by a deep, burning sensation. The area around the wound was starting to heat up, and the pain wasn't far away. And he was losing a lot of blood.

He had a decision to make: Did he drive directly to Barbara's house, with the bullet wound in his shoulder making him weak and vulnerable, and try to persuade her and the kids to run with him? Or did he get medical attention before he went to them?

He was worried that blood loss would leave him unconscious at the wheel of the car, Clyde's family stranded. Helpless. He headed for the dump.

Billy draped his leather jacket over his bad shoulder, stuck the Glock in his waistband, took the bag of money, and went up to Doc's door.

He banged, hearing the mutter of the TV in the sitting room.

Eventually the door inched open, and the familiar wet eye blinked at him.

"Doc." Billy stepped inside, and the door closed after him.

He shrugged off his jacket, and Doc stared at the bleeding shoulder.

"Fucken mess," Doc said.

"I'll pay."

Doc found a rusted pair of scissors lying next to a fly-infested plate of food. He cut away Billy's shirt, exposing the wound.

Doc shook his head, slow as a tortoise. "Ja. You'll pay, okay. Come, sit your ass down."

Billy sat on the arm of a tired sofa.

Doc prodded the wound with a yellow finger. "I'm gonna have to knock you out."

Billy shook his head. "No ways. I got things to attend to. Can't you give me a local anesthetic?"

The old alky lifted a half-empty bottle of brandy from the floor and held it out to Billy. "This is local. And it takes my pain away."

Billy hesitated, then took a swig. Grimaced. Rotgut.

The drunk man lurched into the kitchen and came back with a scalpel that looked as if it'd been used to skin animals. Or detach body parts.

Doc fished a filthy handkerchief from his pocket. "Bite hard on the hankie," he said, palsied hand getting closer to Billy's flesh with the blade of the scalpel. "This is gonna hurt like a motherfucker."

It did.

IT WAS THE first time Disco had raped a girl.

He'd never needed to. His pretty face had always been a magnet for women. He was irresistible. And he'd never craved the power so many men on the Flats felt when they took a female by force.

After Piper killed the mother, slit her throat, and sliced her from the belly up like he always did, he turned to the daughter. Disco expected him to put his blade to work, but instead he punched the girl in the face, sending her sprawling across the bed, her robe riding up on her thighs.

"Dip her," Piper told him.

Disco stared at him.

"You heard me. Rape her."

There was no arguing with Piper. Even though Disco knew why Piper wanted him to do it: to leave something of himself inside her, absolute proof that he'd been part of this slaughter.

Piper would love Disco as long as he obeyed him. He obeyed, or he joined the bodies on the floor. Simple.

Disco tried, and failed, to hold on to some fragile sense of reality. His world had been blown apart since Piper sailed back into it on a wave of blood. Even the madness of tik withdrawal seemed mild compared to where he'd been taken in the last few hours.

Left bloody and torn after Piper rid himself of his lust.

Watching Piper kill the cop.

Just managing to stop him from killing the blondie and the kid.

And when Piper told him his plan, Disco knew the nightmare would never end. Piper saying how he'd figured out a way for them to be together back in Pollsmoor. Forever.

And forever started now.

"Do it, Disco." Piper shoved him toward the girl, who was panting, eyes wide, trying to crawl away from him up the wall. Mute with hysteria. Sobbing soundlessly.

He didn't think he could. Didn't think his body would respond. But he saw Piper's eyes, and he pushed himself down on the writhing girl.

Disco did it.

MANSON CROUCHED ON the floor beside his daughter's body. Instinctively he kept his white Pumas out of the way of the blood. He looked down at Bianca, something sallow and gray—like dirty drain water—already washing the bronze color from her skin. Manson couldn't put a number to the corpses he'd seen over the years. Or how many people he'd killed.

But this hurt like fuck. This was his flesh. His blood.

Bianca's eyes were wide, staring up at him. Her lips twisted in what looked like a smile, like she was going to say something naughty. She'd had a mouth on her, this kid. Girls on the Flats grow up giving dialogue, lightning fast. Ready to cut a man down to size or make another woman feel cheap and beaten. And Bianca had the gift. Make you laugh your ass off and feel like shit at the same time.

But there wouldn't be no more dialogue.

He wished she could say just one more thing, then he'd let her go. Whisper the name of the fucker who did this to her.

He heard his sister, Charneze, sobbing behind him. She reached down and touched him on the shoulder.

"Sorry, boy." She was older than him, thought she could play big sister.

He slapped her hand away and stood. Wiped the weakness from his face.

Manson pushed past her and went into the sitting room. His guys, Arafat and Boogie, waited, standing over the prone form of Smiley. Arafat was big and slow, couldn't meet his eye. But Boogie, skinny and wired on more than tik, pressed up on the balls of his feet, like a greyhound straining to chase a rabbit.

Manson nudged Smiley with his shoe. "Get him to Doc. Tell him to do whatever to make him talk."

Arafat reached down and dragged Smiley to his feet. Boogie stepped in, took some of the weight, Smiley dangling from their shoulders like snot between two sticks.

"And then, boss?" Boogie asked, little rat nose sniffing for blood.

"And then you tell me. Got it?"

Manson watched them haul Smiley out to the car. Then he sagged down onto a chair.

Charneze stood over him. "What you want me to do, boy?"

"I want you to clean her. Dress her up in her nice clothes. Put her makeup on."

"What about the undertakers?"

He looked up at her. "You fucken crazy? You know what those bastards do to the girls? They fuck them. That what you want? Some dirty cunt to get his jollies on her?" She just stared at him. "My daughter died a virgin, and she'll go into the ground a virgin. Now get in there, close the door, and do what I tole you."

She left him.

He was alone with the bodies of Popeye and the cooker. But he didn't cry. He didn't dare. Not yet. Not until this was over.

SHE'D FREED THE boy's hands. It had taken forever, her fingernails breaking as she tried to work the cord loose from Robbie's wrists. The wire had been pulled tight, and Roxy had to claw at it to win each millimeter. The blood that ran down her fingers from the torn nails making it harder.

She'd had to stop every few seconds to wipe her hands on her dress, then start again. The muscles in her shoulders were in spasm and throbbed, sending burning pain down her arms.

But Robbie's hands were loose, and he pushed himself into a sitting position, his bound legs thrust out in front of him, crying as his chubby fingers rubbed his wrists, purple bracelets cut deep into the skin by the cord.

The boy's face was a collage of tears and mucus. And his father's blood.

She had to get him to remove the tape from her mouth. She grunted through the rancid underwear. At last he understood and grabbed the tape and pulled. His fingers slipped. He pulled again. It felt like her skin was tearing, but the tape was off.

She spat out the briefs. Drank air. Got too much of the dead cop with it and had to fight back the bile.

"Robbie." Roxy rolled herself away from the dead man, so that she faced the boy.

The child stared at his father, body shaking, rattling teeth scaring away the flies that buzzed near him.

"Robbie, look at me." The boy looked at her with eyes that had seen too much. "I want you to untie my feet. Do you hear me?"

He nodded but made no move toward her.

"Robbie, if you untie my feet, then I can go out the window and get help. Do you understand?"

"They kill my daddy."

Roxy was sliding herself away from the dead cop, so Robbie had to turn his back on the body of his father to look at her.

Roxy said, "You don't want those men to hurt us, do you?"

He shook his head.

"Then come and untie my feet, Robbie. Please."

He scooted across to her, pushing his bound ankles in front of him. Took hold of the cord that wrapped her legs, trying to find purchase with his small fingers.

It was going to take time. Time they didn't have.

PIPER STOOD AT the window of the bedroom watching the sun choke itself dead on the smog. Night was coming, like an animal stalking the day. Piper was a man of the night. A 28. A soldier in the army of Nongoloza. A descendant of the legendary black bandit who, a hundred years before, had formed the number gangs to fight the oppression of the white man's prison system.

Piper had spent many hours in the Pollsmoor laundry with Moonlight, listening to the old man spin tales of how the gangs had come to be. Telling him that the 28s worked by the light of the moon.

The moon that even now faded up out of the evening, yellow as a dog's eye.

It was time. Time for the ritual.

He turned and saw Disco sitting on the bed, finished with the girl, who lay sobbing, her head buried in a pillow. Piper crossed to the dead woman, sprawled on the frayed carpet beside the bed. He bent and dipped two fingers into the thick blood that pooled beneath her, oblivious to the flies that were drawn to his hand.

He knelt before the white wall of the bedroom. Using his fingers as a brush, he traced a crude hand cocked in the 28 salute. Piper stood and admired his artwork; then he turned to Disco and threw him the Okapi knife. He was about to show the depth of his love for Disco. Show him the greatest respect. Elevate him beyond the ranks of a sex-boy, a mere wife.

Let him do the work of a man. A soldier.

"Up bayonet." The command of a 28 general sending a soldier into battle.

Disco stared at him, bewildered.

"Finish the girl."

Disco looked at him, then down at the knife, blade folded into the handle. Disco's fingers shook as he opened the blade, still sticky with the blood of the boy and his mother. Disco's eyes on Piper. Pleading.

"Do it," Piper said.

And, again, Disco did it. Closed his eyes and plunged the knife into the girl's heart. Piper felt a rush of affection for his soldier wife. The girl groaned and thrashed on the bed.

Piper said, "Another time."

Disco stabbed once more.

"Last time."

The blade sank into flesh.

Piper pushed Disco aside and took the fresh blood from the girl onto his fingertips and wrote on the wall above her head: *The blood has saluted.*

Then he let the love he felt for Disco guide him, and he found his fingers tracing a shape on the wall. Dipping back into the palette of blood when his fingertips ran dry, finishing his work with a flourish. He stood back, satisfied, wiping his bloody hands on his jeans. The ritual was complete.

Piper knew that what he had done in this room would assume the proportions of myth by the time many mouths had carried the story back to prison. Ensuring him prestige and even more power when he and his wife returned to Pollsmoor.

chapter 34

DOC WALKED INTO HIS FETID KITCHEN, CARRYING THE BRANDY bottle like it was a pacifier. He took a long pull, wiped his mouth on the back of his hand. Removing the slug from Billy Afrika and stitching him up had leeched Doc's energy.

You had to concentrate when you worked with the living. He preferred the dead.

But Billy had left him a thousand bucks, good money for what he'd done. Doc had told him to come back in a couple of days, and he'd remove the sutures. Billy had smiled like a man who wasn't sure he was going to be around in a couple of days.

Easy come, easy go.

Doc set the bottle down on the kitchen table, shifting a few dirty dishes out of the way. If the squadrons of flies that swarmed over the greasy plates bothered him, he gave no sign.

He crossed to the old box freezer. The black garbage bag Maggott had fished out the day before lay on the closed lid. He'd put it back on ice after the cop and his brat had left. Taken it

out an hour ago, in the mood to work. But Billy Afrika had interrupted him, and he'd forgotten to make the trip back to the
kitchen and return the bag to the freezer. Doc prodded at the plastic with a nicotine-stained finger and found that the contents
hadn't thawed much.

Good.

He set the bag down on the kitchen table, shifting a few
dishes out of the way. Had another slug of brandy and untied the
bag and shook the arm onto the table. Doc reckoned that the arm
had belonged to a black man in his twenties. Well enough mus-
cled, with all the fingers intact.

He was as incurious about who the man had been as he was
about what had caused his death. He never questioned the cops
who worked at the police morgue when they arrived with body
parts. Just checked the merchandise and paid them. Judging from
the tooth marks at the point of amputation, one of the cops had
used a wood saw to take the arm off postmortem.

Doc opened a kitchen cabinet and lifted out a handheld cir-
cular saw. He plugged it in next to the kettle and flicked the
power on, letting the blade spin and howl for a second before he
killed it and regarded the arm.

He was about to harvest what he could from the limb, for
use as *muti.* Traditional medicine. Despite Cape Town's Western
veneer—cell phones, satellite TV, superhighways—it was still
Africa, where people believed that good luck was limited, and
you had to steal the luck of another. The most powerful way to
do that was to use medicine made from their body parts.

Doc thought about his clients, the *sangomas*—witch
doctors—in the shack settlements sprawling alongside the airport
road. What would make him maximum profit?

He could saw off the fingers and thumb and sell them
individually—would have done it if the hand hadn't been in such
good condition. No, he decided, he would sever the hand just
above the wrist. Sell it as a complete item.

He'd known a darky butcher once, over in Guguletu across the freeway, who had kept a human hand in his freezer along with his sides of meat. Each morning before dawn, he'd open his store and enter the freezer to enact the same ritual: walk among the hanging carcasses and slap them with the hand. Swore it called the spirits and helped him attract customers.

Fucken darkies.

Still, he shouldn't bitch. It made him a decent living.

So he'd detach the hand; then he'd saw what was left of the arm into a couple of pieces. Let the meat thaw and debone it. Package and wrap the flesh to be sold separately. Sell off the pieces of bone as singles.

A nice score.

Doc was about to get to work when he heard banging on his front door. He set down the saw and left the kitchen, closing the door behind him. Went to the drapes and peeped. Recognized two of Manson's crew, supporting a third man who slumped between them.

Shit.

Doc opened the door, and the gangbangers sloped in out of the gloom. They let the unconscious man slide to the floor. Doc could see fluid seeping from his nose. The skinny one, Boogie, gave Doc that look. The one that said: Do something. And fucken do it *now*.

"What's up with him?" Doc nudged the man with his scuffed shoe.

Boogie shrugged. "We find him like so."

Doc groaned as he lowered himself to the floor. He lifted each of the man's eyelids, saw the unequal pupil size. Turned the head, revealing blood clotted in the short, fuzzy hair. Somebody had beaten the 26 unconscious with a couple of well-aimed blows.

"He's probably got a fractured skull."

"Can you wake him up?" Boogie asked.

"Depends. It's going to take some time."

"We don't got no time. Somebody shoot Manson's kid dead. This one know who did it."

Doc sighed, rubbed his eyes. Paradise Park was looking at another gang war.

"Leave him with me. Come back in a half hour."

"We just want the fucker to tell a name. Okay?"

Doc nodded, locked the door after the men left. He stood staring down at the man on the floor. It didn't take a witch doctor to work out what name would emerge from that mouth if he regained consciousness.

Billy Afrika.

BOOGIE WAS AMBITIOUS. So when they got into the green Honda Civic outside Doc's house, he decided to show some initiative.

"Make a turn by Shorty Andrews's place," he said.

The driver, Arafat, was slow, but not that slow. "What you scheming now, Boogie?"

"Who you think killed Bianca?" When Arafat shrugged, Boogie said, "Nobody but the 28s is going to hit the tik house, brother."

Arafat stared at him. "Maybe we should wait . . ."

"Tell your mother to wait. Drive."

Arafat sighed, knew from experience that arguing with Boogie was a waste of time. He could break the little fucker like a chicken bone, but Boogie was a dialogue merchant, made his head spin with his endless yakking.

Arafat cranked the Honda—low rumble of the V6—and they slid off into Dark City.

SHORTY ANDREWS LOVED Céline Dion. When he was hanging with his 28 crew, they listened to gangsta, maybe a bit of R&B if they were chilling and smoking Mandrax. But when he was in his car, it was Céline all the way.

Shorty sat in the Beemer, parked in the driveway of his house, watching the last light fading from the sky, singing along with Céline. Effortlessly reaching those impossibly high notes as "The Power of Love" built to its climax. When the song ended he felt uplifted, as always.

Then he thought about Billy Afrika walking around Paradise Park with a Glock in his hand. That worried him. Things had been nice and quiet for a while, the uneasy truce between him and the Americans still holding. He didn't want nothing to fuck that up.

The quieter life suited Shorty, now that he was getting older. Killing, raping, that was all young man's stuff. He had a family. Responsibilities. He jabbed the CD player with a banana-sized finger and shuttled forward to another ballad to restore his good mood. He joined Céline in "Because You Loved Me," his voice as sweet and pure as a choirboy's.

He was waiting for his wife, who was in the house dressing the younger kid, Keegan. His other boy, the older one—his favorite—clambered into the rear seat and sat fiddling with a toy gun. A Christmas present. A .38 Smith and Wesson. Looked all too fucken real.

They were going across to Canal Walk Mall to eat, catch the latest Eddie Murphy, and maybe buy clothes for the kids.

Shorty stopped singing. Impatient now. "Whitford, go see where your mommy is."

The boy opened the car door, and the dome light kicked in. Right then Shorty heard the sound he knew so well: small-arms fire at close range. The rear window of the Beemer starred, and Shorty threw himself out of the car, 9mm Taurus already in his hand, firing at the Honda that was taking off down the road.

He hit the driver, and the car slowed and stopped. Two wheels up on the sidewalk opposite, under a yellow sodium light. His guys were coming out of the house, Osama and Teeth, blasting away at the Civic.

Shorty got to the car and saw the driver was dead. Boogie, that skinny little fuck, gut-shot but still alive in the passenger seat. Shorty finished him, sending his tik-fried brain onto the side window, slowly leaking down like a lava lamp.

Shorty stood up, catching his breath.

Teeth was beside him. "Boss."

"I'm okay."

"Boss." Teeth said again, and Shorty saw where he was looking.

Whitford was walking toward them, bandy and already chunky, his toy pistol stretched out in front of him—the two-handed grip—firing at the car.

Just like his daddy.

Shorty saw his wife standing in the doorway of their house, impassive. He walked over to the boy, gently turned him, eased him back across the road. "You go to your mommy, okay?'

The boy was reluctant, looking over his shoulder at the wrecked car and the blood.

Shorty knew he'd have to watch this one. Send him to a school in the suburbs. Make sure he became a fucken accountant or something.

Shorty turned to Teeth. "Get all the manpower. Now."

Teeth nodded, and he was reaching for his cell, speed-dialing. Calling the soldiers to the war. Céline still pumped from Shorty's car, telling him that *good-bye* was the saddest word.

ROBBIE SAT CROUCHED before Roxy, tongue protruding from his mouth, as he concentrated on releasing the knot that secured the cord wrapped around her ankles. She'd had to keep talking to him, keep encouraging him as his fingers slipped, and tears flowed and tremors rocked his small body.

It was dark in the hut by the time he had worked the knot loose. Which was a blessing, the Technicolor horror of the dead cop now a muted monochrome.

Her ankles were free. Roxy shook her legs, trying to restore the circulation.

"You're a brave boy, Robbie."

He nodded, sniffing.

Now that her legs were untied, there was an outside chance she could work her handcuffed arms around her legs and bring them to the front of her body. She lay on her back and pulled her arms down toward her butt, her shoulders screaming on the edge of dislocation as she forced her hands past her thighs.

She lifted her left leg into the air, straight as a dancer, kept the right leg bent, and pulled the knee toward her chin. Her shoulder muscles were tearing, but she just managed to get the cuffs past her right foot. Then she could lower her left leg and slip her wrists past it. Her hands were in front of her.

She lay on the wooden floor for a few seconds, catching her breath. Her shoulders throbbing.

Roxy stood and found a three-legged wooden stool lying on its side next to the dead cop. She swung the stool at the window and smashed the glass. The flies massing on the outside of the pane lifted off in an angry chorus, before entering the room in thick formation. Roxy grabbed the reeking blanket that lay on the skinny mattress and used it to cover the shards of glass that spiked up from the window frame.

"Where you going?" Robbie asked. Panicked.

"To get help."

"Don't leave me here. Please, missus."

Roxy grabbed him in her cuffed hands and lifted him through the window, grunted at his unexpected heft. She dropped him onto the sand below.

Then she dragged the stool under the window, hitched up her dress, and sent one leg through the broken window and straddled the frame. She gripped the wood above her head as best she could, handicapped by the cuffs, trying to lift the weight off her leg, but she felt the glass pierce the blanket and slice into her thigh.

She bit back the pain and brought the other leg up, then pushed herself out of the window, landing hard on the sand.

Roxy got to her feet, feeling the blood flowing down her leg.

"I wanna come *wiff*," Robbie said.

She had no time to untie his ankles.

"Please, Robbie, be a big boy and stay here. I'll be back soon."

She ran off toward the street, her cuffed hands held in front of her, the sand still hot on the soles of her bare feet.

The small houses, huddled in the pools of orange streetlight, were quiet. A snatch of laughter and a thump of percussion reached her. Then silence. Lights burned in a house to her left, and she headed that way.

Then she saw two men walking toward her. They were minstrels, like the ones she'd seen by the ocean when she'd gone running with Billy Afrika. Dressed in the gaudy festival outfits: satin trousers and tailcoats festooned with stars and stripes, more stars dancing on the brims of their top hats. She almost laughed. A pair of Uncle Sams. Sent to rescue her.

She ran to the men. "Help me. Please."

The one nearest to her put out gloved hands to steady her, caught hold of her shoulders directly under the streetlight.

And as Roxy looked up at his face covered with red, white, and blue stripes, she saw that the makeup didn't quite conceal the black teardrops that dripped from his eyes.

chapter 35

BILLY CROSSED MAIN ROAD, DRIVING INTO WHITE CITY, FIGHTING the wheel and the stick shift. His left arm was in a sling fashioned from a dirty T-shirt. It stank of Doc: booze-sweat and tallow from corner-store fries. And something stale that Billy didn't want to identify. But at least the alcoholic had dug the bullet from Billy's shoulder and stitched him up, sweating from the effort that it took to force his shaking hands to obey him.

Billy never drank—couldn't afford to be out of control—but he'd sipped at the brandy bottle, feeling its warmth burn deep into his gut. Dug his teeth into the handkerchief and welcomed the pain. Billy had learned about pain young. Learned that it was pointless to try and wish it away. Better to stare it down.

Say you were ready. Tell it to do its fucken worst.

And having a slug dug out by a drunk was a minor annoyance compared to the months of agony after Piper had made him into barbecue boy. That was hell.

Billy found his way to Barbara's street. Nobody had followed him, but he stopped a block from the house, parked the car between the widely spaced streetlights. He stuck the Glock into his belt and left the Hyundai, carrying the bag of money. No way he was going to leave it in the trunk and let it disappear when some tik head decided to boost the car.

It was fully dark now, a killer moon swelling over the grim houses and ghetto blocks, and Paradise Park was starting to make good its Friday-night promise. A car screamed by on the next street, hip hop and testosterone-rich laughter washing over to where Billy walked. He heard the moan of a siren in the distance. And gunshots, coming from Dark City side, enough for a twenty-one-gun salute.

The first notes of the symphony that was to come.

The streetlight outside Barbara's house flickered and buzzed like a dying moth. Sent flashes of orange into the dusty night, then shrank back into darkness. Billy stood awhile, taking in the snapshots of the house the strobing light allowed him. A lamp burned behind the drapes in the bedroom nearest to the street. Barbara's room. A TV set pulsed blue in the sitting room.

Nothing moved in the house.

Billy went through the rusted gate and walked up to the front door. He was about to knock when he saw that the security gate was unlocked, and the door was open a crack. He set the bag of money down and reached for the Glock. Used his foot to edge the door open, swept the sitting room with the gun barrel. Empty.

A half-eaten plate of chicken and rice, seething with black flies, sat in front of the TV. An animated action figure was stuck in a violent loop on the screen—blood spraying from its decapitated head. Grindhouse graphics with thrash metal on the soundtrack.

Billy nudged the bag inside with his foot and elbowed the

door closed. Stood in the sitting room. Sniffed. A smell came to him, fighting the rendered fats and spices on the greasy plate. It was a stink he knew too well. The stink of death.

Looked down at the worn carpet, saw a spoor of footmarks leading from the closed bedroom toward the front door. Tracks that on a wet winter's day might have been mud. But it hadn't rained on the Flats in months. Whoever had walked out of the room had tracked blood.

Billy walked toward the bedroom, stood by the closed door, steeling himself. He pushed the door open. It stopped against the body of the boy, legs in jeans and feet in Nikes. He could see Barbara's face as she lay on the floor. She seemed to be staring up at him. Her mouth was closed, yet her tongue protruded. It took him a moment to understand: her throat had been slit and her tongue yanked out through the gash in her neck, hanging long enough to lick her clavicle.

He shoved hard against the door, shifted the dead boy, and saw the girl on her back on the bed, her white robe sodden with blood, her thighs spread and sticky.

Manson, he thought for a crazy moment. *Manson has been here already and taken these lives in payment for his dead daughter.*

Then Billy saw the Okapi knife lying on the vanity table beside the hair dryer and the brush. Blade open and wet. Left there deliberately. Posed like a still life. Saw the graffiti on the wall. The red hand pointing like a gun. The scribbled words. And lastly, a bloody valentine, a crudely rendered heart framing two names: Disco and Piper.

The room rocked beneath his feet, and Billy had to grab on to the door to stop himself from falling.

He felt a long-ago blade pierce his flesh before the flames took him.

Saw Clyde sinking to his knees, trying to contain his guts with his fingers.

Saw Piper smiling.

Billy Afrika knew in that instant what he was dealing with. And who.

Piper was out. Out to renew his wedding vows in blood, ready to take his bride back to Pollsmoor. What had been staged here would ensure that. There was no way Billy could allow it. Allow prison to keep Piper safe and alive again. This time he wouldn't hesitate.

He stepped over Barbara, hearing the soles of his church shoes suck on blood thick as pudding. Reached for the knife, folded the blade back into the handle, and pocketed it.

Then he moved fast.

Through the kitchen to a small garage, an oil stain on the cement floor where Clyde Adams had once parked his car. The neat shelves still held paint, tools, and the jerrican of gasoline Clyde had used to power his lawnmower. A joke between them: *Where was the lawn to mow, out here on the sand of the Flats? Like a bald man asking for a haircut,* Billy had said, mocking his friend.

He grabbed the jerrican with his good hand and shook it. Still full.

He left with the can, pocketed a box of matches from the kitchen on his way through, and went back into the bedroom. Closed his eyes for a moment and tried to find a prayer. Couldn't. So he forced himself to do the dead the honor of looking at them as he soaked their bodies in gasoline.

Then he swung the jerrican at the walls, splashing the graffiti. Finally, he took Doc's handkerchief from his pocket, still moist from his own sweat and saliva, and emptied the last of the gasoline onto it. He stepped back through the bedroom door and lit the handkerchief, seeing it flame blue and orange as he threw it into the room.

Closed the door on the explosion of heat he remembered too well.

Billy took the drug money and left the house. He stood a moment beneath the strobing street lamp, watched the flames already climbing the bedroom drapes. He felt his hand on the knife in his pocket. He'd promised the dying Clyde that he'd take care of his family. He'd failed. Now he made one more promise: he'd use this knife on Piper.

Finish it once and for all.

DOC EASED THE saw across the arm, just above the wrist, the blade screaming. He kept his head back, but a fine mince of bone and flesh patterned his face and glasses. He killed the saw and heard a moan. The 26 was moving, trying to get up from the dirty tiles. Groaning.

After the others left, Doc had dragged the scarred man into the kitchen and shot him full of adrenaline. Risky stuff. Knew it would either kill the fucker or shock him awake. Doc crossed to the man and lowered himself into a crouch, his arthritic bones clicking out a Cape Flats flamenco.

The scarred man's eyes were fluttering. Then they opened. And opened wider. Doc realized he still held the severed hand. He reached up and put it on the table. The man was blinking, looking around, like he was trying to decide what kind of afterlife he'd checked into.

"Who hit you?" Doc asked.

The man tried to focus his eyes. "It were Barbie."

Doc stood up in stages, using the table for support. He reached for the Eriksson in his back pocket and speed-dialed 26 for Manson. He lived by the good graces of these gangsters, and it always paid to keep building credits in the game. Especially when a war was coming.

He'd get points for passing on the news.

And a few more for telling Manson that Billy Afrika was wounded.

* * *

HER EYES OPENED. A yellow lightbulb, dangling naked from the ceiling, smeared and lagged as she turned her head. Pain. A fire behind her eyes.

Pain was her friend. It meant she was alive. Barely conscious, struggling to stop herself from sliding back into darkness. But alive.

Roxy lay on the floor of the wooden hut again, on her right side, her hands still cuffed in front of her, her legs splayed where she had been thrown. At the extreme of her vision she saw a blur that was Disco slumped on the mattress, Piper standing over him. A shape, like a bundle of discarded clothes, lay near her. Robbie. Unmoving. She had no way of knowing if he had survived his birthday.

She tasted blood in her mouth. And bile. The neckline of her dress was wet with vomit and blood. She sent her tongue exploring her teeth. None missing. Her lip was swollen, and stung when her tongue found a gash.

Piper had punched her under the streetlight. Smashed his gloved hand into her mouth with enough force to whiplash her neck and send her flying, her skull hitting the curb. Then he took his foot back and kicked her in the head. Darkness was already closing in, like a black shroud enfolding her, when she had felt him lift her slack body and sling it over his shoulder. As she passed out she'd drawn his stench into her lungs.

The stink of death and decay.

Now Roxy felt a cough rising in her lungs, fought to stifle it. As she lay there—the lightbulb multiplying, blurring, then resolving into focus—she heard his voice, low and guttural. Insistent. Hammering at Disco, whose halting replies were crushed by the force of Piper's words. She turned her head an inch, saw Piper's shadow move against the wall. Quickly shut her eyes. But he'd caught the movement.

She heard him coming, felt the wooden floor sagging under his weight, her body bouncing slightly as he loomed over her. From the whisper of fabric, she knew he had squatted at her side.

"Blondie." Like a dog growling low in its throat. She didn't move. *"Blon—dee."* His hand on her neck. She willed herself to be still.

Something clicked beside her ear, the sound of a catch locking home.

As she understood what she was hearing she felt the pain, a searing burn as the tip of the blade pierced the flesh of her left thigh. Her eyes opened wide and with them her mouth, ready to scream. His hand clamped down on her face, squeezing the scream away. She sucked air through her nose, panted into the gloved hand that imprisoned her jaw like a vise.

Saw the painted face close to hers, felt his breath like the stagnant fumes of an exhumation as it touched her cheek. He worked the knife into her flesh, twisting with delicately calibrated movements of his wrist, playing her wailing nerves like a minstrel's banjo. She felt a hot stream of piss rush down her thighs, and she writhed and brought up her legs and tried to kick out at him. He laughed, easily evading her limbs, never once taking those eyes from hers. Eyes so dead they needed coins laid on them.

Then he withdrew the knife. Slowly.

She gasped, her screams still choked back into her lungs by his hand. Piper held the knife up for Roxy to see. A stream of her blood traveled down the blade, flowed into the groove, and then dammed against the guard, before a drop fell onto the white glove. He moved the blade away from her face, and she felt it cool and sticky against her thighs, the tip of the knife sliding the fabric of her dress high up on her hip.

He ran the blade softly over her flesh. Caressing her. Teasing her.

She waited. Steeled herself for the agony that was coming.

"Fucken Jesus, Piper." Disco's voice, urgent, spooked. "Come check this out."

PIPER, IN HIS Stars and Stripes outfit—top hat cocked at a jaunty angle—walked from the *zozo* to the street, already smelling the smoke. The minstrel costumes had hung above the dead woman's sewing machine like they were waiting for him and Disco. The moment he saw them, Piper knew the disguises would buy them time, keep them—especially him—hidden in plain view.

To surrender before the tabloids got hold of the story would be suicidal. Piper had no gang protection outside prison. The cops would kill the men who had slaughtered the family of one of their own. He had no intention of joining the dead just yet. No, let the scandal sheets be his insurance policy. Lie low until the bodies were discovered. Wait until the *Sun* screamed out the headlines in nice fat letters across the front page, the story rolling across the Flats, picking up momentum.

Then take Disco, go to Bellwood South, and surrender. Smiling for the cameras, the glare of publicity shining too bright for the cops and the courts to do anything but send them back to Pollsmoor.

For life. Until death did them part.

But now, as Piper saw the blaze consume the dead cop's house, he knew his plan had changed. Seeing the inhabitants of Protea Street running like headless chickens, the people in the neighboring houses wetting down their roofs with hoses to stop the fire leaping through the tinderbox air.

As he watched the flames he saw another body burning twenty years ago. Heard the name Disco had spoken to stop him from cutting the blonde woman's throat: Billy Afrika.

He felt a moment of rage so hot, it was as if he was on fire in that house.

Piper knew who had torched the house. He put all questions

aside. It didn't matter how he knew. All that mattered was what he did next. He would have to start all over. Enact another ritual. Understood now why he wasn't meant to kill the blonde. Not yet. She was the key, and her connection to Billy Afrika carried a weight that he could not ignore.

For Piper there was no God. But there was order. From action came control, and things left incomplete accumulated their own power and lay in wait out in the darkness, ready to ambush you.

His failure to kill Billy Afrika when they were teenagers was such a thing. A failure that had given Billy the opportunity to shoot Piper as he stood over the body of the cop two years before. That Billy had been too weak to do it didn't change the fact that Piper had left himself vulnerable. And now, again, a line of connection joined the blonde to the same man. Time to grab hold of that line and reel Billy Afrika in. Shut his squealing mouth forever.

Piper tilted his head back, closed his eyes, and sniffed at the smoky air, sensing shifts in the atmosphere, looking for readings. Like a predator.

Billy Afrika sat behind the wheel of the Hyundai and fed rounds into the magazine of the Glock. He had fired twice in the tik house, and he wanted a full load of seventeen when he drove to Disco's hut, two blocks down the road, and finished what needed to be finished.

It wasn't easy work, one-handed. He clamped the magazine between his knees and inserted the bullets with his right hand. Then did the same with the body of the Glock, while he pushed the magazine home. The magazine missed the grooves, and he had to grip it with his fingernails and pry it loose. He forced himself to be patient. Freed the magazine and aligned it. Heard it click home.

Billy looked up. He was still parked near Barbara's house.

The flames had spread now, licking the roof, fanned by the wind. Neighbors were yelling. A man tried to open the front door and was forced back by the inferno. Billy lay the Glock beside the bag of money on the passenger seat, started the car, and drove.

Everything had a simplicity now. A symmetry. He cared nothing for his own life. If it ended tonight, it ended. As long as he took Piper with him. Billy slowed, avoiding people streaming into the road, drawn by the fire.

He sped up as he hit the crossroads before Disco's *zozo*. He never saw the other vehicle. Just felt the impact as it T-boned his car on the passenger's side. Glass rained down on Billy, and the Hyundai rolled, shaking him up like he was in a snow globe, banknotes floating around him as the bag split open.

The Hyundai rolled twice, came to rest on its roof like a dying beetle.

Billy hadn't bothered with his seat belt, and he found himself covered in money, lying on top of the dome light of the flipped car, looking at the chrome wheels of a Hummer. He felt for the Glock. Found nothing.

The Hummer's rear door opened, and Billy saw white Pumas step out onto the blacktop, followed by legs in shiny gold sweatpants.

chapter 36

THE CANNIBAL WATCHED THE HEAVY YELLOW MOON RISE OVER THE apartment blocks in Sea Point. Back home his people believed that the full moon was the eye of God watching over the sinners below. God would have a lot to observe in this low-rent part of Cape Town.

From where he sat on the cramped balcony, the cannibal could see into the apartment opposite, only partly obscured by three lines of washing. Loud music blared, and men and women danced their knocked-kneed *kwasa-kwasa* dance.

His name was Bertrand Dubois Babakala. He was a prince, educated at the Sorbonne. Now reduced to living in a backstreet apartment, surrounded by these Congolese refugees with their loud clothes. Cocaine dealers who stood too close in the elevator, treating him with overfamiliarity. As if he were a fellow countryman. He was not.

His country wasn't even a country. Not on any map, any-way. Rather a province of a larger entity that had shape-shifted countless times since the French fled, borders redrawn in blood as alliances formed and split. In truth, if he was pressed, he couldn't give a coherent reason for his belief that this toe of land—no mineral wealth, a population decimated by poverty, warfare, and AIDS—would be any better off independent. But he would give his life for that dream.

Or, rather, the lives of the ragtag army of boys who had come to believe in him as some kind of hip-hop Selassie. A bunch of weed-crazy kids wearing everything from women's bathrobes to the ragged remnants of camouflage, decorated with human body parts. They ran wild in the jungle, slaughtering everyone in their path, chopping off heads and using them as soccer balls.

He'd made good use of the photo-ops during his few brief sojourns with them in the jungle. Made himself infamous when he ate that human heart. He'd just smoked some fabulously powerful ganja—part of a prebattle ritual the boys enacted—and the drug had given his actions the surreal flavor of a dream.

The heart hadn't tasted that bad, really. A little like carpaccio. And his actions had whipped his boys into a fervor.

The briefcase of cash he gave to Joe Palmer was the last of the money fraudulently obtained from a gullible food aid organization based in Paris—anxious to assuage postcolonial guilt. Money to buy weapons for his jungle boys. Boys who had sworn to overthrow the government and usher Babakala to power. And, by God, wouldn't he look grand in a tailored uniform, with a leopard skin sash and a fly whisk, as he stood in the back of an open Mercedes, riding into the capital?

He sighed a very Gallic sigh. Today had not been a good day.

Earlier, while it was still light, they had taken the whore's dented little Fiat Uno up to the big house in Bantry Bay. Babakala, of course, didn't drive. But the whore, Tatiana, did. Badly.

Hunched over the wheel, peering ahead, shortsighted but too vain to wear glasses. Tatiana hadn't told him where she had got the address, but he guessed that one of her clients at the massage parlor was a policeman, and a phone call and a whispered promise would have been enough to secure the information.

It was difficult for Babakala to accept his loss of status. Exiled in Cape Town. Living off the earnings of a Ukrainian whore. He had felt so optimistic that night he had dinner with Joe Palmer and his beautiful American wife. It seemed that the money from the aid organization would flow merrily, improving his prospects. But then, yesterday, he had intercepted that brusque e-mail at the Internet café in Sea Point. Making it clear that no more funds would be made available. Ever. And that he had been blacklisted throughout the international aid community.

Merde.

The little car had strained up the hill, the whore talking incessantly. "We must kill that bitch."

"We just want the money, *cheri*."

"But when we get it, we kill her. Then I want to get into that closet of hers."

He sighed, tuned her out. How he missed his bodyguard, Jean-Prosper, working now as a waiter in a Congolese restaurant in Johannesburg. The man had stayed loyal for months, without pay, but eventually Babakala had to let him go. This would have been Jean-Prosper's job, scaring that blonde into making good on her husband's debt.

They arrived at the house, and the whore bumped the Uno to a halt, just past the open gates. A removal van was parked in the driveway, men loading the contents of the house.

Tatiana was fighting her way out of the car. "The bitch she is running!"

Babakala held her back. And they both saw the uniformed cops milling around. The cannibal understood these things. He knew what was happening and explained to the whore as best he could that the property had been seized.

"Drive on, *cheri*. There is nothing for us here."

She had started the car and taken off back toward Sea Point, casting furious glances in the rearview mirror.

Not a good day.

Now he took his eyes from the yellow moon as Tatiana came out and stood on the balcony, dressed in a low-cut top that accentuated her breast augmentation. He'd paid for that, back when times were good, and he could keep her at home to tend to his needs.

"I go work, Bert." His skin crawled, as it always did, when she called him that. But there was no stopping her.

"*Au revoir*, my dear. Don't work too hard." *Don't enjoy it too much* was what he really wanted to say.

She bent to kiss him, battling the jeans that sliced into her flesh like a delicatessen blade into cold cuts. "Don't worry, my darling. This bitch, I will still have her."

He flapped an elegant wrist. "It's over, Tatiana. *C'est la vie.*"

"Over, my fucking ass."

She clumped off in her high heels, and he sat on the balcony, contemplating his future. Perhaps a job as a doorman at one of the exclusive hotels that encircled the Waterfront like stones in a Cartier necklace? There had been offers.

He sighed, and the rubber-legged people danced and laughed and cavorted like monkeys.

Roxy was at the wheel of Joe's Mercedes, driving through Paradise Park in the direction of Cape Town. The top was up, and Disco sat next to her, still dressed in his full minstrel outfit. Piper was squeezed into the rear, his top hat bending against the low roof. He had Robbie on his lap, the knife held to his throat.

The night had moved into a zone beyond reason.

Yet Roxy felt a strange sense of calm. A weird detachment, as if she was hovering up near that heavy moon, looking down at herself. Maybe that's what happened when you came close to death and survived. She kept on waiting for the shock to hit her, but it didn't. Not yet.

She'd known, as Piper had played the knife over her body, that he was about to kill her. She could see it in his eyes. He was already looking at her as if she was dead. Then Disco had spoken, rapid-fire local patois, and the two of them had left the hut. She'd lifted her cuffed hands and reached across and touched Robbie's neck. Said a silent prayer when she felt his pulse trembling against her fingertips. How badly hurt he was, she had no idea.

Roxy stood, looking around the hut, searching for a weapon. She saw something shining, catching the yellow light. A sliver of the broken window. Most of the glass had exploded outward when she'd smashed the pane with the stool, but this piece lay inside, on the wooden floor. A shard about the size of her index finger, tapering to a sharp point. She had the glass in her hand when she heard them in the yard, and managed to lift her dress and slip it into the elastic of her panties before the weight of the two returning men rocked the hut.

She sat down, watching as they came back inside. Agitated. Disco speaking more now, as if he was trying to convince Piper of something. Piper's voice hammered back at him, but Disco never shut up as they smoked another meth pipe. And it seemed he had gotten his way.

Piper grunted, shrugged. Then he walked across to Robbie and kicked him. The child opened his eyes and sobbed. Piper kicked him again.

Roxy stood. "Leave him. Leave him alone."

Piper laughed at her, kicked the boy again, harder. Roxy shut her mouth, knew that her protests would only make things worse for Robbie.

The child sat up. Piper grabbed him by his T-shirt and lifted him, kicking and twisting, into the air. The knife was in Piper's hand, and he placed it against the boy's throat, his eyes fixed on Roxy.

"Do how I say, or I cut him. Okay?"

She nodded.

Piper lowered the child, who was sobbing, gasping for air, but the man still held on to the T-shirt, blade flirting with the skin of Robbie's throat. Disco came and unlocked Roxy's handcuffs. Brought her a bucket of tepid water and a cloth that stank of piss. He shoved her in front of the broken mirror leaning against the wooden wall.

"Make you look nice."

She obeyed as best she could. Wiped the blood from her mouth. Her lip was swollen, and she saw the beginning of a black eye.

She stood and lifted her dress. Her leg was cut in two places. Once from the glass, the other from Piper's knife. The glass cut was superficial, and the blood had already clotted. But the other wound still bled, and when she moved, it gaped and bubbled, and fresh blood flowed down her leg.

Piper left the boy and came over to her, grabbed the cloth from her hands. He cut a strip with the blade, then he shoved her onto her butt on the floor. He pulled up her dress and placed the cloth over the wound. She was terrified his hand would find the sliver of glass, but her dress veiled it.

"Hold it there," he said, pressing the cloth to the wound as he reached for the tape and wound it around her leg, tight. It held the blood, for now. "Stand," he said.

She stood. Her dress covering the tape and the cloth.

He looked her over. "Ja. That's okay."

"Can I clean up the boy?"

"No."

"At least untie him."

Piper stared her down: the terrifying clown face. Then he swiped his blade though the cord at Robbie's ankles, and the boy sat and rubbed at the flesh where the wire had bitten.

Roxy touched the kid's head. "It'll be okay, Robbie. I promise."

The boy stared at his dead father, not responding to her lie.

They went out to the car, Disco finding Roxy's shoes lying in the dirt and flinging them at her. She slipped them on, and they all got into the Mercedes.

"Close the top," Piper said.

She flicked the switch, and the top oiled seamlessly into place, with little whirrs of the servos.

Piper said, "Okay, now we going to Cape Town."

As she reversed out, she saw a house on fire lower down the street, flames leaping high into the darkness. The roof collapsed, releasing sparks. A million fireflies in the night. A block away, a white car lay on its roof. The street was crowded with people. She heard their excited shouts and the chorus of emergency vehicles in the distance.

A voice ground in her ear, telling her where to drive. Mr. Handsome, breath sour. They were nearing the last of the streets of small houses, and Roxy could see an industrial park and a main road ahead. Seemed to remember driving along that road on her way to the lineup. Felt like years had passed, but it was only two days ago.

Roxy saw a car coming up behind her, expected it to overtake the Mercedes. Then she heard the whoop of a siren and the roof lights of a cop car strobed in her mirror.

chapter 37

"**W**HAT DO I SAY TO THEM?" ROXY ASKED, AS SHE PULLED OVER. Seeing Piper with Robbie held close, seeing the two cops coming, one on each side of the Mercedes.

Piper said, "Say what you like. Just better be good; otherwise, s'trues fuck, I kill him."

The one cop was at her door. The other at Disco's. Both had flashlights. She squinted up at the cop leaning into her open window, and he lowered the beam.

"What you doing out here, lady?"

She was on the verge of speaking—screaming—telling them she had been kidnapped, until she looked in the rearview mirror and saw Piper's hand up near the child's throat, the sleeve of the Uncle Sam outfit hanging long over his fingers.

Knew what was in the hand . . .

Roxy could save her own life. But Piper would kill the boy. Slit his throat before the cops could reach for their weapons.

She heard words. Took her a moment to realize she was speaking them. "These men work for my husband, and they're late for the carnival. So I'm giving them a ride."

The flashlights were raking the car. Disco. Piper. Robbie.

"You American?" The cop at her door asking as he peered into the Mercedes.

"Yes."

"Show me some ID."

It was in her purse. In the trunk of the dead cop's car.

"I'm sorry, Officer, I left it at home. I was kinda in a rush." She tried her best smile. Wondered if he could see the damage to her face. It was on the left side, away from the beam, and she tried to sit so her hair covered her cheek.

"Whose kid is that?" The cop on the passenger side speared Robbie with a flashlight beam. For the first time Roxy noticed she was a woman, androgynous beneath her bulky Kevlar vest.

Disco smiled up at her. "He's my little brother."

And Robbie said, "It's my *birfday*." The first words he had spoken in a long time. They saved his life.

The woman cop laughed. "Why you so dirty then? You must tell your brother to clean you up nice."

The male cop looked at Roxy's breasts, then up at her face. "You know I should give you a ticket for driving without your license on you?"

"I know, Officer. I'm sorry."

He was giving her the eye. Another cappuccino-colored Cape Flats Romeo. "Where you live?"

"Sea Point," she said. First place that came to mind.

"Well, you watch your head now." He laughed. She dug up a girlish giggle from somewhere and even did that little thing with the eyes that always got the guys going.

The cops stepped back, and Roxy started the car, pulled away.

She had no idea where the men were taking her.

* ★ *

DISCO KNEW. THEY were going to the place Roxy had just spoken of: Sea Point.

He'd nearly kissed that kid when it came out with the *birf-day* thing. Disco had to hold on to himself not to piss his pants as they drove away, the cops getting into their Opel and throwing a U-turn and heading back onto the Flats.

Jesus.

Disco wished he had a straw to smoke. He'd just have to take it easy. Step by step. It was a crazy fucken stunt he was pulling here. Piper had been ready to cut the American blondie dead that afternoon, right there where she was handcuffed in the cop's car.

Until Disco had spoken the four magic words: *"She know Billy Afrika."*

A desperate attempt to keep a lifeline dangling. After Billy's visit to his *zozo*, Disco had remembered who the ex-cop was. Remembered Piper talking about him in the cell at Pollsmoor. Calling him Billy Fucken Afrika. The Missing Teardrop.

When Disco spoke the name at Maggott's car, Piper had looked up at him, then he'd removed the blade, a thin trickle of blood tracing the blondie's neck and disappearing between her tits. Piper had smiled his 28 smile as he stashed the Okapi knife and they took the woman and the boy to the *zozo*.

For later, Piper had said.

Disco needed to keep the blondie alive. Billy Afrika seemed to work for her. Protect her. He was a hard man. Not as hard as Piper—who wasn't a man, more like a wild animal—but maybe tough enough to stand up to him. Disco had to get Billy Afrika and Piper together. It was the only chance he saw of coming out of this.

And for that he needed some good luck.

He'd had a shit life. Bad luck had been closer to him than his own shadow. But he'd always hoped his luck would change. The way the wind changed in Cape Town in April. All summer it blew in from the south, lifting off roofs and sending dust and crap into the air. Blowing in even more heat. Driving people crazy.

Then, at Easter time, it changed, came in off the sea from the north. It brought the rain, and the windswept sand was wet down like bloody sawdust after a car wreck. Even the Flats cooled and went green, grass coming up in clumps between the garbage dumps and the pit toilets and the rusted motorcar bodies and the shacks.

That was Disco's favorite time. When he hung out in his *zozo*, lying on his bed getting *zooked* on tik, watching the rain flow down the glass of his window like tears, washing away all the mess and pain out there. Felt as if it was washing Disco's heart.

Disco had done some bad shit in his day, was ashamed sometimes to look his mommy's picture in the eye. He'd stolen. He'd lied. God knows he'd sucked the life out of more than his fair share of tik pipes.

But raping. Never.

And just when he thought that was the worst, Piper made him kill the girl. He could still feel the blade going into her heart, a sick wet sound when he pulled the knife out. The girl crying, begging him for mercy. And Piper standing over him, talking slow and steady. Making him stick her again and again and again. Till the girl was dead.

And fuck, he felt that something in him had died with her.

The fire that came had burned away all the evidence. But not his guilt or his fear. Anyway, there was still the fat woman and the dead cop. And the kidnap of this blondie and the kid. More than enough to get Disco's bleeding ass back in Pollsmoor with Piper. Forever.

So Disco had cooked up a crazy plan, and it had taken a lot

for him to sell it to the wild thing with the knife, back there in the *zozo*. He'd said Piper should cut the blondie's head off out Sea Point side. And then they go surrender to the cops, tell them they were the Barbie Doll killers.

Piper had stared at him like he was fucken insane. "But they know I was still in Pollsmoor when those two blondies was chopped."

"Ja, but I say I did it. That you come out and did the third one with me." Disco had nodded his head toward the blondie, who lay on the floor near the kid. Knew she couldn't understand a fucken word they were saying.

Piper had thought for a long time; then he'd smiled. Knowing they'd get on the front pages of all the papers. Get on TV. Even better than taking out the cop's family. Kill people on the Flats, nobody but the coloreds gave a shit. But nail some blondies on the white side of town, and the whole city went fucken crazy.

The two of them would go back to Pollsmoor as heroes.

So Piper had said, "Let's do it."

Then Disco heard the words that nearly made him cry and rush across and kiss the place where his mommy's picture used to hang.

"And we can use those two"—Piper had looked over at the woman and the kid—"to get Billy Afrika to come that side, too. I want that fucker dead. Finished." He'd pointed to his face. "Get me that missing teardrop." Smiling his 28 smile.

If Billy Afrika was coming, Disco still had a chance. And so did the blonde and the boy. He rubbed the crucifix in his pocket as he watched Voortrekker Road, long and straight, leading toward Cape Town. The street lamps, just for a moment, looked like party lights. Yellow and happy.

THE STINK OF rotting garbage that hung over Paradise Park was overwhelming here at the source. Billy lay at the edge of the landfill, staring out across the sprawl of junk that was almost pretty in the moonlight. Lying in something soft and wet, something with a stench beyond description. After what had happened to him that night, he neither noticed nor cared.

His useless left arm, still in the sling, was wedged beneath him. Shoulder bleeding again. Hot, red pain torching his nerve ends. His good arm was twisted behind his back, and Manson stood on his hand, pinning him, gun to the back of his head. The only weapon Billy had was Piper's knife in his pocket, and he had no way of reaching it.

Manson was going to kill him. He was going to die before he'd had a chance to put things right. He was going to leave Piper alive. Again.

Billy wondered if there was a hell. And if he'd done enough bad things in his life to get sent there once Manson shot him. At least that meant he would meet up with Piper someday. Finish this thing.

Manson was speaking to him, the barrel of a .44 cold and hard at the base of Billy's skull. "Barbie, reckon you gonna go to heaven?"

Like the fucker was reading his mind. Billy said nothing.

"Maybe see your old connection, Clyde? 'Cause Clyde's definitely up there wearing a nice set of angel wings and a fucken halo, isn't he, my brother?"

Nothing back from Billy, who was trying to figure out a way to get his hand to his side pocket. He couldn't. Then he felt the gun barrel withdraw.

Manson squatted beside him. "Look at me."

Billy kept on staring straight ahead, over the trash. Two of Manson's crew sat on an old fridge, rising like an iceberg out of the sea of garbage. One of them lit a bottleneck, face glowing in the light of the match. They'd kicked the shit out of Billy when they hauled him from the wreck. Felt like his nose was broken, and he'd heard his ribs crack beneath a boot.

Not that it mattered.

Manson used the barrel of the .44 to lift Billy's chin. The gun Manson's daughter had shot him with. The gangster's idea of a tribute to his dead child, Billy supposed. The thug was smiling at him, one side of his face orange from the spill of streetlight.

"How you feel about letting Piper walk? Still think you did good?"

Billy looked at him, couldn't stop himself. Manson cunning enough to know how to send Billy to his grave with a dark question mark tattooed on his heart.

"Fuck you, Manson. Just get on with it."

"Ja, I'm wasting my time." He stood. "I gotta go sit vigil with my daughter. You fucker." Manson kicked Billy in the face. Then he leaned down and applied the barrel to Billy's head.

"You ready to go, Barbie?"

"Do it."

"Say your prayers."

Billy heard the shot. Waited to die.

chapter 38

BILLY DIDN'T DIE.
Instead he felt the barrel of the .44 lift from his skull. Heard more shots and turned to see Manson pumping blood from his abdomen, leaking life all over his brand names.

Manson's crew scattered across the dump, firing at the men who came at them from the road. Shorty Andrews navigated the trash, 9mm Taurus still pointing at Manson. The big 28 stood over the American and emptied his pistol, Manson's body jerking like a breakdancer. Then lying still.

Billy started to ease himself to his feet, got as far as his knees, when he heard another shot. Felt a concussion of air. One of Manson's men firing over his shoulder as he fled into the mountains of garbage. Shorty coughed and sank to his knees like he was joining Billy in prayer.

"Fucken mess you started here, Barbie," the giant said, around a mouthful of blood.

As he pitched facedown in the filth, Shorty stretched out his arm like he was offering Billy the Taurus.

Billy took the gun and ran.

THE WHORE, TATIANA, was no philosopher, but she had a theory about the difference between coincidence and destiny.

Coincidence was the small stuff, something that blipped across your radar screen for a moment and then was gone. Like walking into the hair salon and seeing some ugly bitch wearing the same dress as you. Or going on dates with two johns in one night who had silver bolts in their balls. Just things she could chat to Bertie about as they sipped samovars of lemon tea before falling asleep.

But destiny was different. That was life-changing stuff.

Like Chernobyl. Or the time she had her first date with Bert.

She was fresh from the Ukraine, brought out to Cape Town as a mail-order bride by some Greek bastard. He dropped her after he screwed her stupid for a month. Her English was as poor as her teeth—she'd made sure she'd smiled tight-lipped for the snapshot on her MySpace profile—and she didn't have many skills. So she ended up escorting, working out of a massage parlor in Sea Point. When they'd billed her as Russian, she'd thrown a thick-accented shit fit. The Taiwanese owner, a man wrinkled as a shriveled penis, shrugged. Said Russian was exotic. Who the fuck knew where the Ukraine was?

Bert had been one of her first customers, back when he still had money and lived in the nice house in Newlands, with the Jaguar in the garage and the chauffeur to drive him around. She hadn't known much about black men. Had seen only a handful before coming to Cape Town, and he was her first *shokolad* trick. She was terrified, but he'd been sweet and fast. And surprisingly small.

Best of all, he'd paid. No problem.

Soon she was seeing him a couple of times a week. It was easy being with him, and when Bert asked her to move in and give up her job she didn't hesitate. For a while life had been a dream. Days spent at Cavendish Mall buying up every label she saw. Getting the breast enhancement she had always fantasized about. Ready to get her teeth fixed, when Bert's money ran out and he lost the house. They had to move to the shithole in Sea Point. He explained to her—ashamed—that she would have to go back to work. At least for a while.

Tatiana was tough. Hell, she'd absorbed enough of Chernobyl to set radiation testers clicking like frenzied rattlesnakes. And she was still here, large as life. She was used to rolling with the blows, and she'd become fond of her *shokolad* teddy bear. So she dusted off her address book and got to work, sure that the good times would come back again.

Got seriously pissed off, though, when she found out about the money Bertie had given to the South African that night in Camps Bay. It could have kept them living high and happy for a year at least. And there was no way she could deal with the idea that the American bitch had those dollars. With her blonde hair and her teeth and her tits. All fucking real.

So when Tatiana stepped out of the luxury apartment block in Sea Point, where she'd just finished a two-hour date—nice guy, Swiss, clean—and saw that Benz drive past with the bitch at the wheel, that wasn't coincidence.

That was destiny.

She sprinted in her high heels, almost spraining her ankle, to get to her Uno. It took a while to start, but the Benz was caught at a light, so Tatiana had time to get the smoking car cranked and take off after the blonde. She had nailed a couple of lines of blow in the Swiss's bathroom, and her blood was running hot.

The blonde bitch drove for about another minute, past the lighthouse, then turned into the parking lot at Three Anchor

Bay, next to the miniature golf course. Tatiana was fumbling in her purse for her cell phone, digging past the K-Y Jelly and the condoms and the .32 Beretta Tomcat.

Desperate to call Bert and tell him to get over here. He'd have to walk—which he normally refused to do—but it was only a few minutes from their apartment. By the time she located her phone the American was out of the car with a little boy—light *shokolad*—and two guys in weird fancy dress.

Tatiana hid her Uno behind one of those massive SUVs people drove in Cape Town and tried to speed-dial Bert. Nothing. Squinted at the phone, catching the light of the colored globes that hung all gay and festive along the beachfront at this time of year.

Her phone battery was dead. *Shit.*

She knew there was a pay phone at the gas station across from the parking lot, but there was no time. The blonde and her companions were moving, walking toward Three Anchor Bay. Tatiana kicked off her heels and followed, barefoot, holding the shoes in her hand. Her feet hardy from the years growing up peasant-poor near Pripyat before Chernobyl sent her family fleeing to Kiev.

BILLY CUT ACROSS the fringes of the dump, oblivious to the decomposing matter that clung to his shoes and left his jeans and bandaged shoulder wet and reeking. Gunshots rolled across Paradise Park. Way more than usual for Friday night. Sirens serenaded the ghetto, and a chopper hovered like a mosquito over Dark City, a searchlight slicing the night sky. They would make a noise, the cops, but they knew well enough to stay back and let the blood flow.

Billy had ignited a gang war. It would rage until enough young brown men lay dead in the streets, in cramped rooms, and on the seats of chopped-down rides for new leaders to emerge and call a truce. He cared fuck all for the gangbangers, but he felt for the innocent. The kids with bullet wounds—collateral damage of drive-bys. And the mothers cradling the broken bodies of their dead sons. Just another bad thing to add to his tab.

He was sweating, from more than the heat. He felt sick. Dizzy. The wound in his shoulder throbbing with a life that seemed separate from his own. Billy forced himself on, focused his mind, as he emerged from the dump at the bottom of Protea Street, heading up to Disco's hut.

Passed the smoking ruin that had been Clyde and Barbara's house. Saw a group of neighbors tracking through the wet, black mess, looking for anything of value to salvage. A kid in his early teens emerged carrying a singed microwave, warped but intact. The boy looked at Billy, then scuttled off with his prize.

Billy remembered that he held the Taurus in his good hand. The kid had probably thought he was about to be shot as a looter. Billy shoved the gun into his waistband and walked on up the street. Came to the Hyundai, still lying on its roof. All four wheels and the side mirrors were gone. The blind eyes of the empty headlamp sockets stared at him as he passed.

If the Cape Flats ever had a symbolic bird, it would be the vulture.

When he reached Disco's place Billy drew the Taurus, checked the safety was off, and walked up the driveway. The main house was dark and still. He stepped into the yard. Nothing moved. No lights in the *zozo* hut.

His feet crunched on broken glass, and he saw that the window had been smashed. He tried the door. Locked.

Billy stepped back and kicked, high and hard. The plywood door slammed open, and he went in, Taurus ready. In the moonlight he saw a body on the floor, heard a frenzied buzzing.

Billy used his elbow to flick down the switch next to the door, and the naked bulb bloomed. Ernie Maggott lay with his guts spilling out in front of him, covered by a black shroud of meat flies that whined and boiled in the light. Billy saw the coils of cord on the wooden floor, a bowl of water stained pink, and a twist of rag, dark with blood. He didn't know how many people Piper had held in this hut.

Or how many of them had survived.

When Billy's cell phone rang—forgotten in his back pocket— his first impulse was to ignore it. He'd given the number to only two people: Barbara and Roxanne. Barbara wasn't making any calls, and he had enough of his own problems without hearing about Roxy's.

Still, he answered. "Ja?"

"Billy Afrika." A voice as cold and empty as death itself. Piper's voice.

chapter 39

ROXY SAT ON A BOULDER, THE SURFACE DAMP AND SLIMY AGAINST her bare legs, the gentle breeze teasing the ends of her hair like a stylist looking for inspiration. Robbie slumped beside her, asleep, his head resting on her shoulder.

The hot night was rich with the smell of salt water and rotting kelp. And something else, something fetid, that wafted over from the homeless woman with the junk-encrusted cart. The woman who had stared right through her, those days on the oceanfront. Not staring now. Asleep in a stinking pile on the sand next to her cart. Roxy almost wanted to laugh at how she'd projected her fear onto that poor woman.

Now her fear had a name: Piper.

And she was the bait on the hook he dangled for Billy Afrika.

Piper stood at her side. Unmoving. His painted face ghostly in the moonlight as he watched Disco, who kicked at a bottle embedded in the sand close to where the gentle waves lapped. The unwavering gaze of an obsessive lover.

Roxy heard a laugh and looked up to see two men walking on the sidewalk above—just a shout away. One man was tall and fat, T-shirt riding high on the belly that jutted over his belt. He was licking an ice cream cone, listening to the short man at his side. The fat man laughed again, tonguing the cone. And the little bantam laughed, too.

If she screamed, how long would it take this Laurel and Hardy pair to react? Her fingers felt for the shard of glass, still wedged beneath the elastic of her panties. Roxy's eyes were on the men. They were directly above her, still laughing.

"Shhhhh, now Blondie," Piper hissed, reading her mind. Satin sighing as he folded down beside Robbie. She could see the hard gleam of Piper's blade as he brought it close to the sleeping boy's throat.

The men were walking away from her, leaving a trail of laughter that was drowned by the bray of a passing Harley. The bike woke Robbie, and he whimpered, disoriented.

Roxy put a hand to his hair. "It's okay, Robbie. I'm here."

His fingers clutched at her dress. "Are we gonna go to the Spur?"

"Yes, Robbie. I promise. I'm going to take you to the Spur."

"And they'll sing 'Happy *Birfday*'?"

"We'll all sing it."

He leaned his head against her, and she put her arm around him, recoiling as her bare flesh brushed against Piper, who was pressed up close against the boy.

Piper laughed. Like a cat puking a hairball.

THE ORANGE LIGHTS that followed the snaking freeway blurred and multiplied into glowworms, exploding against the windshield.

Billy was sweating, his scar tissue alive with a million cigarette ends. He felt the wound in his shoulder throbbing, and he knew the bandage was wet with more than his sweat. The sling stinking of garbage. And blood. Not all of it his own. He was feverish, on the verge of delirium. Burning up.

Then he was sixteen again, Piper throwing the flaming cloth at him. His flesh bubbling on the bone as the boys rolled him into the grave. The sand in his eyes and his nose.

Blackness.

He passed out for a moment, felt Maggott's Ford drifting away from him, until the blaring horn of a truck scared him awake. He forced his eyes open, fixed them on the road ahead. Trying to keep the broken white line in focus. But the segments were like squirming larvae, and a wave of dizziness hit him again. He fought it hard, pulled the car into the breakdown lane and then onto the shoulder, driving one-handed.

Hauled himself out of the car and gagged, buffeted by the wind of passing vehicles, another horn warning him that he was about to become roadkill. He staggered around to the passenger side and leaned against the car. Doubled over and spewed a hot stream of puke onto the scrappy grass. Felt the sweat dripping from his forehead.

He sagged to his haunches, vomited again. Gasped and wiped his mouth on the back of his hand. He looked up, straight at a white crucifix dangling in front of his eyes. Thought he was hallucinating again, then realized it was a wooden roadside cross, caught in the lights of a passing car. A wreath hung from the cross, flowers dried and dead as the victim. Then gone with the headlamps.

Billy gently tested his shoulder. Agonizing to touch. Bloated and suppurating. Remembered something from his medic's course before Iraq, about gunshot wounds going septic: infection caused gas gangrene that could lead to septicemia and shock and death. Within hours, sometimes.

Saw Doc's filthy scalpel lancing his flesh. Felt the ooze of the waste from the dump as he lay with the wound open and weeping.

Billy lifted himself to his feet. Slowly. He was still feverish but felt clearer after puking. The white lines lay still. The orange lights marched in twos toward the city. He got back into the car, waited for a gap, then allowed the Ford to drift into the flow of traffic.

His phone rang.

Roxy's number, but Disco's voice. "Where you?"

"Past Century City."

"You know the ramp by Three Anchor Bay?"

"Ja."

"We's there. Piper say you come alone or we kill them. The blondie and the kid."

"I'm alone."

The line went dead.

Billy drove, suddenly cold, tremors dancing his hands on the steering wheel. He gripped the wheel tight. The shakes were okay. They'd keep him awake.

He saw Piper with Roxanne Palmer and Maggott's boy. Piper sure that the woman and the kid would make Billy weak. They wouldn't. This wasn't about saving Roxanne and the child. It was about saving what was left of himself.

PIPER SAT WITH the stillness that is born of years of incarceration. The stillness of a man who has nothing but time. The child was asleep again. The woman was sitting with her arm around the kid. She was still, too, but awake. Tougher than she looked, that one. Needed watching.

The oceanfront had emptied. Maybe a walker every few minutes. The homeless darky down the other end of the sand was slumped next to her cart like a sack of shit. She wasn't seeing nothing. Plenty of time now to finish the blonde and the kid. But he resisted the impulse. While they were alive they gave him power over Billy Afrika. Billy was soft that way. Weak as a woman.

It had been Piper's intention to kill them as soon as they walked down the ramp that led to the small beach at Three Anchor Bay. He'd never been down here before, but this was where the Barbie Doll killings had happened, so Disco said. He was ready to finish the blonde. Looked forward to cutting the boy.

Jesus, he hated kids.

He'd had to sit with the little snot-head close by him in the Benz all the way over, to keep the woman in line. Piper had spent too much time in close proximity to death and other men's foul bodies to be sensitive to smell, but there was something the kid gave off that disturbed him. Underneath his dirty clothes there was a sweet scent. A smell he couldn't name. The smell of a young body. Of a child. Something that stirred memories of his brutal early years. Couldn't call it a childhood. The family who had taken him in from the orphanage had done things to him that still woke him up in the night, in Pollsmoor, like obscene lullabies.

Things with lit cigarettes and barbed wire and broken bottles. And their bodies.

He'd erased most of these memories, but some of them still came to him, hot, fevered snapshots projected onto the air above his bunk. Of course he had grown up to do the same things himself. It was in his blood.

But he didn't need these memories. Not now. Not on his honeymoon.

So he waited to kill Billy Afrika. Finish that shit once and for all.

Then he could kill the kid and the woman.

And take the blonde's head and walk across the road to the cop shop and smack it down on the counter of the charge office. Say loud and proud that he and Disco were the Barbie Doll killers. He could already see the flashbulbs detonating, see him and Disco on the TV together. Piper giving the 28 salute, Disco looking like a model. Knew that the D section of Pollsmoor would go befuck when they saw them. Didn't matter if the cops found the real killer, him and Disco would have done enough to be sent home.

Together. Forever.

Piper stood and walked away from the blonde and the kid, but keeping close enough to stop any trouble before it started.

"Disco."

His wife stood looking out over the ocean, watching the little pockets of mist that drifted in. The mist had triggered the foghorn, and it was moaning low and deep, still building up to full voice. Disco didn't hear Piper.

"Disco!" Louder this time. Rough. Like boots on gravel.

Disco turned and came over, face catching the light from the sidewalk above. Piper could see his beauty. Even under the makeup. Piper's stone-killer heart was soft for this boy. He still didn't know why, just knew it was so. Like he knew all this would be worth it when they got home to Pollsmoor.

He took Disco's face in his hand, squeezed it hard enough to bring pain into the boy's eyes. His idea of affection. Piper smiled at his wife and withdrew his hand. Disco rubbed his face, looked at him from under his hat. Terrified. Piper didn't mind that. The thing you loved should be scared half to death of you. That's the only way you kept it.

"I'm going to trust you. Understand?"

Disco nodded. Piper took Maggott's Z88 from the pocket of his tailcoat and held out his gloved hand toward Disco, offering him the weapon. Disco looked at the gun. Looked up at him. Did nothing.

"Take it."

"Why for?"

"Take it, I said."

Disco took it. Letting the weight of the gun droop his hand to his side.

"I want you to sit by them." Jerked his head toward the

blonde and the kid. "You hold that gun on them while I deal with Billy Afrika. If they move, you shoot them. You got me?"

Disco nodded. The top hat almost falling, catching it with his free hand and setting it straight. Piper smacked the hat off Disco's head, grabbed him by the throat, pulled him so close he could see the spidery cracks in the face paint.

"You do what I say, or I cut you. Understand?"

Disco nodded again. Piper released him, bent and picked up the hat off the sand, dusted it clean, and set it back on the boy's head. Looked at it, then adjusted the angle a little to make Disco look prettier.

"Okay, go to them now."

Watched as Disco sat next to the blonde, the gun black against his white glove.

Piper walked across the sand and found himself a spot beside the locked door of one of the boathouses, in deep shadow. From here he looked straight up to the parking lot. Hard streetlight hitting the ramp. He'd have a perfect view of Billy Afrika, who would be looking at the blonde and the kid on the rock as he came down toward the beach.

Wouldn't see Piper in the dark.

TATIANA, STILL BAREFOOT, ran across the road toward the pay phone at the gas station's twenty-four-hour store, carrying her slingback shoes. She was almost hood-mounted by a red Ferrari, gave the driver the finger, then hurried to the sidewalk.

She couldn't figure out what was going on over at the beach. They were doing nothing, didn't even seem to be talking to each other. She had stood for what seemed an hour now, up above the beach, in the shadows, watching and waiting for some action. Nothing. So she decided to take the gap to call Bertie. Tell him to come on over.

She slipped on her heels and walked into the brightly lit store, clacked over to the pay phone on the wall next to the corn chips. Tatiana saw that the phone was card operated, swore, and went across to the counter.

"Gimme a fucking card."

The *shokolad* guy at the cash register, dressed in a stupid red outfit with a yellow cap, took his time. She tapped her peep-toe high heel, shooting anxious glances out the window toward the beach opposite. Not that she could see down to where the blonde and her friends in their bright costumes sat. What was it, this circus shit? She knew the American had been some kind of a fancy model. Maybe this was a shoot. Were they waiting for the cameras?

She needed to hurry, before more people arrived.

The *shokolad* man slid her the card, and she hobbled over to the phone.

Billy Afrika left the Ford. There were four other cars parked in the lot. In two of them he saw the telltale movements of lovers eating one another's flesh. Or hookers working. A dented Fiat Uno, parked under a streetlight, was empty. The fourth car, a Benz 500 SLC, faced the ramp. Also unoccupied.

Billy heard the foghorn, a low bass rumble that got you in the gut, building into a higher-pitched moan like something dying. He crossed the parking lot and saw the concrete ramp falling away from him toward the sand below, contained on each side by stone walls. The ramp just wide enough for an SUV to drag a boat trailer down to the bay.

Near the bottom, under the narrow bridge formed by the sidewalk above, public bathrooms had been carved into the stone. Locked at this time of night. There was nowhere to hide. Once he walked down the ramp he would be backlit, a perfect target.

But he knew that Piper would want him close. Blade length.

So Billy started walking, the Taurus held at his side, shoulder throbbing beneath the sling. His legs still unsteady, the sweat rolling freely—from the heat and the fever and the fear. Not fear for his own life; he was long over that. Fear that he was close to Piper once more, and that he wouldn't be able to finish him.

As he walked, his shadow stretched tall as a tree in front of him, far more solid and substantial than he was. He saw the sand, heard the soft hiss of the ocean, the water hardly moving in this protected little bay. When he reached the bottom of the ramp he saw a bundle of rags lying beside a supermarket cart that had its wheels planted in the sand. It took a moment for the bundle to take on human form: a black woman sagging up against the cart. Asleep.

Blonde hair caught his eye at the far end of the small beach. Roxy and Maggott's kid sat on the rocks. Roxy had her arm around the boy. Billy blinked, fought off a moment of nausea and dizziness, sure he was hallucinating again. Opened his eyes. Saw he wasn't. Roxy was being guarded by Uncle Sam.

Billy stepped forward, crossed beneath the walkway.

A voice came from deep in the shadow to his left, from a place where the streetlights couldn't reach. "Drop the gun."

Billy let his fingers open, and the Taurus slid from his grasp and hit the sand with a wet slap.

"Put your hand on your head."

Billy obeyed, and a figure sucked itself out of blackness. Another Uncle Sam. But no minstrel costume or makeup could disguise the man walking toward him. It was more than a physical thing. It was an atmosphere. The way he poisoned the air around him. A being soaked in death.

The man stopped and smiled, gold teeth glinting like the blade in his hand.

"Billy."

"Piper."

chapter 40

SHE SAW THE SHADOW FIRST, A LINE OF INK DRAWING ITS WAY DOWN the ramp. Roxy sat up, took her arm from around Robbie. She needed to be ready. Saw feet, legs, and then finally Billy Afrika's face, his close-cropped bronze skull haloed by the street-light behind him. He moved into shadow as he crossed under the sidewalk. It was only for a second, but he disappeared. As if she had conjured him up and then lost him.

Until he stepped out onto the beach.

It shocked her to see his left arm in a sling, and even from where she sat she could tell that he was moving slowly, his steps unsure as his feet found the sand. She heard Disco, pressed close against her, suck in a breath, his eyes fixed on the approaching man.

Roxy slid a hand under her dress and worked the sliver of glass free, palming it. She brought her hand back to her lap, cupping the jagged edges.

Waiting for her moment.

*   *   *

BILLY STOOD WATCHING the man who had scarred him. Killed his partner. Butchered Clyde's family.

Piper glanced across at Disco and Roxy and the child before he turned his gaze to Billy Afrika, like an animal sensing his prey. Then he was coming.

Billy saw there wasn't going to be a preamble. Piper's blade lifted higher than his shoulder, blade briefly yellow in the street-light. Billy was about to make his own move when a wave of dizziness rocked him and his legs buckled. He fell like a condemned man through a gallows trapdoor. Took forever for his knees to hit the cool sand.

Instead of taking him in the heart, Piper's blade struck Billy's skull, slicing deep into the scalp above the right ear, glancing off bone. Blood flowed, thick and immediate, over Billy's forehead, blinding his right eye and dripping down onto the sand.

He looked up, and through his good eye he saw Piper recovering his balance, setting himself, raising the blade like he was the reaper about to harvest.

DISCO KNEW HE must act. He had to use the gun in his shaking hand. Shoot Piper. A voice told him you couldn't kill a thing that was already dead. That even if he emptied the gun into Piper, he'd just keep on coming with his Okapi knife and his 28 smile. That was crazy. Even Piper was flesh and blood and shit like any other fucker.

But just in case, as Disco brought the gun up from his lap, he leaned closer to the blondie, ready to tell her that she should take the kid and go, make for the ramp. Run.

*   *   *

Roxy saw Billy Afrika go down, saw Piper fall upon him. The creature next to her leaned in, his breath hot on her neck. Before she could think, she gripped the sliver of glass, swung her arm, and buried the tapering shard deep in his left eye.

Disco screamed, his voice filling the night in the lull of the foghorn. He stood, for a moment still holding the gun. Then he released the weapon, both his hands flying up to the glass, trying to pull it from his eye.

The gun seemed to hang in space. Roxy reached out, ready to grab it, fingers closing on the hot night air as the pistol rippled the water and disappeared.

The knife sank to the hasp, deep in Billy's chest.

He felt blood well and flow, spurting down his shirtfront. Spurting meant his heart was still beating. Maybe. Piper withdrew the knife, Billy's blood beading the air as he lifted it high again. This would be the killer blow.

A scream. Wrenched from deep. Full of pain and the animal fear of death.

Piper paused, the knife frozen at the apex of its backward arc. He looked over his shoulder, toward his dying wife.

Billy thrust his right hand into the folds of the sling, his fingers slick with his own blood. He found the handle of the Okapi, set his grip, and pulled the knife free, blade already extended and locked. Positioned before he'd left Maggott's Ford.

He rammed the blade home low in Piper's gut, just above his pubes. Piper turned to look at him, as close as a lover, stale breath sighing from the mouth like a gaping wound in that painted face. Using the last of his strength, Billy forced the knife upward, feeling the blade lay open viscera, sinew, and flesh. Dragged the blade until it jammed against Piper's sternum, jarring Billy's hand.

Piper sagged toward him, lips working as if they wanted to form words. Words that were drowned in the blood that spewed like black water from the mouth of a gargoyle. In the end, Piper died like any other man: coughing blood and breath as life slid from him with his voided waste.

Billy sagged onto his back, feeling the weight of the dead man pressing down on him. When he tried to move, his clothes slipped across his skin, thick with blood. His blood and Piper's. Billy managed to roll Piper onto the sand, lay fighting for breath, staring up at the moon fixed on him like an accusing eye.

A face blotted out the moon. A face fringed by blonde hair. Roxanne.

She was touching him. Speaking. He couldn't feel her touch. Couldn't hear her words. Saw her running toward the ramp, the child at her heels. The world was losing focus at its edges, darkening like an iris toward the middle of his vision. Before blackness closed on him, Billy saw one last thing.

Another knife blade catching the streetlight.

The homeless woman who had been sleeping next to her cart was on her feet, standing at the mouth of the ramp. She forced Roxy back against the wall and had a knife held high. Billy understood who she was. And what she was about to do.

He tried to shout. But the tide of darkness took him as he saw the long blade fall.

THE SILENCE WOKE HIM. DOC, SPRAWLED BENEATH THE KITCHEN table, the empty bottle of brandy lying next to him like an old lover, felt the familiar hangover throb at the base of his skull as he sat up. He tried to fit the pieces together. Why had he passed out under the table? Couldn't remember.

He eased himself to his feet, aging bones serenading the dawn, and walked out into the sitting room. The shattered window was a reminder. And the line of high-caliber bullet holes stitching the wall. His TV lay on its back, tube smashed.

No cricket today.

Doc's house was a bad place to be during a gang war. Sitting as it did in this bit of no-man's-land, between the 26s and the 28s, it was strafed by both sides as they lay down covering fire for the soldiers crossing Main Road into enemy territory. But now it was quiet.

Doc edged to the broken window and peered out. In the dawn light he could see all the way up Main. It was strewn with barricades of wire and rocks, and a burned-out car lay on its side not far from his front gate. The body of a man sprawled face-down near the car, his blood dark on the sand. A woman in a Muslim headscarf scuttled across the road, carrying a plastic shopping bag and a tub of Kentucky chicken, and disappeared into Dark City. Otherwise the road was empty and silent.

Then Doc heard the flat slaps of an automatic rifle. Snipers were on the roofs of the houses on the White City side, firing across the road. He heard answering fire. Shouts. Breaking glass. Screams.

He wandered back into the kitchen, which had small, high windows that looked out over the dump. The safest place to be. He crawled back under the table and tilted the empty bottle, the last drop of brandy burning sweetly on his tongue. He was out of booze, and these gang wars had a way of dragging on. The cops were happy to let them take their own course, looking on them as a culling process. A way of getting shit off the streets. If a few innocents died, who gave a fuck?

It was going to be a long day.

Billy Afrika, if he wasn't dead in a ditch, had a bucketload of blood on his hands.

IT WAS BAGHDAD revisited, Billy fading up out of darkness, a pale face swimming in front of him. But this was a man in a white coat, gray-haired and expressionless. Billy tried to speak, but he had something shoved down his throat. Knew he had to pull it out, tried to move his hands. Couldn't. He faded out again.

Sometime later he floated back.

He was alone in ICU, with the machine hum of the monitors and the suck and click of the respirator, persistent as an obscene caller caught in a loop. His throat was dry and inflamed from the ET tube shoved down into his air passages. Two chest tubes poked out of holes in his right side, near the ribs, draining rust-colored fluid into a plastic container near the foot of the bed. The fluid bubbled like a hookah pipe as the machine inflated his lung. He lifted his arms, saw the IV lines disappearing into the veins of his hands.

There wasn't a part of his body that didn't hurt.

A dark-skinned woman in nurse's gear came in. Gave him the once-over.

"Can you hear me?" she asked. He croaked a reply. "Don't try and talk. You've got a punctured lung. And that bullet hole in your shoulder went septic. Bloody near killed you. Next time you have backyard surgery, don't come here to make it nice."

He wanted to ask her about Roxanne Palmer. But the nurse was gone. He lay taking stock of the pain. Feeling the emptiness inside him now that Piper was dead. Nothing like hating somebody to give you a reason to go on living.

Billy did the arithmetic. Added up the tab. He had been back home four days. He'd killed two men and a girl. And he'd caused the death of many others. But he had survived. So what did that mean?

Maybe it was a sign. Or maybe it meant sweet fuck all.

He listened to the respirator. *Suck. Click.* Felt his chest expanding, despite himself. Felt life go on.

As sleep ambushed him, Billy Afrika saw a road ahead and him on it. His feet sucked and clicked as he walked, the blacktop tacky with blood.

THE CANNIBAL WATCHED the dogs, three of them, the size of small ponies. Muscle and sinew playing beneath their shiny coats, their long tongues lagging and flapping as they wrestled on the grass. He stayed well back, near the railing on the oceanfront.

Bertrand Dubois Babakala didn't trust white men's dogs. The animals often barked at him, sometimes tried to nip his black flesh, the proxies of their masters. Giving expression to what was now forbidden in this country, but decrees and laws could never contain what seethed beneath.

He was relieved when the dogs ran off and started worrying at the frayed blanket that hung from a wire cart stranded under a shriveled tree, wheels akimbo. A bulky homeless woman lay facedown a short distance from the cart, unmoving, arms spread wide, as if she had been dropped from a height.

Babakala lit another Gitane and leaned on the railing, watching the activity down in the little bowl of Three Anchor Bay. Groups of uniformed cops like jellyfish washed up on the sand. Figures in suits and white coats. Cop vans, ambulances, morgue vehicles parked on the ramp. Media clotted the parking lot above, and a white helicopter swooped down low, like a scavenging gull. The door was open, and a man with a video camera leaned out, the lens flaring for a moment as it caught the sun.

Babakala had started his day the way he started every day. He had brushed his best suit and put it on over a white shirt, trying not to notice the fraying at the sleeves. He shined his loafers, bought in Milano some years before. The leather was cracking, and the sole of the left shoe sported a hole the size of a dog's puckered anus.

He left his apartment and wandered down to the main road in Sea Point, to the little coffee shop where he took his morning café au lait and read a page or two of André Gide's *Travels in the Congo*. The cannibal found the Frenchman's loathing of his colonial countrymen bracing.

He sat at a table on the sidewalk, not because it seemed more Parisian, but because regulations forbade him to smoke inside. After a few sips of coffee, he listened to his voice mail messages. He'd slept with his phone off, unperturbed when Tatiana hadn't returned. She sometimes had what she called "sleepovers," where she spent the night with a client. These earned her more money.

He had to play the message from Tatiana twice to understand it. She was at Three Anchor Bay. She had found the American woman. Babakala felt the coffee curdle in his gut, and he pushed the cup away, half full. He left change in the saucer and hurried down to the oceanfront.

Where he now stood. Smoking.

He feared the police even more than he feared the dogs that were tugging at the blanket, one of them up on his hind legs, long snout rooting inside the cart. There was no way that Babakala was getting any closer to the action down there on the beach. He tried Tatiana's phone, for the tenth time that morning.

And for the tenth time heard her recorded voice: "This is Olga. You leave for me a message after the beep." Olga was her working name. The clients seemed to find it easier to remember.

He slipped his phone back in his pocket.

"Hey, Blackie! Come here!"

Babakala heard one of those white voices, dripping with entitlement, and thought at first he was being addressed. But the voice belonged to the owner of the dogs, a man with sandy hair, two small children, and a tired-looking wife sitting with him on a picnic blanket on the grass.

All three dogs were now up on their hind legs, desperate to get at what was in the supermarket cart. One of them—the darkest of the three—jumped higher, his hind paws finding purchase on the wire frame, trying to climb inside. The weight of the dog's body toppled the cart onto its side, and the contents spilled out.

The dogs jumped back, startled. Then they pounced, and each dog grabbed something in his mouth and they ran back to their owner, side-by-side like the hounds of hell, and proudly deposited three stinking, fly-covered, decomposing human heads in the middle of the picnic blanket. The white woman screamed and gathered her children. The man stood, backed away, tripped over his own feet, and ended up on his backside.

Something drew Babakala closer to the blanket. One of the heads was fresher. It lay looking up at him, framed by hair dyed the color of egg yolk.

Tatiana.

The cannibal blinked, fought rising vomit, and walked away quickly, feeling the brick of the sidewalk through the hole in his shoe.

Heading toward the Waterfront and that job as a doorman.

chapter 42

AS THE SUN BLED OUT AND DIED, THE SKY WAS TOUCHED BY A streak of emerald. The fabled green flash. Roxy remembered reading somewhere that this was the green of paradise. The green of hope.

She sat with Robbie at a window table in a Spur steakhouse. The boy was demolishing a double cheeseburger and fries. Washing it down with a chocolate shake. If appetite was any indicator of recovery from trauma, he was doing just fine.

Roxy had made a trip to the salad bar—the place where leaf vegetables went to die. Anything that was fresh and green was hunted down and drowned in a rich, sweet dressing. She filled a bowl with lettuce and a few potato wedges, color-coding her food to keep it away from the shades of blood and guts that had painted the backdrop of the last few days.

They were at the Spur in Hout Bay, across from the harbor, watching small fishing boats chugging in with their catch. There was a Spur in Sea Point, but it was within sight of the beachfront, too close to the carnage. So she'd put Robbie in the rental car and driven away from the city, along a road that wound around the peninsula, mountain above them, ocean below. The boy fell asleep beside her, clutching the pink bear she'd bought him at the Waterfront. A replacement for the one that lay somewhere in the dust of Paradise Park.

Roxy hadn't slept in two days. The idea of sleeping, even though her body was wilting with exhaustion, terrified her. As if the monsters who'd failed to destroy her during the waking nightmare would finally succeed if she closed her eyes. So she stayed awake. Focused on the road. Robbie whimpered in his sleep, and she lay a hand on his head, stroked his hair.

He had saved her life the night before.

The homeless woman had come at Roxy out of the shadow beneath the bridge, mumbling something as she sent her left shoulder into Roxy's chest, smashing her back against the wall. The woman's right arm was raised, knife etched in silhouette against a streetlight, and Roxy realized who she was. The blade dropped.

Roxy lashed out, managed to deflect the blow. Then the woman fell against her, heavy and stinking. Roxy couldn't move, her right arm pinned at her side. The knife was lifting again, and Roxy screamed. The scream lost in the bellow of the foghorn that suddenly found its voice. Roxy managed to twist her left arm free, tried to grab the woman's wrist, to stop the knife arm. It was like trying to halt a slowly falling tree trunk. The blade came down toward her with a terrible inevitability. Roxy heard herself panting in the silence as the foghorn died.

Then the woman made a sound too strangled to be called a cry. Something wet and glottal escaped her lips, and the knife stalled. Roxy saw Robbie punching and kicking at the woman's leg. A leg that, even in this light, was fat with swelling. Roxy lifted her own leg and pushed her foot against the woman's belly, shoved with all her weight, bracing herself against the brick wall at her back. The woman toppled, falling against the cart, knife clattering to the concrete.

Roxy grabbed the boy, plunging on up the ramp.

She saw someone standing above, another woman—pale hair hot under the streetlight.

"Help!" Roxy's voice sounded raw and foreign to her ear. "Help us!"

The light-haired woman was coming down the ramp. Coming toward them.

"Thank God. Please, help us!"

The woman held out a hand. Roxy saw what was in the hand: a small, black gun.

The Ukrainian whore said, "Where it is? The money?"

Roxy almost laughed as she edged around the Ukrainian, who circled with her, back to the ramp, weapon extended, dye job burning like a beacon in the streetlight.

The homeless woman, leaning on her wire cart for support, inched her way up toward them like some hellish wind-up toy, the sound of the wheels on the ramp masked by the blare of the foghorn.

The whore shoved the gun in Roxy's face, shouting. "I say, where it is?"

The madwoman pushed away from the cart, wobbled, raised the long-bladed knife. Roxy, wrapped in shadow, had time to think that the whore wasn't even a real blonde, then the knife was falling . . .

Roxy scooped Robbie up and ran for the Mercedes. She sped the city block to Sea Point police station. Her memories of the next few hours were like snapshots from a stranger's photo album.

A hospital emergency room, smelling of disinfectant, booze, and blood, the cops jumping Roxy and Robbie to the head of a line of torn and broken brown bodies.

Billy Afrika motionless beneath a ventilator mask as he was

rushed by, gurney wheels tracking blood into a scuffed chrome elevator.

A young Cuban doctor stitching Roxy's leg, staring up at her through sleep-deprived eyes, as if he was surprised to be entrusted with a skin as pale as hers.

After the medics were through with them, the cops took her and the boy back to Sea Point police station. A woman constable showed Roxy into an interview room and disappeared with Robbie. Roxy met her interrogator, a dark plainclothes cop with a mouth that sagged at the corners, as if it was being dragged down by all that he had seen men do. He drank coffee from a foam cup, listened to her, spoke hardly at all.

She fed him a version of the truth: how the detective, Maggott, had asked her to drive with him out to Paradise Park, to do a face-to-face with one of the men he believed had hijacked them and killed her husband. Thought that seeing Roxy might shock the man into dropping his guard. The dark cop stretched the side of his mouth in a sour smile. Shook his head.

Roxy saying that, after Piper killed Maggott, he and Disco abducted her and the boy. Left them in the hut, then came back and forced her to drive the men to Three Anchor Bay. Told him how Billy Afrika had tried to save her and Robbie. How she had stabbed Disco with the spike of glass. Last saw him lying facedown in the shallow water like he was snorkeling.

Then she stopped, sat silent, watching the dark man.

He stared at her, tapping the foam cup with his ring finger. "Know anything about the dead woman down there?"

Roxy shook her head. She'd edited out the attack by the woman with the knife and the whore's ironic death. Let them make some sense of it. She couldn't.

The cop said, "Beheaded like the other Barbies. Only difference is, she isn't a blonde. Not a genuine one, that is." He took a sip of coffee. Shrugged. "Maybe the carpet doesn't match the curtains, if you know what I mean?"

Roxy did. But she played it all natural blonde and dumb. Shook her head, again.

The cop was staring at her again. Sensing there was more. Not pushing, for now. There may be further questions later. But she could go.

Go where? Roxy wondered as she walked down the empty corridor. She passed an open door, glimpsed Robbie curled up on a wooden bench, asleep under a blanket that looked as if it had been dragged up from the cells. He sucked his thumb.

Roxy stopped. Felt the cop watching her, saw him framed in the doorway of the interview room, foam coffee cup still in his hand. She asked what was going to happen to the boy. He shrugged, saying the police were unable to trace any of his relatives. The mother had a bad history with social workers, and she'd disappeared. The kid would have to go to a place of safety.

Roxy heard herself speaking. "Can I take him with me? Care for him until you find his family?"

The mournful man took a while to nod his assent.

It was light by the time she left the police station with the groggy child. As she buckled Robbie into the Mercedes, Roxy saw that the oceanfront swarmed with blue uniforms. She started the car, then killed the engine. Went around to the rear and opened the trunk. Took a moment to convince herself she wasn't imagining the small silver case lying where Joe had left it. Roxy popped the two catches and cracked the lid far enough to see the crisp, new hundred-dollar bills in neat piles.

She felt life's current tugging at her again, ready to move her along.

Roxy took a deep breath, closed the case, and slammed the trunk. She drove down to the Waterfront, into the underground parking lot. This early, the Mercedes was the only car on the vast grid of white lines and oil stains. Roxy parked and retrieved the case from the trunk. The boy watched as she sat behind the wheel and counted the cash inside. Exactly two hundred and fifty thousand dollars.

So she had gotten away with murder. And she had a chunk of money. The only person who knew she had killed Joe Palmer was lying in ICU. She'd go see him, tomorrow maybe, and give him fifty thousand dollars. More than he was owed, but she figured he deserved it. Believed Billy Afrika would keep his mouth shut, money or not. If he lived.

Roxy took the chrome case, held the boy by the hand, and headed into the Waterfront, the white confection that encircled Cape Town's dockland. Cleaners buzzed the tiles with polishers, and brown girls on impossible heels clattered in to open the luxury stores, their breathless Cape Flats chatter channeling the ghosts of Disco and Piper.

Roxy led Robbie into a bathroom, sat him on a row of basins beneath the mirrors, and cleaned him up as best she could. A woman in a Stella McCartney dress walked in, took one look at them, and walked right out again. Roxy scrubbed at the blood on her face and dress, arranging her hair so that it covered most of the black eye. Stared at herself in the mirror: Courtney Love after a busy night.

At American Express, Roxy changed enough dollars into local currency to do what needed to be done that day. Buy clothes for herself and Robbie. Take him bear shopping. Pay for a nondescript rental car.

Roxy checked the two of them into a hotel at the Waterfront, hard cash and her American accent lowering the raised eyebrows of the desk staff. She locked the chrome case in the hotel safe and took Robbie up to their room, an off-white rectangle with a wall of glass framing the harbor and the distant Cape Flats. She closed the drapes.

Roxy spent a long time in the shower, scrubbed her skin and washed her hair. Came out in a clean white robe, towel turbaned around her wet hair, to find Robbie asleep on the double bed, arms wrapping his bear. She lay beside the boy, watching the mute TV, listening to his soft snores. Whenever his breathing grew quiet, she found herself touching his throat. To convince herself he wasn't dead.

Her body begged for the painkillers the bruised-eyed doctor had given her. But she didn't touch them. Knew they'd make her sleep. She stared at the flickering tube—tennis and fashion and Thai beaches and men climbing Everest—but she saw blood and bone and fire. The AC seemed to suck the stench of death into the room.

Somehow the day slid toward dusk, and at around six Roxy roused herself. Sat at the makeup mirror and painted away the external damage. She undressed Robbie and carried him into the bathroom. Washed the boy and dressed him in his new clothes. Told him it was time for his birthday treat.

As they parked outside the Spur, he looked afraid for the first time that day. She thought it was the trauma taking hold.

Roxy held his hand. "What's up, Robbie?"

"We not gonna get in trouble if they find out my *birfday* was yesterday?"

She laughed. The sound shocked her. She hadn't laughed in days.

Roxy had reached over and kissed him on his forehead. He'd smelled of soap and small boy. "It's okay; don't worry. It's our secret."

Now that it was fully dark, the sparklers on the cake fizzed brightly, lighting Robbie's face as the young waitress put the plate in front of him. All the serving staff, maybe ten guys and girls, gathered around the table and sang "Happy Birthday" to Robbie. He grinned up at them, and across at Roxy, through the fountain of sparks, and he looked delighted.

In that moment Roxy knew what she had to do. Knew it smacked of celebrities shopping for kids in the Third World— *think I'll take a brown one to go with the yellow one*—but she would adopt the boy. Then get the hell out of this country. Put a couple of time zones between them and the horror of the past days. Start a new life.

A reflection in the window caught her eye. A big man with dark hair, in a black suit and white shirt, bearing down on her. But when she turned, she saw he was just a guy with his wife and his kids, smiling as they passed. Roxy smiled back.

She took Robbie's hand and joined in the singing.

acknowledgments

I would like to thank my agent, Alice Martell, and my editor, Webster Younce. I am indebted to Sumaya de Wet for sharing with me her extraordinary accounts of growing up on the Cape Flats.

ROGER SMITH was born in Johannesburg, South Africa, and now lives in Cape Town. He is the author of the thriller *Mixed Blood* and is writing a third novel. Visit his website at www.rogersmithbooks.com.